DOUBLE CROSS

STEPHANIE HARTE

B

Boldwood

First published in Great Britain in 2025 by Boldwood Books Ltd.

Cover Design by Colin Thomas

Cover Images: Colin Thomas

A CIP catalogue record for this book is available from the British Library.

Paperback ISBN 978-1-83533-197-2

Large Print ISBN 978-1-83533-196-5

Hardback ISBN 978-1-83533-198-9

Ebook ISBN 978-1-83533-195-8

Kindle ISBN 978-1-83533-194-1

Audio CD ISBN 978-1-83533-203-0

MP3 CD ISBN 978-1-83533-202-3

Digital audio download ISBN 978-1-83533-199-6

This book is printed on certified sustainable paper. Boldwood Books is dedicated to putting sustainability at the heart of our business. For more information please visit https://www.boldwoodbooks.com/about-us/sustainability/

Boldwood Books Ltd, 23 Bowerdean Street, London, SW6 3TN

www.boldwoodbooks.com

For Betsy
Whose young life came so close to ending
Here's to not taking tomorrow for granted and making the most of
second chances!

1

DAISY

Friday 9 January

The unexpected sound of my mobile ringing startled me, waking me from my sleep. I opened my eyes and blinked several times as I tried to adjust to the darkness before I stretched my arm over to the bedside cabinet and picked up the handset. Mum's name was illuminated on the screen. That couldn't be a good sign. Something must have happened. She was hardly likely to call me in the early hours of the morning for a casual chat.

'Hello,' I said.

My voice was husky from the booze and fags I'd had before I went to bed, so I coughed to clear my throat.

'Daisy, you need to come to the hospital right away. Your dad's taken a turn for the worse.' Mum didn't attempt to hide her panic.

My heart started pounding in my chest.

'Oh no! I'll be with you as soon as I can, but I'm in Kent...'

'What the hell are you doing in Kent?'

I opened my mouth to reply, but Mum steamrolled on before the words had time to leave my lips.

'You had no business leaving the hospital. You should have stayed by your dad's bedside. Your selfishness astounds me,' Mum shouted before she slammed the phone down on me.

When the call disconnected, I glanced at the screen. It was quarter to three in the morning. Even though I'd had good reason to desert my post, Mum found my absence unforgivable, and she was stubborn to the last, so no amount of grovelling or sucking up was going to help. Not that she'd given me an opportunity to apologise. Mum was gunning for me, so it wouldn't have mattered what I'd said.

The call left me shell-shocked. Momentarily dazed. I needed to act fast, but it was as though I'd been glued to the bed. Thoughts raced around in my head as I scrambled out from the warmth of the quilt. The temperature had dropped since I'd gone to bed, so I shivered as I threw off my pyjamas and pulled on a pair of skinny jeans and a hoodie.

I was up to my neck in shit. I didn't know what to do for the best. Mum didn't realise I'd rescued Lily, and my twin sister had no idea that our dad had been brutally attacked by the scumbag he owed money to, Warren Jenkins.

My intentions had come from a good place, but I wasn't sure Mum or Lily would see it like that when they realised I'd been keeping them both in the dark. In my defence, Lily was still trying to come to terms with the ordeal of being kidnapped. She already had too much on her plate without worrying herself sick about Dad. Mum was doing enough of that for all of us. She was so preoccupied with him fighting for his life to notice anything going on around her, so I'd taken advantage of that. I'd done a cowardly thing and buried my head in the sand. Even though I knew I was being deceitful, I wasn't going to beat myself up over it. I'd done what I thought was right. It was a judgement call. A sudden knock on the bedroom door interrupted my train of thought.

'I'm sorry to come bursting in on you, but I heard the phone ring,' Bernice said as she pushed the door open. 'Is everything OK?'

Bernice Allen had been looking out for me from the first moment she'd met me. She had my back. She had my respect. I didn't want to burden her with my problems, but she had a knack of coaxing things out of me.

'You know you can tell me anything, don't you?' A worried look was carved into Bernice's features.

I bit down on my lip. Tears began stabbing my eyes, threatening to fall.

'What's wrong, darling?' Bernice reached for my hand as she crossed the room. 'Is it your dad?'

I nodded my head. I couldn't bring myself to speak. Emotions had welled up inside me, and it was all I could do to hold them in. It wouldn't take much for the floodgates to truly open.

'Has he passed away?' Bernice's blue eyes bored into mine.

My silence made her jump to conclusions as she tried to piece the puzzle together and fill in the blanks. I forced myself to find my voice and set the record straight.

'No, but he's not doing good. He's gone downhill. Mum wants me to get to the hospital straight away.'

'Oh no. That's awful. Give me a couple of minutes to get dressed and I'll drive you,' Bernice said.

'I can't ask you to do that. It's the middle of the night, and King's College Hospital is hours away from here.'

'What sort of friend would I be if I let you go alone? It's not up for discussion. I'm going with you,' Bernice insisted.

To be honest, I was glad she'd taken charge of the situation. My head was all over the place. I wasn't in the right frame of mind to make a mercy dash to the hospital on my own.

'We'd better wake Lily.'

My heart sank. Tempted as I was to slip out of the house while she was sound asleep, blissfully unaware of the danger Dad was in, I knew that was the wrong thing to do. Bernice could sense my hesitation, so she started trying to talk some sense into me, but her words were having trouble getting through my thick skull.

'She's going to find out at some point. The longer you leave it, the harder it's going to be.'

Bernice was right. I had to come clean. Now that I'd been backed into a corner, I didn't really have another option. But I had a horrible feeling there wouldn't be a good outcome. Guilt wedged itself into my chest. I'd been counting the minutes, the hours, the days until this moment came.

'I've been dreading having to do this.'

'I know you have, but it needs to happen. Don't look so worried. Everything will be all right.' Bernice gave me a sympathetic smile.

I wanted to believe what she'd just said, but Bernice didn't know my twin, Lily, like I did. My sister was highly strung. Emotional. Dramatic. She could turn on the waterworks in an instant. Whatever the occasion, she could find a reason to blub. And for once in her life, she had a very good reason. I couldn't dispute that.

2

LILY

My breath caught in my chest when I opened my eyes and saw the outline of two people hovering over me. I froze, heart pounding as I struggled to focus. For one horrible moment, I thought I was back in the warehouse with Smithy and Tank, the two heavies who'd been holding me against my will in the bedroom on the mezzanine level. I could still picture it so clearly.

'Are you OK, Lily?'

The sound of Daisy's voice broke the spell and dragged me back to the present. Then I realised it was her and Bernice standing over me. Imagination was a powerful thing. The threat had felt real, but my mind was playing tricks on me.

'Shit! I'm sorry I scared you,' Daisy said with a guilty look on her face.

That was an understatement if ever I'd heard one. I was absolutely terrified even though I knew I wasn't in danger. I doubted I'd ever feel safe again. Daisy would be unimpressed by an emotional display, so I dug deep and kept a lid on things. I wanted to build bridges. I didn't want to do anything to piss my sister off. I clamped my lips shut and did what came naturally. Retreated into my shell.

'You've got to get up. We need to go to the hospital.' Daisy's words had a sense of urgency about them.

'Why? What's the matter?' I asked.

'Your dad's not well,' Bernice piped up.

Then she glanced sideways at Daisy, who met her gaze, and a silent exchange passed between them. I had the strangest feeling they were being economical with the details they were sharing and weren't telling me the full story. I wanted to quiz them more about it, but being woken from my sleep made me feel disoriented, and the opportunity passed before I had the chance when Daisy began to speak again.

'Mum wants us to get to King's College as soon as possible. We need to get on the road. It's a long way from here,' Daisy said as she pulled back the quilt, exposing me to the cool night air.

I wrapped my arms around myself in a bid to keep warm. The old house hadn't retained a scrap of heat since the boiler went off.

'What did Mum say? It must be serious for her to call you in the middle of the night.'

My question hung in the air between us. It was clear Daisy had no intention of answering it. She just stared at me with a weird look on her face.

'Can you stop the interrogation and get some clothes on? We need to get out of here,' Daisy snapped.

'You don't need to bite my head off.'

Her abruptness took me by surprise. She was wearing her don't fuck with me face, so I wasn't brave enough to challenge her further. It didn't take much to push her buttons, and this wasn't the time to start a pointless argument.

I could see Daisy wasn't going to fill in the blanks no matter how much I wanted her to, so I threw my legs over the side of the bed and sat up. Bernice grabbed some trackies and a sweatshirt from the chest of drawers in the corner of the room and brought them over to me. I felt like I was in a trance as I put them on. As soon as I finished dressing, they herded me out of the door.

I'd barely fastened my seat belt when Bernice's red Jag roared down the drive. Gravel sprayed from its tyres, which pelted up at the sides of the car. Even the risk of damaging the shiny paintwork wasn't enough to make her take her foot off the accelerator.

Anxiety coiled itself around me as my heart started pounding in my chest. I didn't need to be told something was terribly wrong to know that was the case. I was desperate to find out what was wrong with Dad, but after Daisy's earlier response, I knew better than to ask any more questions.

The silence in the car was deafening as Bernice sped along the windy country lanes at breakneck speed like she was a competitor in the Monaco Grand Prix. She needed all her wits about her to negotiate the narrow tracks and hairpin bends in the pitch dark, or Dad wouldn't be the only one requiring a hospital bed. The last thing I wanted to do was divert her attention away from the road by having words with Daisy. I could feel the waves of hostility radiating off my twin, so I read the signs and kept my mouth shut. But my curiosity was killing me. We couldn't get to King's College soon enough for my liking.

3

DAISY

Mum looked haunted as she sat by the hospital bed with Dad's hand clasped in both of hers. His freckled face looked flushed, and an angry-looking rash covered both of his arms.

Mum barely tore her eyes away from him when we walked into the ICU. Several moments passed before she realised Lily was standing next to me. She was so absorbed by the gravity of the situation that her response was underwhelming, even when Lily rushed forward and dropped down on the chair next to her.

'Oh my God, what happened?' Lily asked, covering both of my parents' hands with hers.

Before Mum had a chance to answer, a doctor came into the room and approached the end of the bed.

'Are these your daughters?' she asked, glancing at Lily and me.

'Yes,' Mum replied in a tiny voice.

'I'm a family friend,' Bernice said to explain her presence in the room.

I wasn't sure how her comment would go down, but either Mum didn't hear her or she chose to ignore her because it didn't provoke a reaction, which surprised me. They weren't each other's biggest fans. Bernice had been like a surrogate mum to Lily and me, but my mum and dad had no time for her. I was surprised Mum was being so reasonable. But it didn't last.

'We've got the results of the lumbar puncture and I'm afraid it's confirmed what we feared. Desmond has meningitis,' the doctor began.

The word meningitis rattled around in my brain. I didn't know much about the illness, but I was pretty sure it sometimes had deadly consequences.

'Oh my God, that's serious, isn't it?' Mum's dark brown eyes glistened with tears as she trembled from head to toe.

'I'm afraid so. It's a potentially fatal complication of his traumatic brain injury. The penetrating wounds Desmond suffered in the attack tore the protective tissues surrounding his brain, which allowed bacteria to enter and cause the infection,' the doctor explained.

Lily turned away from Dad in slow motion. I felt the weight of her stare as her glare settled on me, and she fixed me with a black look. She'd obviously put two and two together and realised I knew more than I was letting on. A feeling of dread swirled inside me. But then Lily turned her attention away from me and looked up into the doctor's face as she concentrated on what she was saying.

'We've already started Desmond on intravenous antibiotics to help fight the infection and we'll also treat him with corticosteroids to reduce the inflammation and swelling. But the next twenty-four hours will be critical. We don't know if he'll respond to the treatment.' The doctor had a comforting bedside manner. Her voice was gentle and oozed sympathy.

It was hard enough for me to take in the enormity of the situation. I couldn't even begin to imagine the turmoil Lily was feeling. Up until a few hours ago, she'd been oblivious to the danger Dad was in. But it was too late to regret my decision. I pushed the guilt from my head so that I could try to decipher exactly what the latest development in Dad's fight for life meant for our family.

'Do you have any questions?' the doctor asked.

'No,' Mum said, fighting back her tears.

The minute the doctor left the room, the atmosphere changed. Mum unravelled herself from Lily's grasp and got to her feet. She looked daggers at me before she walked over to where I was standing.

'So nice of you to finally show your face. I'm disgusted with you. What could be so important that it kept you away from your dad's hospital bed?' Mum seethed.

'I would have thought that was obvious,' I fired back, my tongue getting the better of me.

Emotions were running high, so I should have known my rudeness would go down like a slab of meat at a vegan dinner party.

'Don't you dare use that tone with me,' Mum replied, acid coating her words.

'You wanted me to find Lily, didn't you? So that's what I've been doing. This might come as a huge surprise to you, but unfortunately, I can't split myself in half and be in two places at once!'

My response was intentionally abrupt. Sarcastic. I knew I wasn't being very diplomatic, but I couldn't help myself. My temper had spiked, so the words galloped out of my mouth before I could stop them.

'Don't you dare try and talk your way out of this! You haven't got a leg to stand on. I find it very hard to believe that you've been tied up every minute of every day since you left me here to deal with this on my own. There's no excuse for the way you've behaved.' Mum's eyes were blazing.

'This isn't getting you anywhere. Why don't you both take a step back,' Bernice suggested, holding her hands up in front of her in an attempt to calm the situation.

But her stint as a peacemaker was short-lived when Mum tore into her with both barrels loaded.

'Why don't you mind your own fucking business.' Mum spat the words out like they were burning the inside of her mouth.

Bernice was no shrinking violet, but she had the good grace not to react.

'You shouldn't even be in here. In case you hadn't noticed, my husband's gravely ill, so he doesn't need all and sundry spreading their germs around him.'

I felt my mouth drop open. The way Mum was carrying on, anyone would think Bernice had crawled out of a gutter.

Bernice slipped her arm around my waist, so I turned my face towards hers. 'I'll be outside if you need me, darling,' she said.

Her voice was soothing. Oozing empathy. I could feel my bottom lip begin to tremble in response. I didn't usually cry at the drop of a hat. That was Lily's department. But I appreciated her show of support more than words could say.

'Thank you,' I mouthed, not trusting myself to speak.

Bernice gave me a slight squeeze, then she flashed Lily a half-smile before she turned on her high heels and walked towards the door with her head held high and her long, dark brown ponytail swishing behind her.

Even though Mum had basically told Bernice to sling her hook, she seemed surprised by her departure. I should have known Mum wouldn't be able to help herself. She always had to have the last word.

'Don't bother waiting. My girls don't need you,' Mum said to Bernice's retreating back.

Bernice didn't lower herself to reply, which was the best thing she could have done because her silence seemed to rile Mum up more than any words she could have uttered. There was nothing more frustrating than being blanked, was there?

It was strange, but almost as soon as the door closed behind Bernice, the fight seemed to seep out of Mum. I let out a deep breath as I tried to slow my racing heartbeat. Bernice was right. This was neither the time nor the place to get into a slanging match.

'Is somebody going to tell me what's been going on?' Lily asked once we were alone.

'Warren Jenkins broke into the house and attacked Dad with a screwdriver. He forced it into his ear canal over and over again, which left him with a brain injury. He's been in a coma ever since,' I said.

When I saw Lily's shock and her tears start to fall, I cast my eyes down on the floor. Guilt gnawed away at me like termites in a piece of rotting wood. It was hollowing out my insides, making me feel sick.

'Why didn't you tell me?' Lily's tear-stained face was pained.

'It was a judgement call...'

I knew I'd been deceitful, but I thought I'd done the right thing by keeping the news from her. I was wrong. So wrong. If Dad didn't pull through, she was never going to forgive me, so I could kiss goodbye the opportunity to rebuild our relationship and put things right between us.

'Is that the best excuse you can come up with?' Lily asked as her expression darkened. 'That decision stopped me from spending time with Dad.'

I felt bad enough without her making me feel ten times

worse. 'I did it for your own good. You needed time to heal. Knowing Dad was at death's door would've been too much for you to handle. You were too fragile. Too emotional...'

'I can't believe you lied to me!' Lily wailed.

'I didn't lie to you. I just didn't mention that Dad was sick. Warren Jenkins still poses a massive threat to us. He's bound to be sniffing around, waiting to see if Dad pulls through. Mum and I witnessed what he did. I didn't want to put you at risk by bringing you here to the hospital.'

I'd honestly thought what Lily didn't know wouldn't hurt her. Big mistake.

'I don't care about Warren. All I care about is that my dad is in ICU fighting for his life...'

Dad's machine let out an unusual sequence of beeps, cutting her off mid-flow. Mum rushed back to take up position next to him. I pulled up a chair on the opposite side of the bed and plonked myself down. My eyelids were growing heavy. I was exhausted from the lack of sleep, but we were in for a long night. There'd be no shirking my responsibilities this time. Much as I hated being in a hospital setting, I had to do the right thing and stay with my mum and sister so that we could put on a united front and will Dad to fight the infection with everything he had left to give.

Hard as it was going to be, I had to bitterly resist the urge to run away. The sounds. The smells. The noises bothered me. I found all of them equally disturbing. Unsettling. But I had to suck it up and get on with it.

While we waited, my thoughts turned to MacKenzie. He was never out of them for long. I'd only known him a short while and much as I hated to admit it, he'd already stolen my heart. Days had passed since I'd last heard from him. Worry had wrapped itself around me like a creeping vine. I didn't want to think the worst, but if he was alive, why hadn't he contacted me? How long did it take to send a text and tell me he was OK?

Samson owned Eden's, the club I used to sing at. When I'd asked him yesterday what he'd done with MacKenzie, Samson had insisted he was dead. I thought he'd just said that to upset me, so I'd been determined not to believe him, but maybe he'd been telling the truth for once.

I'd been clinging to the hope that MacKenzie was just lying low, waiting for the dust to settle, and that he'd resurface when the time was right. He'd done a disappearing act before, hadn't he? He was an expert at dropping off the radar. But my faith in that theory was diminishing with every day that passed. The weight of all this doom and gloom was crushing my fighting spirit.

4

SAMSON

I woke with a start, then glanced at my watch. It was quarter to five in the morning. What the fuck was going on? It was unheard of for me to get up before lunchtime. This was the second night in a row I'd had trouble sleeping. Bernice Allen, the widow of my arch-enemy Roscoe Allen, had taken it upon herself to barge into my house yesterday and shoot me with a full metal jacket in an attempt to get even for me executing her hubby. The injuries she'd caused made it impossible for me to get comfortable. It had taken me ages to drop off. I'd been tossing and turning for hours, and every time I moved, shooting pains ripped through my insides and out the top of my arse.

Bernice was going to die for what she'd done to me and my hired muscle, Gary. The poor bastard had had more lead pumped into him in his final days, thanks to Bernice and her gammy-eyed husband. They'd been using him as target practice. But his luck ran out when he made the ultimate sacrifice and dived in front of me to protect me from the 9 mm FMJ Bernice fired from a concealed pistol. The bullet killed Gary, entering his chest and exiting his back, then went into my gut and came out the top of my rump.

I thought I was a goner, too, when I hit the deck and smashed my head off the marble floor, knocking myself unconscious. Gary landed on top of me, so when I came around, I had barely any air left in my body. His twenty-stone bulk had forced most of the oxygen out of my lungs. It took a monumental effort on my part to find the strength to push the fat bastard off me. Nobody wanted to find themselves pinned to the ground by a corpse. Now I knew what hookers complained about when fat fuckers popped their clogs doing the deed while the girl was flat on her back. Talk about going above and beyond the job description. What a way to make a living!

If Gary hadn't sprung into action when he did, I'd be the one who was six feet under. I'd heard people say when they'd had a near-death experience, it made them take stock of their life and change their outlook. I wasn't about to find religion or inner peace or become more tolerant and less interested in material possessions. And I certainly wasn't going to get all nostalgic and start ticking things off my bucket list in case my time ran out. I only had one thing on my mind, and that was to get even with the bitch who was putting me through hell.

But that would have to wait until later. I needed to get some kip. As I tried to find a position that wasn't excruciatingly painful, an unpleasant thought suddenly burrowed its way into my brain. I'd been so preoccupied with the ache in my guts and throbbing arse cheek that I'd forgotten all about MacKenzie's decomposing corpse rotting away in my dungeon. Fuck. I'd have to get one of my guys around to clear up the mess before it stank my sprawling mansion out.

My housekeeper was a very discreet woman who valued her job and knew the importance of not seeing or hearing anything, but even she had limitations. She prided herself on keeping my place spick and span and was very particular, which ticked all the boxes of hired help if you asked me. She followed my instructions to the letter and did everything just how I liked it. If a putrefying honk suddenly started permeating its way through the structure of my gaff, she was bound to notice. Even if she didn't ask awkward questions, a stench like that travelled. I couldn't risk a nosy neighbour getting wind of it. If they stuck their beak in, I could end up with the Old Bill sniffing around, literally.

Choosing the right men for the job would be a massive ball ache. Like I needed anything else going on below trouser level at this moment in time. I'd lost four members of staff in a matter of days. I supposed I could outsource the job, but I preferred to keep issues of a delicate nature like this in-house where possible. Whoever I chose would need to have cast-iron stomachs. Not only did they have MacKenzie's rotting remains to deal with, his piss and shit were splattered all over my porcelain tiles. It was going to be ripe in my torture chamber, there were no two ways about that.

As I mulled over the options, Hamish and his younger brother, Angus, sprung to mind. They were two big Scottish lumps who looked like contestants in the caber tossing at the Highland Games. They'd both done time, which was a win-win as far as I was concerned. Prison provided a great education. Cons were banged up for one offence but learned how to turn their hands to many other things while they were doing a stretch in the company of other lags.

The brothers grim hadn't been on my payroll long on account of them being banged up, but I reckoned they'd fit the bill. I couldn't imagine either of them would shy away from a bit of rubbish removal. There was only one way to find out.

'Hamish, I've got a job for you and Angus. Can you come over to my house asap?'

'Yes,' he replied in his broad Scottish accent.

I didn't apologise for calling him at an unearthly hour of the morning. If he was bothered that he'd been rudely awakened, he didn't express it. But then again, Hamish was a man of few words, which was just as well because I couldn't understand what the fuck he was saying most of the time.

The brothers had grown up on a deprived council estate in Paisley and had seen a lot of hardship in their short lives. They were dream employees as far as I was concerned. When people were desperate for money, they'd pretty much agree to do anything.

* * *

Some gentle knocking on my bedroom door refocused my attention.

'Come in,' I said.

'I'm sorry to disturb you so early, Mr Fox, but there are two gentlemen at the front gate asking to see you,' my housekeeper said a short while later when she poked her head around the door.

She seemed surprised to find me awake. She started work at 5 a.m., but our paths wouldn't usually cross until late afternoon. Her assessment of the brothers brought a smile to my face. I wasn't sure I'd describe the Desperate Dan lookalikes as gentlemen.

'Hamish and Angus?' I asked just to be on the safe side.

You couldn't be too careful these days. The last time I'd had unexpected guests, I'd let a killer into my house. It beggared belief that Bernice had had the balls to waltz into my property and blow a hole in Gary while trying to get to me.

'Yes.' My housekeeper nodded.

'Tell them to park their van around the back of the house and show them into my study, please,' I replied. 'And stay with them until I get there. I don't want them nicking anything.'

It was going to take me a while to waddle from my bedroom at the back of my mansion to my office in the east wing. But I needed to show the guys how to access the dungeon in the basement, which was strictly off-limits to everyone apart from my trusted close circle. Hamish and Angus hadn't previously been in that coveted position, but this seemed like as good a time as any to elevate their status. I always found it difficult to take the leap of faith and allow somebody into the inner sanctum, but sometimes circumstances forced my hand.

As soon as I walked into my office, my housekeeper made herself scarce without me even having to dismiss her.

'Thanks for coming so quickly. I have a clean-up job that needs your immediate attention,' I said once we were alone in the room.

'What d'you want done with it?' Hamish asked.

'That's your call. But make sure you leave no trace of it behind,' I replied.

I didn't give a flying fuck about the technicalities. I just wanted MacKenzie out of my house. I hobbled over to the far side of the room and pressed my forefinger on the sensor so that it could read my print. A second later, the door unlocked. 'The rubbish is down there. But I don't want you to bring it through the house. There's a separate entrance that leads into the grounds. Let me know when you're about to leave, and I'll show you the way out. Did you park around the back of the house?'

'Yes,' Hamish replied.

'Good. Everything you'll need is in the cupboard down there.'

Hamish and Angus didn't bat an eyelid as they stepped past me and started to walk down the stairs – *rather them than me*, I thought as I watched them go. Expecting to be in for a long wait, I limped over to my drinks cabinet and poured myself half a tumbler of single malt before carefully settling into my office chair, resting most of my weight on my good arse cheek. I was only halfway through the measure when Hamish appeared in the doorway.

'Angus is just finishing off the floor. Was it the mop and bucket you wanted us to dispose of?'

His accent was so strong for a minute I thought I'd misheard his question. 'Come again?'

'The rubbish you were talking about. Was it the mop and bucket?' Hamish reiterated.

A red mist descended in record time, and if I hadn't been quick to swallow the expensive whisky I'd been savouring, I'd have spat it all over the desk. Did the big lummox have shit for brains?

'What the fuck are you talking about, you dopey bastard?'

Hamish might have been the size of a house, but when something riled me up, I had the strength of ten men.

'You said you wanted us to take the rubbish out the back entrance. Was it just the mop and bucket?'

Was this guy for real? Was there nothing going on inside his dome? Were all his brain cells out to lunch? More likely on the piss! I'd heard the brothers were partial to a bevy or twelve. What they did in their spare time didn't concern me as long as it didn't affect their performance at work. But the booze must have addled the contents of their nuts. I hadn't anticipated they'd be incapable of following simple instructions.

'Yeah, that's right. Dispose of the cleaning equipment but leave the rotting carcass where it is.'

Hamish stared at me, slack-jawed, and I shook my head in disbelief. Then I put the crystal tumbler down on my desk so that I could clench and unclench my fists. I didn't hide my actions. I wanted Hamish to know how close he was to receiving a knuckle sandwich. He seemed unperturbed by the threat. He was preoccupied with mulling over what I'd just said and stared at me with a look of confusion on his face.

'Carcass. What carcass?'

My mouth dropped open as I processed his reply. I couldn't believe what I was hearing. When Hamish had stuck his big ugly mug around my office door, I hadn't realised news that warranted trashing the place was about to be delivered. I only just managed to resist the urge to tip over my desk because I was in such a hurry to see if MacKenzie had done a disappearing act.

I shoved my chair back and got to my feet. A stab of pain ripped through my insides as I bore my weight. But I gritted my teeth and pushed through the agony.

'Get out of my way,' I snapped when I reached where Hamish was lurking in the open doorway.

Every step sent red-hot waves crashing through my body. The descent into my dungeon was excruciating but necessary. My nostrils twitched as I inched closer. I didn't want to inhale too deeply. But there didn't appear to be even the faintest honk of eau de 'toilet'. A sweet-smelling floor cleaner had replaced the stink of MacKenzie's crap. Angus had done an excellent job eradicating every trace of the piss and shit from my porcelain floor. I was delighted to see it was no longer battle-scarred. I'd thought I was going to blow a gasket when MacKenzie Cartwright dropped his load all over my white tiles after I'd sent a series of electric shocks through his bollocks. What a selfish bastard!

My eyes fixed on the chair equipped with leg and wrist straps where MacKenzie had been slumped the last time I'd been in this room. It was empty. How could that be? I was sure he was dead. Nobody could have survived what I'd put him through. But he must have. Either that or a miracle had occurred, and he'd been resurrected like Lazarus. I wasn't a big believer in the power of the man upstairs, so I dismissed that theory as soon as it entered my brain. It was much more likely that he'd tricked me by playing possum. MacKenzie was vermin, and everyone knew they were almost impossible to eradicate.

Thanks to Bernice distracting the operation before it was fully completed, he'd slipped through the net again. If she hadn't darkened my doorstep, I'd have realised he still had breath in his body. Somehow. That fucking woman had a lot to answer for. When I caught up with her, she'd wish she'd never crossed paths with me. I was going to make her suffer. Make her death long and painful.

I couldn't believe MacKenzie had managed to escape from my clutches. I'd well and truly had him cornered. But he was a slippery bastard. His time would come. And when his moment of reckoning finally arrived, I'd make him beg for mercy before I finished him off once and for all.

5

MACKENZIE

I couldn't believe my luck when I'd come to and found myself alone in the dungeon. My last memory had been of Samson flicking the switch on a box that had wires running from it to a couple of metal crocodile clips attached to my gonads. The pain from the electric shocks hit me in agonising waves. I'd never felt anything like it. It was off the scale. Watching me writhing in agony made Samson grin with delight. He'd turned the lever over and over again. Then everything went black.

As I went to stand up, my trainer slipped on the floor. The legs of the chair were surrounded by crap. A vague memory stirred at the back of my mind. In my hurry to escape, I'd forgotten I'd lost control of my bladder and bowels. Samson was so particular about everything he'd have been disgusted at the violation, which would have brought a smile to my face if I hadn't been in so much pain.

My eyes scanned the scene. I'd done a real number on my old boss's pristine tiles. But I didn't have time to gloat. I needed to get as far away from here as possible before Samson and Gary came back and finished the job.

I wasn't sure why Gary had opened the chair's straps, but I knew I had to take full advantage of the position I'd found myself in. I heaved myself out of the seat using my good hand and held on to one of the armrests as I pulled my boxers and jeans up with two fingers of my bandaged hand.

I was having the week from hell. In the early hours of Tuesday morning, Arben Hasani, an Albanian drug lord, and two of his guys had broken into the Old Mill House while I was sound asleep. They'd come to issue me a warning and I was dragged out of bed and frogmarched into the kitchen. One of the guys forced my palm onto the glowing red ceramic hob. My flesh had stuck to the hot plate like steak on a griddle. Arben had called it a taster punishment for paying with counterfeit notes for the cocaine he'd supplied. The notes were genuine. I'd stake my life on that. He'd given me a week to come up with a hundred grand, or he was going to let his guys get stuck into me.

I shuddered at the memory, then pushed it to the back of my mind. I had to focus on my current predicament and try to navigate my way through the piss and shit without injuring myself further. It stank to high heaven. I was glad I wasn't the mug having to clean it up. I was pretty sure the unenviable task would fall to Gary. There was no way Samson would get his hands dirty. He'd burn the house to the ground before donning a pair of Marigolds and setting to work with a bottle of bleach.

My heart was pounding as I made my way to the door. My progress was slow. I was moving at a snail's pace. A combination of unsteady feet on a hazardous surface and a barely functioning body hindered my bid for freedom. When I finally got to the back entrance, I glanced over my shoulder to check the coast was clear. I'd had visions of Gary grabbing me by the scruff of the neck and pulling me back to the chair, but he was nowhere to be seen. I pushed down on the bar, half expecting the door to be locked, but it swung open, and I stumbled out into the darkness.

Fresh air had never tasted so good. I gulped lungful after lungful, but when the ultra-bright light on the wall above flashed on, illuminating a large patch of ground in front of me, I had to flatten myself against the edge of the house. For my sake, I hoped nobody inside had noticed that that part of the garden had suddenly lit up.

I couldn't afford to get caught now. I was in no condition to make a run for it. Samson's house was set in sprawling land-scaped grounds. It would take every ounce of strength I had left within me to stagger to the main road. I'd have to take the long way around and hug the perimeter wall to avoid the security lights and cameras. Samson had spared no expense when it came to protecting his mansion, so I'd have to keep my wits about me and tread carefully to avoid triggering any of the devices.

I'd only been limping for a very short time when I spotted headlights on the driveway in the distance. My heartbeat started galloping in my chest when I realised they were coming towards me. I dropped down behind a large shrub and watched with my pulse pounding in my ears as a white transit van crept along the gravel. It was travelling so slowly that time seemed to stand still. I saw two dark-haired guys inside as it drew level with me. It was difficult to tell from the distance I was at, but I was almost sure I didn't recognise either of them. But Samson must have known them. Otherwise, they'd never have been granted access to his fortress.

I was scared to breathe in case I gave myself away, so I held my breath until the van passed me. What was wrong with me? It wasn't as though the occupants were close enough to be able to hear me. But I did it all the same. My ears pricked up when the engine stopped. Then, two doors opened and closed. The sound of footsteps on gravel rang out in the darkness. Echoey. Threatening. My senses were heightened. When it dawned on me that they were coming this way, my pulse sped up again.

The men had parked their van around the back of Samson's house, close to where I'd been tortured, but they were heading back down the driveway. I let out a huge sigh of relief when they veered off onto a different path and approached the front door. A few seconds later, they disappeared inside. I stayed in my hiding place long after they'd gone. I was frozen with fear, terrified to move a muscle.

It was cold and damp in the bushes. My short-sleeved T-shirt wasn't generating any heat, so I rubbed at the goose-pimpled skin on my arms to try and warm myself up, but it made no difference. My teeth were beginning to chatter. I'd probably end up with hypothermia if I didn't keep moving. Besides that, Samson might realise any minute I'd shot through, and the first thing he was likely to do was search the grounds. An involuntary shiver ran down my spine, giving me the incentive to pull myself off the muddy floor. Hard as it was going to be, I had to push on.

Every inch of ground I covered was torture. I was weak; battered and bruised. But it wasn't just my body letting me down; my brain was scrambled. I was finding it hard to concentrate. On more than one occasion, I had to stop myself from curling into a ball and hiding in the shrubs again to have some much-needed rest. But desperation kept me edging closer to the finish line.

I was nearly delirious by the time I reached Sutton Lane. The street lights seemed to be winking a silent encouragement to me as I drew closer. The sense of freedom made me feel light-headed. I'd come so close to losing my life. I shoved my numb, unbandaged hand into all the pockets of my jeans, searching for my mobile, but Samson must have emptied them when I'd passed out. My wallet and cash were missing, too; so much for my plan to go and buy a lottery ticket and call an Uber.

There was no way I could walk home from here. Even if I'd been fighting fit, it would take at least an hour and a half. In my present condition, I'd have to triple the time. I wasn't strong enough to endure gruelling exercise like that. My only hope was to try and blag a free ride on the train.

Getting to the station was going to be an uphill battle. My resolve was slipping as I plodded along the empty pavements. I wasn't sure what time it was. It was still dark, but it was the depths of winter, so it could be early morning or evening. There was no way of knowing. All this effort could be in vain. I was breathing out of my arsehole by the time I reached Clapham Junction. My lips lifted into a hint of a smile when I saw the station was open. Thank fuck for that! I walked into the forecourt and glanced up at the digital display. It was 7 a.m. So it was morning, but I had no idea what day of the week it was.

'Excuse me, mate,' I said to the first member of staff who came into view. 'I've just been mugged. The guy nicked my phone and wallet...'

'Oh, that's terrible! What's the world coming to? Just give me a moment and I'll call the police,' he replied, interrupting me mid-flow.

That wasn't the answer I'd been hoping for.

'There's no point. The bloke's long gone,' I said to stop him calling out the filth. I needed them poking their noses in like a hole in the head.

'You look pretty badly injured. Would you like me to call an ambulance?' The man's eyes scanned my face and arms as he drank in my wounds.

I dreaded to think what I looked like, so I tried to gloss over it. 'It's just superficial,' I lied. If he saw the state of my nether regions, his eyes would pop out of his head.

He eyed me suspiciously as he weighed up the situation.

'Honestly, mate, it doesn't warrant tying up the overstretched emergency services for a few cuts and bruises.' I channelled my inner stiff upper lip and fixed him with my best brave face.

'Are you sure? It's no trouble,' he replied.

'I just want to go home. But the guy stole my wallet and phone so I can't buy a ticket. I don't suppose there's any way you could let me through the barrier, is there?' I fixed a set of pleading eyes on him.

'Where are you trying to get to?'

'Denmark Hill Station.' It was only three stops from here, so I was hopeful he'd take pity on me.

I could tell the idea made him uncomfortable. His eyes darted left and right to see if anyone was watching, and then he opened the gate and waved me through.

'Thanks, mate, I really appreciate this.' I smiled.

He nodded an acknowledgement and then made himself scarce.

After everything I'd been through with Samson, my faith in the human race had been restored. It was good to know there were still people out there who were willing to do things to help out a total stranger. I felt lighter, buoyed up by the fact that a good Samaritan had stuck his neck out for me.

6

DAISY

Dad looked peaceful, but the atmosphere was charged. Mum and Lily clung to each other on one side of his bed as I sat alone on the other. In between sobs and emotional displays, they looked daggers at me. It wasn't my fault Dad was in this position. Warren had inflicted the injuries, but I suppose I had to shoulder the blame for not telling Lily about the attack sooner before he'd deteriorated. And I doubted Mum would ever forgive me for deserting my post at the bedside vigil she'd been keeping since Dad had been admitted. Grudge-holding was her favourite pastime.

As time inched by, I tried to get to the bottom of what made my mum tick. She was a complex character who, once crossed, cut people adrift. I could sense I was dangerously close to her turning her back on me. Motherhood didn't come naturally to her. It was no secret that her pregnancy wasn't planned, and finding out she was having twins was a lot to cope with. Dad was elated, but behind closed doors, he wasn't much help. He made himself scarce, leaving Mum to do all the hands-on work: feeding, changing and getting up in the night. Mum got on better with Lily because she could manipulate her. Whereas I knew my own mind and wouldn't be bossed around, which didn't go down well. My mum liked to call the shots. So did I.

The beep, beep, beep of the machines was strangely hypnotic. I'd almost go so far as to say I was enjoying the background sounds of the heart monitor and blood pressure device until one of Dad's vital signs either rose or fell outside a healthy level and rang out a warning, which made me jump out of my skin. An alarm started getting louder, faster, and changing pitch as lights began flashing.

'Get the doctor,' Mum said, leaping to her feet. Her panic was palpable.

Before I had a chance to go for help, the doors burst open and in rushed the doctor and three nurses who asked us to wait outside while they attended to Dad. After what seemed like an eternity, we were called back in. We gathered around Dad's bedside as the doctor began to speak.

'We're going to send Desmond for a CT scan to see what's going on inside his brain. If you'd like to wait in the relatives' room, I'll come and find you when I have the results,' she said.

With one of the nurses showing us the way, Mum, Lily and I filed out of ICU, one behind the other. Bernice caught my eye as I walked past her, but we didn't speak. She looked as worried as I felt. Waiting for news was pure torture.

* * *

'You should have told me what was going on. I had a right to know,' Lily suddenly piped up.

She shook her head while glaring at me. After what felt like the longest time, she tore her eyes away and focused her attention on Mum.

'I'd never have left you to deal with this on your own if I'd known Dad was sick,' Lily said, throwing me under the bus.

I let out a sigh. The blame always lay at my feet. Nothing ever changed. I'd heard it all before. The doctor appeared in the doorway, which halted the Daisy-bashing before it had a chance to properly pick up momentum. I knew I should be grateful for her intrusion, but it was only putting things off. Delaying the inevitable. There was no excuse for what I'd done, even though I thought I was acting in Lily's best interests. The jury had reached a unanimous decision. I was guilty as charged. Surprise, surprise.

'I've just looked at the results of Desmond's scan, and I'm sorry to have to tell you that he's had a massive stroke which has caused extensive damage to his brain,' the doctor began.

Mum's hand covered her mouth as she stared at the lady in the white coat.

'It's a serious but common complication of meningitis. I have to warn you in cases like this, the outcome can be fatal.'

Mum gasped. Lily wailed. My insides somersaulted.

Mum and Lily began sobbing in tandem, which interrupted the doctor's flow. I watched her chest rise and fall as she composed herself. Breaking news like this to desperate relatives must be the worst part of the job. I wouldn't want to be in her shoes for anything.

'During a stroke, the blood supply inside the brain is disrupted, which kills brain cells. It can be life-threatening if that happens in a part of the brain that controls the body's life support systems like breathing and heartbeat. Desmond was evaluated using the Glasgow Coma Scale, and he scored three. A score of eight or less suggests a severe brain injury,' the doctor said, regaining her stride.

I was sure I wasn't the only one who'd noticed the second mention of mortality in a matter of minutes.

'Desmond is unresponsive to the outside world. I'm afraid it's only a matter of time...'

Mum let out a howl that made my blood curdle.

'Would you like to sit with him?' the doctor asked.

'Yes, please,' I replied.

Mum and Lily were too distraught to speak.

We filed back into the ICU in a trance and gathered around the bed. Dad looked like he was asleep and I kept expecting him to open his eyes any minute. But I knew that wasn't going to happen. His hand felt cold and his skin was mottled and had a bluish tinge to it. His breathing was noisy and I knew why they called it the death rattle now. Regret swirled around in my brain. Watching him stare death in the face had changed my perception. I wished I could have put things right before he died. But it was too late to turn back the clock.

If I'd been alone in the room, I'd have told him I was sorry we hadn't had a better relationship. I was sorry I always butted heads with him. I wished he'd loved me the way he'd loved Lily. But at the final moment, none of it really mattered. We'd never seen eye to eye, but that didn't mean I didn't love him, and I'd always regret that things hadn't been better between us.

As we sat in silence, me against them, Dad's breathing became shallower. Less frequent. And then it stopped altogether. After he took his last breath, the sound was deafening. We all noticed it. Eyes darted. Pulses pounded. But nobody spoke. Tears fell. The loss was instant. I frantically delved through memories of the past for something comforting to cling to. I couldn't find anything. I'd never felt more alone in my life.

I sat motionless as the doctor checked Dad for signs of life.

You could have heard a pin drop as we waited for the words we knew were coming.

'I'm afraid Desmond has passed away,' the doctor confirmed.

Mum let out a gasp followed by a wail. Lily joined in and started sobbing. What did they think the woman was going to say? It was obvious he'd lost the battle. Dad never regained consciousness after Warren brutally attacked him with a long-handled screwdriver. The doctors had said they were amazed he didn't die at the scene, but when he contracted meningitis on top of everything, his body gave up fighting. He'd stubbornly clung to life by his fingernails, but in the end, there was too much stacked against him.

'He can't be dead.' Mum was in denial.

'I know it must be hard for you to accept that he's gone. In situations like this, it sometimes takes a while for the reality to sink in. We did everything we could to save him,' the doctor said.

'So why didn't he make it?' Mum threw the doctor a withering glance as anger momentarily replaced her anguish.

'I'm so sorry for your loss,' the doctor said before she walked out of the ICU.

I didn't blame her for making herself scarce. She'd done everything humanly possible to help, but Dad was too ill to survive. The last thing she needed was Mum giving her a kicking for trying her best. It wouldn't have mattered what the doctor said. Mum wasn't going to listen. She wasn't thinking straight.

Mum shook her head as she trained her eyes on the doctor's retreating back as though she was negligent. She didn't thank her for taking care of Dad while he'd been so poorly. She was too caught up in her own emotions and didn't want to accept the outcome.

Mum got up from the chair and threw herself across Dad's lifeless body. It was heartbreaking to see her struggling to cope with her grief. She was inconsolable. Her whole body was shaking as she cried her eyes out. His death had hit her hard. She held on to him for several minutes before she peeled herself away. Then she leant forward and planted a kiss on his forehead before she sat back down on the chair.

Silent tears rolled down my cheeks as Lily and Mum attempted to drown out each other with their body-wracking sobs, as though they were in competition to put on the most emotional performance. Meanwhile, I felt empty. Hollow. Numb with grief. Our relationship was complicated, but that didn't mean I wasn't devastated.

It felt weird to no longer have a dad. Even though he hadn't been up to much, I was still going to miss him. It would take time to get used to the fact that he was never coming back. Life was fragile. The future could change in a heartbeat. Warren Jenkins deserved to suffer for what he'd done. I was terrified of him, but I hoped one day I'd feel brave enough to get my own back on the bastard.

7

DAISY

Bernice was pacing up and down the corridor like an expectant father waiting for news of the impending birth when Mum, Lily and I filed out of ICU, wearing grave expressions. She must have the patience of a saint. She'd sat out here on her own for the best part of twelve hours.

'Why are you still here?' Mum asked with spiteful venom in her voice when the two women came face to face. 'You're like a vulture circling, waiting for your prey to die so you can pick its bones clean.'

'I'm doing no such thing. I'm just trying to help,' Bernice replied.

I was glad she still retained her dignity even though Mum had lost the plot.

'We don't need your help. Me and my girls can manage just fine without you.' Mum's voice broke with emotion as she stifled a sob.

After the way Mum had torn into me earlier, I was surprised to be included in the family unit, but it was clear she didn't want Bernice muscling in on her territory, so if it meant keeping me close to prevent that from happening, that was precisely what she intended to do.

Bernice was an intelligent woman. She didn't need it spelled out to her. She knew we wouldn't be leaving the hospital if Dad still had breath in his lungs.

'Let me give you a lift home. It's the least I can do,' Bernice offered.

I admired her generosity. I knew for a fact she didn't suffer fools gladly, but she'd cut Mum a huge amount of slack by turning the other cheek.

'Come on, girls, let's get a taxi. There's a rank outside the main entrance,' Mum said without bothering to reply to Bernice.

I wanted to pull her up for being so rude, but I didn't want to end up having a showdown in the hospital corridor. So, instead, I mouthed an apology to Bernice as I trailed behind my mum and sister.

'Call me,' she mouthed back, putting her manicured hand up to her ear to mimic holding a phone.

I nodded a silent reply. Mum would only get riled up if she'd seen our exchange, so it was better for all concerned that we communicated in secret.

* * *

The taxi dropped us close to our semi-detached house on Crawford Road and we walked the last couple of doors. Mum froze on the pavement outside number forty-one, and the colour drained from her face as her eyes scanned the red brickwork. I stepped past her and started to walk up the path. I glanced over my shoulder when I heard my sister speak.

'It's OK,' Lily soothed, taking Mum by the hand and leading her towards the front door.

Mum moved like a zombie as she shuffled behind my twin. Her reluctance was so apparent anyone would think she was wearing concrete shoes. Mum was visibly shaking when I put the key in the lock. Bernice had arranged for the front door to be repaired after Warren had kicked it in. She'd also cleaned up the mess and the gruesome blood-soaked scene where Dad was butchered, but Mum didn't know any of that. She hadn't been in the house since Dad was taken to hospital.

I stood in the hallway, holding the door open as Lily pulled her over the threshold. She towed her along the hall into the kitchen. I was glad she bypassed the living room. The sofa was long gone. I'd given Bernice permission to dispose of it. No amount of scrubbing would have removed the dried-on stains. Even if Dad's blood hadn't been ingrained in the fabric, I doubted any of us would ever feel comfortable enough to sit on it again.

I could sympathise with how Mum was feeling. I remember having a similar reaction the first time I stepped inside the house. But I'd walked into the aftermath of Warren's visit. The place was still trashed, but now the door had been fixed, and there wasn't a trace of the broken glass littering the hall, or gore all over the living room. Bernice had done an amazing job, not that Mum would ever thank her for her efforts.

Judging by her reaction, I was pretty sure Mum was having flashbacks to the last time she'd been here. Dad's presence was all around us, woven into the structure of the house. Lily and I had grown up in this semi. We'd never lived anywhere else, so it seemed very strange for Dad not to be here.

Thoughts started swirling around in my head. There was a lot to do. We had a funeral to organise. A death to register. Friends and relatives to notify. But before we could do any of that, there was the mother of all arguments to be had. It had been brewing since we walked away from King's College.

'You're such a selfish little bitch,' Mum roared the minute I walked into the kitchen. Her devastation seemed to disappear into thin air as she launched into me. 'Didn't I deserve to have support at a time like this?' Mum's dark eyes were blazing.

Here we go again. We'd already had this conversation. But she wasn't going to let the matter drop. She was furious that I hadn't stayed with her while Dad battled for life, but there was nothing I could do about it.

'I got to the hospital as soon as I could, but it's a long drive from Kent,' I snapped.

'You know damn well that's not what I'm talking about.' Mum's voice was sharp. Hostile. It made me uncomfortable. I wondered what she was going to say next. 'You should have told Lily what had happened with Warren as soon as you found her, not waited days to break the news. I bet she'd still be in the dark if I hadn't forced your hand...'

Mum was seething, so the last thing I needed was Lily piping up and making things ten times worse, but that was exactly what happened.

'Mum's right. You shouldn't have kept this from me. You denied me the chance to sit by Dad's bedside. And now he's gone,' Lily sobbed after she threw in her two-pence worth.

Change the fucking record! I hadn't done this to be spiteful. I'd made a judgement call.

'It's easy for the two of you to lay the blame at my feet. But Lily was broken. She was in no condition to emotionally prop you up like I'd been trying to do. Your negativity was draining. I struggled to cope with it. Lily was in a fragile state. Watching you weeping and wailing would have finished her off.'

Mum looked like she'd been slapped around the face by a

porn star's wet dick. She was horrified. Rendered speechless. It took her a matter of seconds to regain her composure before she reloaded her poison darts and fired them out of her mouth and into my heart.

'You've been nothing but trouble since the day you were born. How dare you speak to me like that. I've just lost my husband. My soulmate. The love of my life. I have every right to weep and wail, as you put it. You're a vile individual. Rotten to the core. No wonder your dad despised you,' Mum shouted before storming out of the kitchen with Lily hot on her heels.

Mum wasn't one to mince her words. But I was shocked by how low she'd stooped. I glanced over at Dad's usual spot at the head of the pine table as Mum's barbs bounced around in my head. She was hurt, I got that, but that didn't mean it was acceptable to lash out at me. I couldn't deny Dad and I had had a difficult relationship, but did he really despise me? There was no doubt about it. The thought of that was going to haunt me. It wasn't as though I could confront him on the matter. He'd taken the answer to the grave with him.

Mum hadn't hung around to face the music. She'd dropped the bombshell and scarpered. It was probably just as well she wasn't here. Otherwise, I'd have retaliated. My temper usually followed the same path. I'd have dragged up the most upsetting thing I could think of and thrown it back at her. I wouldn't have been able to stop myself. It wasn't a conscious choice. The decision wasn't mine to make. It was involuntary. A reflex action. Blind fury took on a life of its own. I was powerless to prevent it. Mum said I was a vile individual. Well, the apple didn't fall far from the tree, did it?

Silent tears slid down my face as I sat on my own, trying to process everything that had just happened. I felt so alone. So vulnerable. I wished MacKenzie was here to throw his arms around me, hold me close and be a shoulder to cry on. Tendrils of fear began creeping through me. His silence bothered me. I had a horrible feeling something terrible had happened. What if I never saw him again? I couldn't bear the thought of losing him, too. My mood had hit rock bottom, but I needed to drag myself out of this negative mindset. I was usually a glass-half-full kind of girl. I'd have to force myself to stay positive, keep a level head and not panic. No news was good news. Right? So why was I struggling to believe that?

8

DAISY

I was no pushover by any means, but I felt like I'd been set on by a pack of wild dogs. I didn't want it to be like this. I wanted us to have a fresh start. A new beginning where we put all the hostility and animosity behind us. But it was clear my mum and sister weren't on the same page as me. The best thing I could do was give them some space. Give the dust time to settle. All of this was so raw. Maybe when emotions weren't running so high, they'd meet me halfway and we could have a truce.

I got up from the table, walked over to the cupboard and took out a large glass. Then I opened the fridge and poured white wine up to the rim. Lily's eyes would have been on stalks if she'd seen it. Being careful not to spill any, I carried it back to where I'd been sitting. After what I'd been through, I needed a drink.

As I sipped the Pinot Grigio, the only sound was the clock ticking, marking the passing of time. Since Mum and Lily had stormed off, I'd desperately tried to block the argument from my mind, but I'd failed miserably. I couldn't seem to stop what Mum had said replaying over and over again. I reminded myself that she wasn't thinking straight. She was grieving. She was bitter. She wanted somebody to blame. I was the obvious choice. But nothing could excuse the things she'd said to me. The mudslinging was too personal. Too hurtful.

I wished I hadn't taken the bait, but everyone had a limit. And she'd pushed me to mine in record time. So I'd retaliated. On the attack in a split second. It was too late to regret my part. Too late to wish I'd behaved differently. What was done was done.

I couldn't sit around doing nothing. I needed something practical to take my mind off the row, so I walked out to the hall and took Mum and Dad's address book down from the windowsill. I ran the pad of my thumb over the embossed cover as I went back into the kitchen. Pulling out the nearest chair, I plonked myself down. I felt like I had the weight of the world resting on my slumped shoulders. This was going to be a horrible job, but somebody had to do it. Volunteering for the unpleasant task might earn me some brownie points.

I took a big gulp of wine to help me compose myself. Then I opened the cover. I'd intended to start working my way through the entries, phoning as many of the friends and relatives as possible to break the shocking news about Dad. But I stopped in my tracks when I saw the first name staring back at me. I did a double take. What a blast from the past! I wasn't sure I'd ever known her surname, but it had to be her, didn't it? Mum's best friend's first name was unusual. I couldn't imagine there were too many Colleens living in Camberwell. According to the address written in Mum's handwriting, her house was only a couple of roads away from ours, which added weight to my theory.

Mum and Auntie Colleen used to be as thick as thieves. That was why she was given the precursor to her name. To validate her importance in our family. She wasn't related to us by blood. Mum and her were childhood friends. They'd lived next door to each other when they were kids. Went to the same schools. Shared the same circle of friends. They had been inseparable.

I was too young to remember the details of what went wrong between them, but one minute, my surrogate auntie was a permanent fixture in my life. The next, she was gone. Auntie Colleen disappeared off the face of the earth overnight, which had been upsetting for Lily and me at the time. We'd adored her. She was always at our house and was part of the furniture. She didn't have a husband or kids of her own, so she always tagged along with us, which suited Mum and Dad. Having twins was hard work, so they'd never say no to an extra pair of hands. Why would they? They all got along well together. It wasn't a hardship having her around.

I hadn't given the situation much thought in years, but the hazy memory ignited a spark of curiosity within me. Something catastrophic must have happened between them because Auntie Colleen suddenly exited our lives, and I hadn't seen her since. To my knowledge, none of us had, which seemed weird as she lived close by. I was surprised we hadn't bumped into each other. Unless she'd moved out of the area without warning, but that didn't explain why we'd lost touch with her.

'What do you think you're doing?' Mum asked.

I jumped out of my skin. I hadn't realised she was standing in the open doorway.

'I thought I'd start ringing around. Let people know Dad's passed away...'

Mum narrowed her eyes. 'Who have you phoned so far?'

'Nobody. I was just about to call the first person in the book, Colleen Ahearn.'

I saw Mum take a sharp breath when the name left my lips. She looked like she'd seen a ghost.

'Well, don't bother.' Mum's voice sounded screechy.

My hunch must have been correct. Judging by her response, they'd had a falling out of monumental proportions.

'But that's Auntie Colleen, isn't it? Surely she'd want to know...'

I'd decided to push her to see if Mum would feel compelled to divulge anything. Fill in some of the blanks. But I soon wished I hadn't bothered. Friction was building between us and I could sense an eruption wasn't far away. The shadow of grief was no longer hovering over Mum. The heat of her gaze bore into me like a red-hot poker before she began shouting at the top of her lungs.

'Don't bother interfering! If I'd wanted you to go snooping through my address book and make calls on my behalf, I'd have asked you to. I'll notify people in my own good time.'

So much for me scoring brownie points! My peace offering was rejected. It looked like Mum was about to beat me with the olive branch I'd extended.

'I'm sorry. I was just trying to help,' I shouted.

I hadn't intended my apology to be heartfelt, but it fell on deaf ears anyway. Mum looked daggers at me and then upped the ante by trying to snatch the book out of my hand. I instinctively pulled it out of her reach and hid it behind my back like a five-year-old child about to have a forbidden bag of sweets removed from their grasp. My defiance fuelled Mum's fury.

'Give that to me right now!' Mum held her hand out.

Her dark brown eyes were blazing. She was fuming, which made me want to guard the precious address book with my life. I couldn't hand it over even if I'd wanted to. My stubbornness wouldn't allow me to back down. We were locked in a battle of wills, and I didn't intend to be the loser.

'Daisy, give it to me,' Mum roared.

Then she shot me a look before she lunged at me. I ducked out of her way, which made her see red. I knew if I gave the book to her, she'd destroy the page with Colleen's details. I could remember the address, but I hadn't memorised her mobile number, so if she'd moved out of the area, I'd never be able to contact her. I was desperate to know what had gone on between them, but Mum wasn't acting rationally. She was behaving like a lunatic.

'I want that back right now,' Mum bellowed, chasing me around the kitchen table like a woman possessed.

I was ducking and diving, doing my best to stay one step ahead of her. We'd done several laps, and she started to look breathless when somebody banging on the front door with their fist stopped her in her tracks. She looked at me with fear in her eyes. We both sensed who was outside.

'For God's sake, keep it down, the two of you. It sounds like World War Three's broken out in here,' Lily called with an authoritative tone in her voice as she bounded down the stairs.

She rushed along the hall before I had a chance to stop her. A feeling of dread swirled inside me. Unbeknownst to her, she was about to let an evil force into our home.

9

LILY

'How lovely to see you again. I hope I'm not disturbing anything,' an enormous man in a long, leather trench coat and flat cap said as he pushed past me and forced his way into the hall.

I'd never seen this man before in my life, but he seemed to know me, or at least he thought he did. He wouldn't be the first person to mistake my identical twin for me. People always found it hard to tell Daisy and me apart.

'It sounds like there's trouble in paradise. I thought you'd be too busy planning Des's funeral to be bothered fighting amongst yourselves, but it seems I got that wrong.' He laughed.

I was shocked that the uninvited guest knew my dad was dead. We'd only been back from the hospital for a couple of hours, and as far as I was aware, only the hospital staff, ourselves and Bernice knew that Dad hadn't made it. While I was trying to work out who the man was, two oversized goons followed him inside. I stood open-mouthed with the door latch still in my hand.

I wasn't sure who I'd been expecting to see when I opened

the door. My head had been spinning from listening to Mum and Daisy arguing about the address book, so I hadn't been thinking straight. I was usually a cautious person, but the sound of the knocking had been frantic. Urgent. I thought it was something important that warranted my immediate attention, so I didn't waste time checking to see who was on the other side before I released the lock. In a moment of madness, I'd kissed goodbye my instinct to be wary. I hoped I wouldn't live to regret that hasty decision.

'I see you've had a tidy-up since I was last here. Treated yourself to a new sofa. The other one had seen better days.' The big man laughed, sending a shiver running down my spine as he stood at the entrance of our living room looking around.

A chilling thought suddenly entered my head. Daisy had told me that Warren Jenkins had broken into the house and attacked Dad with a screwdriver. She hadn't mentioned where the assault had taken place, but I had a horrible feeling I'd worked it out. She'd said he still posed a massive threat to us and was bound to be sniffing around, waiting to see if Dad pulled through. My mum and sister had witnessed what he'd done. Was I staring Dad's murderer in the face? My blood ran cold.

'I haven't come here for a social visit, but I heard on the grapevine that Des had popped his clogs, so I thought I'd drop by,' he said.

His words made tears spring to my eyes. There was no easy way to acknowledge a relative's death, but what a horrible way to put it. It was as though Dad's life was worthless. As though his existence meant nothing. If I'd been a braver person, I'd have loved to call him out on what he'd said, but as I stood shaking in my shoes, the words died in my mouth before they'd even fully formed.

'I'm sure you've got a lot to organise, so I won't hold you up. I just wanted to clarify that Des's debt is still outstanding,' he said, fixing me with an intense glare as he stared into my soul. He paused just long enough to allow the contents of my stomach to flip. 'Now that he's not in a position to repay it himself, it passes to his next of kin. I'll give you some breathing space to arrange his send-off, but I'll be back next week to collect the first instalment.'

Silence hung heavy in the air between us. I could tell he was waiting for me to speak, but I couldn't think of a suitable response. We weren't in a position to pay off Dad's debt. Especially at this moment in time, but there was no point in telling him that. It wasn't what he wanted to hear. Judging by what he said next, he must have sensed what I was thinking.

'I appreciate you've got a lot to pay for at the moment. Coffins aren't cheap, so I'll ease you back into your payment plan. But I'm not running a charity, so don't take the fucking piss. I want a thousand pounds in cash to start with. Do I make myself clear?'

His words hit me like a dagger to my heart, making out he was being so reasonable, and yet I knew Dad had died at his hands.

I hadn't moved position since they'd barged into the house, but Warren suddenly paced up to me and jabbed his giant forefinger in my face. I jumped out of my skin before I started frantically nodding. Then he gestured behind him with a flick of his head to the two heavies filling the hallway, and the three of them filed outside.

As soon as I closed the front door, I turned the key to deadlock it. Then I grabbed hold of the banister to help support my weight. My legs had buckled. I thought I was going to keel over. My heart thundered against my ribcage. Pounded at a million miles an hour. Fear had me in its grip. I was so focused on calming my breathing as I battled to slow my racing pulse that I didn't hear Daisy come out of the kitchen.

'Are you OK?' she asked, her features set in an expression of concern.

What kind of a question was that? Of course I wasn't OK. I was petrified. Beside myself. Trembling from head to toe. Surely she could see that!

'What do you think?' I shouted.

'There's no need to bite my fucking head off,' Daisy shouted back.

'So nice of you to put in an appearance once the coast's clear. I can't believe you left me alone to deal with that maniac.' Now that I was out of danger, my fear had turned to fury.

'You had no business answering the door to him in the first place, so you've only got yourself to blame. It might have escaped your notice, but I didn't see Mum rushing out here either.' Daisy was fuming, too. It didn't take much to push her buttons.

How typical of my sister to try to deflect attention away from herself by throwing my mum under the bus. Don't get me wrong, I was annoyed with her, too. But Daisy never took responsibility for anything. She did whatever she wanted whenever she wanted and only ever looked out for number one.

'I don't know what you're making such a fuss about. Warren didn't harm a hair on your head, did he?' Daisy put her hands on her hips and glared at me.

So much for us having a fresh start. It didn't look as though the tension between us would ever ease.

'Maybe not, but he scared the shit out of me.'

'Why do you think we made ourselves scarce? The last time Mum and I were face to face with that lunatic, he was butchering Dad with a screwdriver.' Daisy threw me a black look.

A knot formed in the pit of my stomach. Even though I hadn't been there, I could picture the gruesome scene in my mind. I wanted to ask if Dad suffered or passed out quickly. I wanted to ask about the new sofa, but I wasn't sure I wanted to hear Daisy's response, so I kept the questions to myself and changed the subject.

'I take it you heard Warren say he'll be back to collect a thousand pounds next week.'

Daisy nodded.

'How are we meant to get hold of a thousand pounds by then?'

Daisy shrugged. Then she stepped past me and walked up the stairs without saying another word. It was almost as though she was washing her hands of the problem, but I couldn't deal with this on my own. We'd been left an equal share of the debt – the unlucky beneficiaries of a non-existent entry to Dad's will.

I was about to call after her to say as much, but I thought better of it. We'd only end up in a slanging match, and I didn't have the energy to deal with another argument, so instead, I peeled myself away from the stair post and walked into the kitchen to check on Mum.

When I stepped inside and saw her huddled on the floor under the table with her head bowed and her knees pulled up to her chest, my heart bled for her. I crouched down beside her and touched her arm. She flinched and whimpered when my fingers made contact with her skin. She hadn't looked up as I came into the room, so she didn't know who had touched her.

'It's OK, Mum. It's Lily. Warren's gone.'

Mum didn't reply, but she started sobbing. I threw my arms around her shoulders to comfort her. How could I be angry with her? She'd been through so much. She needed me to show her some compassion, not give her a hard time.

Daisy was unbelievable. She'd stormed off to her room like she was the wronged party and left me to pick up the pieces. I wasn't in the best place right now to cope with all of this. I was still trying to process having been kidnapped and almost raped on top of the death of my dad, without having to be strong for Mum, too. She was usually the backbone of the family, but she'd crumbled. I'd never seen her like this before. I was doing my best to prop her up, but my efforts seemed to be in vain. I wasn't sure I could reach her. She was lost in a pit of despair.

As I tried my best to comfort her, my thoughts drifted to Warren's visit. Where were we meant to get a thousand pounds from in such a short space of time? We were broke. We didn't have a bean. And now we had Dad's funeral to pay for on top of everything. Fear began swirling inside me. What the hell would happen to us if we didn't pay up? Would he start picking us off one by one?

10

DAISY

I had to get away from my mum and sister. The atmosphere inside the house was charged, so I was going to take refuge in my bedroom. Lily had a fucking cheek tearing into me like that. I got why she was angry, and I felt a slight pang of guilt for leaving her alone, which lasted less than thirty seconds before it evaporated into thin air. She had no idea what we'd been through, so she wasn't in a position to judge. Lily was the biggest coward of all of us, so if the tables were turned, there was no way she'd stick her neck out for me. I knew that for a fact.

I supposed it was a bit selfish of me to let her face Warren Jenkins alone, but the man scared the shit out of me, so wild horses wouldn't have dragged me away from the safety of the kitchen. I was still scarred from the first time I'd met him. I didn't fancy reacquainting myself with him ever again. And I wasn't the only one who'd shied away from providing backup. Mum had dived for cover and shot under the table the minute she'd heard Warren's voice. I didn't blame her. She knew first hand how violent he could be. A vision of him dragging Mum around our living room like a rag doll because he hadn't liked the way she'd looked at him before he'd butchered my dad with a screwdriver forced its way into my mind. Mum was a strong woman, so the thought of her cowering under the table didn't sit right with me. I would have tried to comfort her if I hadn't been so mad at her. The one good thing to come from Warren's visit was she'd forgotten all about her sacred address book.

All the same, I wasn't about to take any chances, so I took a photo of Collette Ahearn's details with my phone and then crept back down the stairs so that I could return the red embossed book to the windowsill. Lily's voice was soft and soothing as she spoke to Mum in the kitchen. I wondered if she'd managed to coax her out from under the table yet, but I didn't let my curiosity get the better of me. I couldn't face another round of arguing over nonsense. I'd had my fill for the day.

Mum had made it perfectly clear that she wanted to do the ringing around, so she could be my guest. I was only too happy to hand over the job. But there was one person I was going to make it my business to call – Auntie Colleen. I was desperate to know what had gone on between them. She'd stopped having contact with my family. With my mum. Her so-called best friend. That hadn't happened for no reason. A skeleton in the closet was about to come out of hiding. I was certain of it.

The suspense was killing me. It felt like an itch I couldn't scratch. The only way I'd get some relief was to reach out to Auntie Colleen. See if there was some substance behind my suspicions. My mum was never going to spill the beans. Auntie Colleen might be reluctant to shed any light on the matter, too. There was only one way I was going to find out.

I didn't want anyone unexpectedly bursting in on me, so I turned the key in the lock once I was back in my bedroom. Then I went over to the far side of the room. I didn't want Mum or Lily to overhear the conversation I was about to have. My fingers trembled as I punched the number into my phone. As it started to ring, my heartbeat sped up. I wasn't sure why I was so nervous. Whatever had happened between them had nothing to do with me. The phone had been ringing for what seemed like an eternity when it suddenly connected.

'Hello?' a woman said when she answered the call.

'Is that Colleen Ahearn?' I asked.

'Is this a sales call?' she replied.

'No, it's me, Auntie Colleen. Daisy, Daisy Kennedy. Des and Tara's daughter. Do you remember me? You used to be good friends with my mum and dad.'

Silence stretched out between us. Awkward. Uncomfortable. The only sound was the rhythmic pounding of my pulse in my ears. It was deafening as it punctuated the stillness. I wasn't sure what to make of the long pause. Waiting for a response was agony. Was she searching through the deepest recesses of her mind, trying to recall the people I'd just mentioned, or was there another reason she was staying quiet? Had my unexpected call rattled her? Either way, her lack of reply was puzzling. I was hoping she'd be delighted to hear from me. I had fond memories of her. She'd been a big part of my life when I was little.

'Are you still there?' I asked.

My question jolted a reaction from her. 'Yes, I'm still here. I'm sorry, I'm not trying to be rude, but I wasn't expecting to hear from you, so I feel a bit shell-shocked,' she admitted, which was perfectly understandable.

I felt my spirits lift. 'There's no need to apologise. It must be weird to suddenly hear from me after all these years.'

I should have realised calling out of the blue might not be the best way to go about things.

'To be perfectly honest, I nearly didn't pick up. I don't usually answer calls from numbers I don't recognise,' Auntie Colleen said.

'I'm sorry to phone you without warning, but I've got some bad news. I thought you'd want to know my dad passed away today...'

'Oh my God! I'm so sorry, Daisy. That's awful. What happened?'

Shit! I clearly hadn't thought this through. How could I answer that question? I wanted to believe Auntie Colleen was trustworthy, but I hadn't clapped eyes on the woman for over a decade, so I'd have to err on the side of caution and be economical with the details. Warren Jenkins wasn't a man I wanted to upset, so I'd leave his name out of the frame.

'Dad had meningitis. Unfortunately, he developed blood clots as a complication, which led to a massive stroke...'

My head had been spinning when the doctor explained what caused Dad's death, but I tried to relay what I could remember in simple terms. The last part of the story was true. I'd just left out the brutal attack he'd suffered at the hands of Warren, which had caused him to contract meningitis in the first place. I felt uneasy. I hoped she wouldn't realise I was hiding something. I wasn't very good at keeping things to myself. Auntie Colleen had no reason to question my account. It was a well-known fact that people died from meningitis. And that was ultimately what would be on Dad's death certificate, so I had nothing to feel guilty about.

'Aww, Daisy, I don't know what to say. Words can't describe how gutted I am to hear about your dad. I'm so sorry, sweetie.'

'Thank you.'

Auntie Colleen seemed genuinely upset, which made me wonder even more why my mum had thrown away a lifelong friendship as though it was nothing. When she realised Dad was dead, her tone instantly changed. At first, she'd been guarded. Suspicious. But her walls had come tumbling down, just like that, as she sent a wave of sympathy crashing towards me. I let it wash over me. Took a moment to enjoy the relief that the initial frostiness had thawed. I was hopeful that in time, I could rebuild a relationship with her. She'd been an integral part of my early life.

'I have to say I'm shocked to hear from you after all this time. But I'm glad you phoned. Does your mum know you called me?' Auntie Colleen asked.

I could sense there was so much more to unearth if I dug beneath the surface. But I had to play it cool. I didn't want to frighten her off, or I'd never get to the bottom of the mystery. I only had a split second to decide, or I'd give the game away, so I followed the same path and bent the facts.

'No.'

I'd told Mum I was going to phone Auntie Colleen before she went ballistic. She didn't know I'd gone through with it, so technically, I wasn't lying.

'I didn't think so,' Auntie Colleen replied.

'It would be great to see you again. Do you fancy going for a coffee sometime? I'd love to catch up and find out what you've been up to. Hear all your news,' I said.

I didn't bother adding, *and I'm a great listener if you feel like unburdening yourself by sharing all the sordid details of what happened between you and my mum all those years ago.*

'I'd love that! Are you free tomorrow?' Auntie Colleen asked, and my heart almost leapt out of my chest.

11

SAMSON

Saturday 10 January

'Aggh! Watch what you're fucking doing, will you? You should have been a butcher, not a doctor,' I bellowed into my private physician's lug hole.

Anyone would think the guy didn't like me the way he was manhandling me. He was scrubbing my wounds with that orange disinfectant stuff, which looked and smelled like the old-fashioned creosote my old man used to paint the fences with. It had better not stain my skin and designer clobber, or there'd be hell to pay.

'Don't be such a big baby, Mr Fox,' the quack said, glaring at me through his Joe 90 specs. 'Believe me, you'll be sorry if you end up with an infection. Foul-smelling pus is one thing, but sepsis can kill.'

With the doc's warning ringing in my ears, I gritted my teeth and let him get back to work, rooting around the gaping hole in my arse cheek with his cotton wool pad. I wanted to headbutt the fucker. The pain was unbearable. I had to grip onto the side of the couch to stop myself from lashing out at him.

'Your wounds are healing nicely,' the quack said when he finally stopped violating me. 'Full Metal Jackets are not designed to stop inside their targets. As you well know, they have enough velocity to injure or kill more than one person. It's not always the bullet that kills you but the damage it causes. You should count your lucky stars the cartridge hit you in the stomach and passed through you without damaging any of your major organs.'

That was easy for him to say, but he wasn't the one with a hole the size of China in his arse. Every movement was excruciating, and trying to get comfortable wasn't getting any easier. My balls were the size of melons, but a shag was out of the question right now. And yet the wanker who was bleeding me dry with his ongoing house calls thought I was lucky. You couldn't make this shit up. The doctor was the one who should be counting his lucky stars. He'd have been on the receiving end of my temper if I hadn't needed his services. Who the fuck did he think he was calling me a big baby? Once I was in the clear, he would pay for that remark.

I'd have to get the quack to give me some strong meds to numb the pain so that the drive to Kent was bearable. I hadn't intended to leave the confines of my mansion yet, but in light of recent developments, there was a very good chance I could finish Bernice and MacKenzie off at the same time, so I needed to strike while the iron was hot. I didn't want to give them time to regroup and come up with a plan. Bernice would still be gloating, thinking she'd got one over on me. She'd be smiling from ear to ear like the fucking Joker. I wanted to catch her off guard while she was revelling in the glow of revenge.

Bernice thought she'd wiped me out. She thought she'd outwitted me. That would have gone to her head. She'd let her guard down now there wasn't a threat looming over her. She was about to learn the hard way that she wasn't as clever as she thought she was. If Bernice had half a brain, she'd be dangerous. But she was just a slut on legs, and an old clapped-out one at that. She looked ridiculous, strutting around in her skin-tight clothes and skyscraper heels. I couldn't wait to dole out the punishment she deserved for the agony she'd caused me.

12

MACKENZIE

I hadn't ventured outside my flat since I'd made it home. I'd been so exhausted I literally dropped into my bed and slept for sixteen hours straight. I was disorientated when I woke up at eleven-thirty last night. I sat up in a panic. My eyes scanned the room. It took me several seconds to register where I was as it was pitch black.

As the fear drained from my body, I reached for the bedside lamp, but my fingers froze on the switch. I decided against turning it on. I'd have to live like they did in the blitz and not use any lights. Adopt a self-imposed blackout for my own safety. Who knew if Samson was watching my property? If he had eyes on it, I didn't want to give myself away. If the place was in complete darkness, hopefully he'd assume nobody was home and that I was lying low elsewhere.

I was taking a huge risk coming here. It was an obvious thing to do, but it was the closest place I could bolt to. I was glad I'd installed a key safe. At least I was able to let myself in without bothering my mum for her key. The last thing I needed was for her to start asking awkward questions. I didn't want to concern her. She was a natural-born worrier and would be beside herself if she knew what was happening.

I didn't want to be a sitting duck. As soon as I was in better shape, I'd take myself somewhere further afield, but in the meantime, my flat was as good a place as any to hide out. I had a freezer full of food and plenty of booze and drugs in the cupboards, so I'd be pretty content while I recuperated. I had a feeling I had a long journey ahead of me. I was drained. I'd never known tiredness like it. But I'd been through the wars and had the battle scars to prove it. My body needed time to heal. I was scared to look at my balls. I knew they were covered in burns from the electrodes Samson had tortured me with. He was a sick bastard. There was no denying that. The saying 'what doesn't kill you makes you stronger' sprang to mind!

It was barely eleven o'clock, but I desperately needed a drink and a few lines of rocket fuel. I was in agony. With any luck, it would dull the pain and take my mind off the throbbing in my bollocks. It was excruciating. Every movement sent waves of agony crashing through my body. I felt like someone had taken a branding iron to my balls. Anything that touched the wounds made me double over. There was only one thing for it – my jeans and boxers had to come off. I needed to let everything hang free.

I hoovered up two lines of coke and then poured a hefty measure of Kraken into a glass. I downed most of it before I plucked up the courage to look below my waist. When I did, I sucked in a loud breath. It was like something out of a horror film. My dick had turned black, and my nuts were like two uncooked meatballs. Large sections of skin had peeled away from them. I thought I was going to puke when I saw the raw flesh. It made me shudder. My inner thighs were bright red, too, and covered in blisters.

I hoped I wasn't going to be scarred for life. But injuries as severe as these were bound to leave their mark. I'd been hoping to rekindle my romance with Daisy, but she'd run a mile if she saw the state of my tackle right now. I was struggling to come to terms with how it looked, too. The black prick and blood-red goolies weren't going to be a turn-on. They'd give her nightmares, that was a certainty. I gulped back the rest of the spiced rum in the glass and poured myself another. My nerves were jangling.

I felt weak from the pain, so I didn't want to move around unnecessarily. Everything I needed was in the kitchen: food, booze and drugs; all of them were within easy reach, so I eased myself onto one of the metal-framed chairs, gritting my teeth as I did. The padded fake leather seat was surprisingly soothing on my nether regions, cooling the painful burns.

I pulled open the drawer behind me and took out an old handset I'd used during my street dealing days. It hadn't seen the light of day for years, so I wasn't sure whether it still worked. Using the table as support, I hoisted myself back onto my feet and rummaged around until I found the cable. I connected it to the base and plugged it in at the wall. Time would tell if the old relic had life in it.

I was fucked without a phone. I couldn't reach anyone. They couldn't contact me either, but I didn't want to go out to buy a new one in case I got spotted. And I couldn't risk having one delivered. An Amazon package being pushed through my letterbox would be a dead giveaway. I knew my old boss was baying for my blood, but I wasn't going to make this easy for him.

I parked my arse back on the kitchen chair. As I waited to see if my old mobile would charge, my thoughts turned to Daisy. I was desperate to contact her, but I didn't know her number off the top of my head, so even if I could get the phone working, I'd be no better off. I wondered if she'd left me any messages. If she had, she'd be calling me every name under the sun for not getting back to her.

Daisy hadn't been impressed when I'd dropped off the radar before. She'd thought I was blanking her. But I never disappeared without good reason. Sometimes, it was a case of self-preservation. When the going got tough, it was every man for himself. I didn't mean that literally. I hoped Bernice didn't think I'd deserted Roscoe in his hour of need.

Time was virtually standing still while I stayed in the flat, feeling sorry for myself. Sitting alone, staring at the four walls, was doing my nut in. As soon as I felt strong enough to travel, I'd head down to the Old Mill House and pay Bernice and Daisy an unexpected visit. I hadn't even been able to offer Bernice my condolences yet. I'd be gutted if she thought badly of me for not getting in touch before now.

Samson had got the wrong end of the stick, thinking my old boss, Roscoe Allen, had intercepted his long-awaited shipment of cocaine. Roscoe had paid the ultimate price for Samson's mistake. Even if he had nicked Samson's gear, he wouldn't have been stupid enough to try and flog it on home turf. Carly Andrews was responsible for that suicidal move. She used to be a barmaid at The Castle, but pedalled drugs as a side hustle. She'd told me she was under strict instructions by the guy she was working for to sell the stolen coke cheap and flood the market. I wouldn't have wanted to be in her shoes when Samson worked out the connection. I felt bad that I couldn't warn her, but I was in shit up to my neck. I needed to concentrate on saving my own sorry arse.

A feeling of dread started welling up inside me. Samson had told me he'd go after Daisy. He wasn't impressed that I'd helped myself to the cash in his safe, and he'd intended to kill her to teach me a lesson. She'd only escaped being snatched because Gary ballsed up and he'd accidentally taken Lily instead – the perils of being an identical twin. He'd threatened to rectify Gary's cock-up even though neither of the girls should have been caught up in any of this. They were both innocent parties. But Samson didn't give a shit about that. He wanted revenge, and he didn't care how he got it. I'd never forgive myself if Daisy was hurt because of me.

I couldn't just sit here doing nothing. Now that the rocket fuel had kicked in, I was beginning to feel half normal. I could hear Kent calling me loud and clear. I couldn't resist the pull. I had to find Daisy and make sure she was OK. I was only a couple of hours away from Dover. If I could grin and bear the drive down, I'd be in a far better position than staying holed up in the flat anyway. Samson's place was too close for comfort.

I dragged myself to a standing position and glanced at the phone. It was 80 per cent charged. Hallelujah! There was a God! But I didn't have time to revel in this moment of good fortune, so I unplugged it, then inched my way into the bedroom and put on the loosest set of joggers I owned. I'd have to go commando. I couldn't bear the thought of a set of boxers rubbing my bare flesh.

I stared at my reflection in the full-length mirror. I wasn't exactly a sight for sore eyes. My skin was grey, and I looked haggard. Nobody would guess I'd had sixteen hours of sleep. I looked like I'd been up all night. I was probably dehydrated. I'd had barely anything to drink and no solid food in a couple of days, but I didn't feel hungry. The pain must have been affecting my appetite.

I briefly considered having a quick shower to freshen myself up but dismissed the idea. I usually loved the feeling of hot water on my skin, but in my current predicament, it would take my agony to another level, so I reached onto the windowsill, picked up my trusty can of Lynx Africa and gave myself a liberal dousing of the stuff, almost choking myself in the process when the fumes went down the wrong way. Then I forced my legs to carry me to the bathroom to give my teeth a good scrubbing. I smoothed down my wayward brown hair with my good hand before rechecking my appearance. I wasn't looking my best, but I wanted to get onto the road before the rocket fuel wore off.

It probably wasn't the brightest idea to drive while under the influence of drink and drugs, but it wasn't as though I hadn't done it before, and I didn't have another option. There was no way I could take the train. Being on public transport would leave me exposed. I'd feel safer travelling under my own steam.

13

DAISY

I lay in my bed staring at the ceiling, lost in a cloud of apprehension. I'd arranged to meet Auntie Colleen this afternoon in a cafe so that we could talk without fear of anybody eavesdropping. But I felt uneasy about going behind my mum's back even though we weren't on good terms at the moment. The move seemed sketchy. Dishonest. Was I doing the right thing?

After I'd spoken to Auntie Colleen, my immediate thought was to pick up the phone and call Bernice. Fill her in on everything that had gone on since we'd left the hospital, but I didn't want to burden her with all of my problems. She had enough of her own to deal with without me piling more stress onto her shoulders. She'd only recently lost her husband and soulmate, Roscoe. Her world had been blown apart.

I felt guilty that I hadn't been checking in on her, but I was no good at hiding things, so if I phoned to ask her how she was getting on and she said the same back, I'd never be able to keep all of this to myself. I had verbal diarrhoea when it came to things like this. I was too easy to read. Even if we weren't face to face, Bernice would know instantly that I was hiding something.

Bad as I felt not checking in on her after she'd been so good to me, I'd have to wait until after I'd met Auntie Colleen.

I couldn't explain why, but I'd felt compelled to reach out to my mum's estranged best friend. She was the closest thing I had to family now that Mum and Lily had cut me adrift. I'd unintentionally alienated them, so they'd formed their own little pack and there was only room for two members. I was an outcast. It was as though I'd been orphaned overnight. I needed some stability in my life. Losing a parent when you were twenty-three was tough, and I was struggling to process the enormity of facing the future alone.

Loyalty meant everything. But Mum and Lily didn't deserve mine after the way they'd treated me. Shunning me at a time like this when we should all be sticking together hurt like hell. I couldn't wait to hear what Auntie Colleen had to say. Mum's ears would be burning, no doubt. Tough shit! I wasn't going to feel guilty about that. It was payback for the way she was treating me. Lily was her shining star and she didn't have the capacity to love more than one child. But she had two daughters. A fact she seemed to have conveniently forgotten.

14

MACKENZIE

The whole time I was in the car, I couldn't get Daisy out of my head. All manner of different scenarios shuttered through my mind. My brain was scrambled, but there was no point in thinking the worst. It wasn't going to help matters. Bernice was looking out for Daisy, so I knew she was in good hands. Staying positive was the way forward. Going into panic mode wasn't the way I rolled.

I made it to Dover in good time, having just about survived the long car journey from Camberwell. My crotch felt like it was on fire. Every time I moved, pain raced around my body. But I was here now, so at least I could stretch my legs and take the pressure off my tender inner thighs. I scanned the car park of the Old Mill House, but there was no sign of Bernice's distinctive cherry-red Jag.

I hadn't driven all this way to have a wasted journey, so I crossed the block-paved parking area and climbed the two flights of steps with the speed of a geriatric tortoise, keeping my legs splayed as I walked to avoid any unnecessary chafing. Eat your heart out, John Wayne! I paused outside the front door for a few seconds to give myself time to paste a smile on my face just in case Daisy or Bernice were inside. Then I buzzed the apartment intercom. When there was no response, I placed my ear to the door and listened. There wasn't a sound coming from the other side. The thought of hobbling back to my car filled me with dread, but it had to be done. I'd have to grit my teeth and think of England.

A short while later, I pulled up outside Roscoe's pub, The Castle. I hobbled towards the door, and when I pushed it open, I saw Bernice standing behind the bar in all her glory. I started grinning like the village idiot. She was a sight for sore eyes wearing one of her trademark black skintight outfits with her long dark brown ponytail hanging over one shoulder. As I walked up to the counter, our eyes met, and Bernice's glossy red lips stretched into a wide smile.

'Oh my God, you're alive!' Bernice said.

She hurried out the door at the back of the bar and rushed over to me with her arms outstretched.

'Yep, I'm still just about breathing.' I laughed as Bernice pulled me into a tight embrace. I coughed as I inhaled a lungful of the cloud of perfume surrounding her.

'I've been so worried about you, darling. I thought Samson had done away with you,' Bernice replied, giving me one last squeeze before she released me from her grip.

'He tried. I'm so sorry about Roscoe.' As I offered my condolences, I caught hold of Bernice's manicured hand.

Tears sprung to her blue eyes, but she somehow managed to hold them in.

'Thank you. I'm still trying to get my head around it. So you know he's dead?' Bernice quizzed, pulling her hand away from mine before crossing her arms over her ample chest.

I nodded. 'I was with him...'

I wasn't going to go into the gory details of how Samson ended Roscoe's life to spare Bernice the horror, but also because I didn't want to have to relive the terrifying ordeal. Watching Roscoe's body contort while Samson pumped him full of bullets would haunt me until my dying day.

Bernice's eyes grew wide. I silently prayed that she wouldn't ask me to tell her what had happened. It would break her heart to know that Roscoe was terrified and in agony when he took his last breath. But at least he wasn't alone.

'I wondered if you were in the car with him. You're lucky you weren't killed, too.' Bernice gave me a weak smile.

A wave of guilt washed over me, so I cast my eyes to the floor. But I knew Bernice wasn't trying to make me feel bad. She seemed genuinely delighted to see me. I didn't tell her the only reason I'd walked away was because Samson had other plans for me.

'I wasn't trying to make you feel awkward, darling,' Bernice said. When I glanced up, she was staring at me with a concerned look on her face. 'I'm just pleased somebody was with Roscoe in his final moments. I was worried he was on his own.'

I was glad Bernice had taken some comfort from knowing I was there. But the whole conversation was making me feel edgy. I didn't like hiding things from her, but there was no way I wanted to get onto the subject of Samson's dungeon. Discussing the sorry state of my tackle with her would be mortifying. The less people who knew about my electrified bollocks, the better. I was crossing my fingers that Bernice didn't start grilling me on the ins and outs of her husband's execution or where I'd disappeared to afterward.

'What happened to your hand? Samson, I bet?'

'It's a long story...'

And one I wasn't prepared to get into, so I started gearing up to ask her if Daisy was OK when she dropped a bombshell.

'As you can imagine, I was beside myself with grief when the police told me Roscoe had been murdered, so I went over to Samson's house and shot him and Gary dead,' Bernice casually dropped in.

'Fuck!' was the only word I managed to say.

'Daisy tried to talk me out of it, but I wouldn't listen. Samson had to pay for what he'd done. An eye for an eye and all that. I was worried I might lose my nerve if I gave things time to sink in, so I decided to seize the moment,' Bernice said.

'Fair play to you. You must have nerves of steel,' I replied.

'I was shitting myself. I hadn't intended to shoot them with the same bullet. I was aiming for Samson, but Gary leapt in front of him, and they both went down like sacks of shit.' Bernice laughed.

'Are you sure they're dead?' I asked, trying to keep a lid on my delight. That would explain why Samson hadn't finished me off.

Bernice nodded. 'I'm sure. My gun was loaded with Full Metal Jackets that could fell a rhino.'

'Well done, you. That's fantastic news!' I grinned. At least I only had one gangster after me now. Things were starting to look up, so I took the plunge and asked the all-important question that had been on the tip of my tongue since I'd arrived. 'How's Daisy doing?'

Bernice's face dropped, and she shook her head. My heart began thundering in my chest, so I had to force myself to stay calm.

'She's not great as it happens…' Bernice paused for what seemed like an endless moment. 'Her dad died.'

I breathed a sigh of relief before my mood took a nosedive.

Not because I was devastated by the news. I wasn't Des's biggest fan. The guy was an arsehole if you asked me, but that was beside the point. He was Daisy's dad, and she was only twenty-three. That was too young to lose a parent – even a useless one.

'Oh, shit! When did that happen?' I asked.

'Yesterday afternoon.'

'Is she back in London with her mum?'

'Yes, and Lily.'

'Lily?'

'I'm so sorry, darling, I forgot you didn't know. Daisy and I found where Samson was holding her, and we broke her out on Tuesday.'

My head was spinning there was so much to take in.

'Jesus. Why didn't you wait for backup?'

'There wasn't time. I didn't mention it to Roscoe because I knew he'd tell me not to go without him.'

I didn't know exactly when Bernice and Daisy sprung Lily, but Roscoe probably wasn't in a position to help anyway. Samson had made sure of that.

'Is Lily OK? Did they hurt her?'

Being kidnapped would be a horrendous ordeal for anyone, but Lily was a highly strung sensitive soul, so I couldn't imagine she'd have coped with the situation well. And Samson was an animal. He took immense pleasure from other people's pain. The fact that Lily was a woman would change nothing. He was all for equality when it came to dishing out punishment.

'Not in the physical sense, but she's very shaken up,' Bernice replied.

After what I'd just been through, it surprised me to hear that Lily was unharmed. Maybe Samson was mellowing with age. Or maybe Lily hadn't told Bernice what they'd done to her out of embarrassment. I could sympathise with that. I wouldn't be sharing the details of my torture with anyone. I hoped she hadn't been sexually assaulted, but something told me there was a good chance she had. Samson treated women like commodities. Forcing Lily to do something against her will would be the ultimate power game. Right up his street. He loved flexing his muscles.

'Lily's bound to be rattled, but at least they didn't hurt her,' I said, even though I wasn't convinced that was the case.

'I suppose we should be thankful for small mercies. The poor girl was absolutely terrified. They had her handcuffed and chained to a ring on the wall. It's going to take her a long time to get over what she's been through, but she's doing as well as can be expected.'

Bernice gave me a small smile to mask her concern, so I didn't like to say that Lily might never come to terms with what happened because I didn't want to worry her further.

'I was beginning to think we'd never track her down. How did you find her?'

'I saw a new development of warehouses being advertised on an estate agent's website. The interiors looked exactly like the ones in the videos you were sent,' Bernice replied.

'Blimey. You did well to spot that!'

I'd spent ages surfing the net, and I'd come up with nothing. Trying to find where Lily was being held was like looking for a needle in a haystack.

'I know. I couldn't believe my luck. I spotted it on Monday night, but by the time I phoned, the place was closed. The guy called me back on Tuesday morning and said all the units were empty except one, so I had a really good feeling about it.'

Bernice looked so happy, but she wouldn't be smiling if she thought more deeply about this. If she'd called Roscoe when she'd found the listing on Monday, he'd have travelled back to

London straight away. So he wouldn't have been in Kent when Samson had gone on the warpath on Tuesday. I decided to keep that to myself, though. It was clear she hadn't given the timeline for Roscoe's execution much thought. Highlighting it would only distress her, and it wouldn't change the outcome. My heart sank. Why the fuck hadn't she just phoned Roscoe?

'I was desperate to take a closer look, but you know what estate agents are like; they're so pushy. The guy was trying to pin me down to do a viewing, so I told him I wanted to see the location before I went any further. Thankfully, he gave me the address. Daisy and I went to check it out, and when we got there, the car she'd seen Lily being bundled into was parked outside. It was clear we were at the right place, so we waited for it to get dark, and then we took them by surprise.'

I was shocked Bernice had done something so reckless. Roscoe wouldn't have been happy that she'd put herself, Daisy and Lily in danger. She was lucky her plan hadn't backfired.

'Was Samson inside?'

'No, but he'd left two of his guys guarding Lily. They weren't going to let her go, so I had to shoot the pair of them.'

My guts rumbled. This was starting to make sense. When I was in Samson's dungeon, he'd been rambling on about us killing two of his men and taking his hostage. At the time, I'd thought, what men? What hostage? Samson clearly hadn't known Bernice was responsible for bumping off his men and taking Lily. He'd accused me and Roscoe of doing the deed. When I wouldn't confess to my involvement, he'd tortured me. But Roscoe had paid the ultimate price.

I felt like I was about to spew and I needed some air. I had to put some space between us. Bernice thought she'd done something good by freeing Lily, but the way she'd gone about it had caused a whole heap of trouble for me and had cost Roscoe his life. My pulse was pounding in my ears.

'Is everything all right, darling?' The sound of Bernice's voice broke my train of thought. 'You've gone very pale,' she continued.

That didn't surprise me.

'I'm not feeling well. I think I need to step outside...'

Even though I was desperate to cut and run, I couldn't leave without giving her my number. I owed it to Roscoe to look out for her, but I was secretly hoping our paths wouldn't cross anytime soon.

'Do me a favour. Stick your number in my phone, will you?' I asked as I handed it to her.

'What happened to your mobile? Did you lose it?' Bernice's heavily made-up eyes searched my face.

'It's a long story. I'll tell you another time,' I replied, gripping the side of the bar to steady myself.

Bernice did as I'd asked, eyeing me suspiciously as she keyed her number into my contacts list.

'I hope you feel better soon,' she said as she handed me back the phone.

'Thanks,' I replied.

Then I turned on my heel and attempted to walk out of The Castle without drawing attention to myself.

15

SAMSON

I was in a foul mood, so nothing could stop the murderous thoughts from rattling around in my brain as I made the uncomfortable drive to Dover. I couldn't get there soon enough for my liking. I tried to prop myself up onto one of my arse cheeks to relieve the pressure on my wound, but I'd been stuck in the car for hours now, so there was no relieving the pain.

I'd got caught in roadworks the minute I turned out of my drive and now the traffic on the A2 was bumper to bumper. One lane was coned off, but there was no sign of any work going on. Typical National Highways bollocks, digging up anything and everything just to inconvenience the general public whether the improvements were necessary or not.

Even when I wasn't in pain, I had no patience behind the wheel. I liked to get from A to B as quickly as possible. Cutting up other motorists and lane hopping was my speciality, but doing some of my usual dangerous manoeuvres was a pipe dream at the moment. This was going to be the journey from hell. My temper was simmering under the surface. I had to vent my frustration somehow. I was bored of sticking my hand on the horn and leaving it there. It wasn't making the tailback move any quicker, so I'd progressed to yelling verbal insults and giving obscene hand gestures to anyone I could make eye contact with to try and pass the time. Engaging in a spot of road rage was the only thing keeping my mind off the past few days. But even hurling abuse at all and sundry had its limitations.

It didn't matter how hard I tried, I couldn't seem to stop my mind drifting back to Tuesday. I'd nearly blown a gasket when I'd learned my coke was doing the rounds in Dover, right in the middle of my old rival, Roscoe Allen's patch. Did he really think I wouldn't put two and two together and find him guilty without giving it a second thought?

But what pushed me over the edge was when I'd discover that two of my men, Smithy and Tank, were lying dead in the warehouse where I'd been holding Lily, and some interfering arsehole had freed her. I was fuming. My blood was boiling. Roscoe and I had been enemies for donkey's years. The red mist had descended and I was ready to settle the score.

After Kyle had tipped me off that Carly was the one shifting my gear, I'd set out to deal with her before she sold off all my consignment at a rock-bottom price. I'd turned up at the hostel, ready to confront her, and spotted Roscoe and MacKenzie sitting in Roscoe's Jag across the road from the shithole where she was living, and the plan changed.

Roscoe's day of reckoning had been a long time coming, so I took him out of the equation at the scene and sent him to meet his maker with a body resembling a sieve. One carefully aimed bullet would have done the trick, but where was the fun in that? I'd given MacKenzie a front-row seat at his boss's elimination so that he'd know exactly what was in store for him.

It was a sad fact, but you couldn't get the staff these days. When I first started out, my guys would lay their lives on the line for me. Credit where credit was due. Gary stepped up to the plate and took a bullet for me. But that was why he was on the payroll. It was part of the job description. And he'd fucked up more times than I cared to remember, so it was about time he did something right.

MacKenzie Cartwright used to be the manager and in-house dealer at Eden's nightclub before he'd done a runner after helping himself to the contents of my safe. What a fucking liberty! The treacherous bastard would be wishing he hadn't switched sides. As if I was going to tolerate him working for a rival. He thought he'd got the upper hand, but I'd had a special treat in store for him. I'd wanted him to die begging for mercy, which I'd had no intention of showing.

The wanker had caused me no end of grief, so it had given me great pleasure to watch him writhing in agony. But somehow the little scrote had survived having an electric current passed repeatedly through his bollocks, which was a mystery to me. His nuts must be made of cast iron.

It cut me to the quick to know MacKenzie had slipped out of my grasp again. How the fuck had he outsmarted me? I couldn't allow that to happen. He'd get too big for his boots. Get ideas above his station. He was a half-wit. An imbecile. I was the one in the power seat. That lesson needed to be brought home loud and clear.

Bernice was already on my radar for using me as target practice, but if she was harbouring the scrawny little runt, she'd be wishing she'd never crossed paths with me.

Bernice had an inflated opinion of how tough she was. She thought she could match me. Stupid bitch. I despised that woman with every breath in my body. I couldn't wait to finish her off. Three of my guys had been snuffed out because of the Allens. It had been a devastating blow to my team and one I wouldn't take lightly. Heads would roll for this. And two heads were better than one.

16

MACKENZIE

It had taken every ounce of strength I had to make it to the car, so I breathed a sigh of relief when I finally eased myself into the driver's seat. As I started the engine, a pang of guilt stabbed me in the gut. I felt bad that I'd lied to her, but my loyalty lay first and foremost with Roscoe. I couldn't bear to think he might have died in vain.

After a quick top-up of rocket fuel to numb the pain, I hit the road. I wanted to get as far away from Dover as humanly possible. The Castle held too many memories of my old boss. I'd wanted to pay my respects, but now I felt worse than before. I shouldn't have come. It was too soon. Roscoe's loss was too fresh.

I'd been on the road for less than ten minutes when my eyes were drawn to the opposite carriageway. I hadn't been giving the road my full attention, so I couldn't be 100 per cent sure, but I was almost certain Samson's Range Rover had just passed me, heading towards Dover. It was a very distinctive car; the black alloy wheels with red brake callipers were an unusual feature. But Bernice had told me she'd killed him, so it couldn't have been him behind the wheel, could it? It must have been a coincidence. Right? Maybe, but I didn't believe in coincidences. It would be easier to convince me that dark forces were at work. Samson was alive. I was sure of that.

'For fuck's sake!' I shouted at the top of my voice, slamming my good hand on the steering wheel. Even though she wasn't my favourite person right now, I'd never forgive myself if something happened to Bernice. I'd have to swallow down the bad feelings I was harbouring. Two wrongs didn't make a right.

Bernice had adored Roscoe, so there was no way she would have knowingly played a hand in his death. It was stupid of me to think that. There was no point in dwelling on the circumstances. Samson had been gunning for him, so logic told me if he hadn't murdered him when he had, it would have been in the not-too-distant future. Roscoe might not be with us any more, but that didn't stop me from wanting to make him proud. I wouldn't let him down.

My head was scrambled. I didn't know what to do for the best. I was in no condition to do much to help Bernice. Even if I turned the car around, Samson had a head start on me. He'd reach her before I did. Hesitation could get a person killed. It had only taken a matter of seconds for him to pump Roscoe full of bullets. When he caught up with Bernice, he'd kill her too. She was likely to be dead by the time I arrived. I had to warn her. I found her number in my contacts list and hit dial.

'Bernice, it's me,' I said when she eventually picked up.

'Hello, darling, I wasn't expecting to hear from you so soon. Are you feeling better now?'

I left her question unanswered. I didn't have time to make polite conversation.

'I've got some bad news. Samson isn't dead. I've just passed him on the road and he's heading your way. Get out of the pub right now. He's only five minutes away...'

'Oh my God! When I saw Samson and Gary drop from one bullet, I should have known it was too good to be true.'

I could hear the fear in Bernice's voice. She had good reason to be scared. Samson preyed on the weak and ate the vulnerable for breakfast.

'Have you got somewhere safe you can go?'

Bernice paused for a second before she replied. 'I'll head to the farmhouse. He won't find me there. It's in the middle of nowhere.'

'Are you sure Samson doesn't know about the property?'

'Yes. We only bought it recently. I stayed there with Daisy and Lily until Des took a turn for the worse, and we had no issues. It's in a very secluded spot. You can't see the house from the road. It's surrounded by that much land,' Bernice said.

I couldn't lie. That sounded like the perfect place to lay low.

'Great. I'll meet you there.'

My earlier hostility was forgotten. I couldn't desert Bernice in her hour of need.

'Thanks, darling. I'll text you the address.'

'OK, but get on the road first. You're running out of time.'

A layby was up ahead, so I pulled the car over and waited. When the message came through, I stuck the postcode into Waze. I was pleased to see the address was a fair distance from here. The app predicted a twenty-five-minute drive for Bernice along the A20, which was a total blessing as she'd be hugging the coast at the start of her journey and driving in the opposite direction to the way Samson was travelling. My journey was about the same length. I didn't need to turn around. I could stay on the A2 and then take a left turn onto Swanton Lane. With any luck, we'd arrive around the same time.

17

SAMSON

I slammed on the brakes of my Range Rover outside the shabby exterior of The Castle and shut off the engine, then ran my fingertips over the Glock nestled in the waistband of my suit trousers. My lips parted into a smile. Sending Bernice off to meet her husband would give me immense pleasure. They'd be able to hold a double funeral at this rate, I thought as I grinned from ear to ear. With any luck, MacKenzie would also be in there. Two for the price of one.

I flung open the door and eased myself off the driver's seat, then paced towards the front door. Adrenaline had chased the pain away, so I was able to move swiftly. The element of surprise didn't have the same effect if executed slowly. Speed was of the essence. If Bernice or MacKenzie had seen my car pull up, I didn't want to give them time to scarper.

I shoved the wooden door with the palm of my hand. To my surprise, it didn't budge. So I barged it with my shoulder to double-check that the decrepit weather-worn entrance wasn't just stiff and swollen from the sea air, but it didn't move an inch. I peered through the grimy stained-glass panel to check for movement inside. The place was in darkness. What kind of a boozer was closed on a Saturday afternoon? A shit one like this, I reasoned. The first stage of my plan wasn't working out as expected, and I felt my blood pressure soar.

Powered by my volcanic temper, I hoofed it along the narrow, litter-strewn passageway at the side of the building, which led to the pub's emergency exit. When I reached it, I swung my leg back and booted the door with my foot. The force sent shock waves straight to my injured arse cheek. Pain ripped through me, which heightened my foul mood. The doors were locked too, but now I was really riled up, so I smashed the large single-glazed floor-to-ceiling panel at the side of one of the doors with the butt of my Glock. Once I'd made a large enough hole, I stepped inside.

With a fresh burst of adrenaline coursing around my body, I tore through the deserted pub, taking out my rage on the tables and chairs. When I got behind the bar, I smashed the bottles and glasses within easy reach and then turned on the taps of the beer kegs. I was determined to make as much mess as possible. I made light work of tearing down the fishing nets and lobster pots decorating the beams before turning my attention to all the crappy seaside memorabilia dotted about.

I was doing everybody a favour by going to work on the place. Captain Pugwash's watering hole was an eyesore and long overdue a refurb. I'd broken into a sweat by the time I'd finished, so I grabbed one of the last remaining pint glasses that hadn't been shattered and ran it under the free-flowing golden stream of Stella. After I downed the contents of the glass, I pulled a face. Even the beer tasted bad in this shithole. I should have guessed as much.

The drawer to the till was open, so I cleaned out the small amount of float inside it. The couple of hundred quid barely covered my petrol, but I helped myself to it all the same. That was when I noticed the box of matches sitting next to a lantern on the front of the bar. An idea sparked in my head. Sometimes, the best plans come to you on the fly. I was impulsive by nature, so I wouldn't fight the urge to torch the place. It wasn't what I'd set out to do, but it would bring me a huge amount of satisfaction knowing how much distress it would cause Roscoe's whore.

I picked up the box and struck the match against the side. The naked flame held me in its spell for several seconds before I paced across the dingy, dark wood floorboards and set fire to a set of heavy, red velvet curtains hanging at the window at the front of the pub. They went up in an instant, which brought a smile to my face. So I repeated the process on the other sets framing the windows on either side of the bar. The wooden whisky barrels they used as tables and chairs contained so much ingrained booze that they acted like firelighters. Pretty soon, the whole place was ablaze.

Tempting as it was to hang around and watch the dump burn to the ground, there was no point. If the emergency services arrived, I didn't want to be on the scene. It was highly likely that some do-gooder would take it upon themselves to alert the fire brigade to the burning building. The sweet taste of revenge would quickly sour if I was linked to the crime and ended up in the clink. My job here was done.

Bernice and MacKenzie would live to see another day. They might think they'd got the upper hand by making themselves scarce, but when they scuttled out from wherever it was they were hiding and came back to the craphole that had been Bernice's old man's pride and joy, they'd find there was nothing left apart from a pile of ash.

When I'd set off from London, this hadn't been the outcome I'd envisaged, but I was OK with that. A blow for Bernice was a win for me. Being the victim of a fire was devastating. All your worldly possessions were lost in an instant. She could buy more of her tarty clothes to replace the ones she'd lost, but everything that belonged to Roscoe was gone forever. A satisfied smile spread across my face. She'd be tormented by that for the time she had left. I couldn't have planned things better if I'd tried.

Emotional suffering was a good substitute for physical pain if you asked me. She was broken without her soulmate. I couldn't wait to see what the bitch was made of. See how much shit she could cope with. She'd be begging me to put her out of her misery by the time I'd finished with her. I'd be only too happy to oblige. And as for MacKenzie, he'd well and truly used up the last of his nine lives.

18

DAISY

I'd been a virtual prisoner in my room since Mum and Lily had let rip at me. I'd only ventured out to use the loo and grab some food. I couldn't live like this. Stuck in a silent void. Treading on eggshells. Swamped by their feelings. Swamped by my feelings.

Mum's words had stung. More than that. They'd stabbed me in the heart. Their sharp edges jabbed deep inside me. They were cruel. She'd intended to hurt me. Cause me as much pain as possible. She wanted me to suffer the way she was suffering. But she'd gone too far. I needed space from her. And Lily. Being in the house was claustrophobic. A ticking time bomb. I could sense another eruption wasn't far away. It was bubbling under the surface. Emotions were running high. Tempers had frayed. It was a volatile situation. Three o'clock couldn't come around soon enough. I couldn't wait to see Auntie Colleen and have a long overdue catchup.

* * *

My earlier excitement had disappeared into thin air, and now a ripple of anticipation ran through my insides, making me feel queasy. I didn't know why I was suddenly so hesitant. I was on the verge of bolting in the other direction when a burst of determination swept through me and carried me along the pavement towards the cafe where we'd arranged to meet. My hands trembled as I pushed open the door. A blast of warm air beckoned me inside, so I cast my eyes around. She wasn't here yet. At least, I hoped that was the case. She could have got cold feet and changed her mind. I'd give her ten minutes. If she hadn't arrived by then, I'd go.

I made my way through the tightly packed floor space and sat at a table in a dimly lit corner with my back against the exposed brick wall so that I had full view of the interior and pavement beyond. Shrugging off my puffer jacket, I hung it over the chair and picked up a menu. I felt self-conscious being on my own. Everybody else was in small groups or pairs, so I slumped my shoulders and lifted the laminated booklet higher than necessary so I could hide behind it.

A few moments later, I heard the door open, and my heart started hammering in my chest. Auntie Colleen gave me a tight-lipped smile when her gaze landed on me. She looked different to how I remembered her. Her hair still flowed over her shoulders in loose waves, but it was platinum all over now. It used to be two-tone; blonde on top, brunette underneath. I'd thought she looked like Christina Aguilera, who I used to be obsessed with back then. The memory brought a smile to my lips.

The sound of her heels echoed on the varnished floorboards as she walked towards me. She was wringing her hands and looked nervous. That made two of us. I could be moments away from discovering something that shaped my whole life. I felt sick. Edgy. But if the secret was buried too deep, there'd be no unearthing it.

I wiped the palms of my hands down the legs of my skinny jeans and got to my feet.

'Hi, Auntie Colleen. It's lovely to see you,' I said. I didn't know whether to give her a hug or a handshake, so I did neither.

'Hey, Daisy, it's lovely to see you, too. But do me a favour, drop the auntie, will you? You're a grown woman, so having that attached to my name makes me feel like I'm a hundred years old.' Colleen laughed, accentuating the fine lines at the sides of her eyes.

That suited me fine. It felt weird to call a woman I wasn't related to auntie. I sat back down, and Colleen pulled out the chair opposite me.

'I wasn't sure I was going to recognise you. You were a little girl the last time I saw you, but you haven't changed much at all,' Colleen said with a smile. 'You're looking well. How are you bearing up?' Her expression changed to one of concern.

'I'm OK. I'm still trying to get my head around everything. It all happened so fast. It's hard to believe Dad's gone.'

Colleen reached across the table and rubbed my forearm with her fingertips. 'I know, sweetie, I couldn't believe it when you told me. Des was always such a character. Larger than life. It's shocking to think he died so young.' Colleen shook her head.

I let out a sigh and cast my eyes back to the menu. I could feel myself welling up, and I didn't want to make a fool of myself in a public place in front of a woman I hadn't seen for years.

'Have you ordered yet?'

I glanced up at the sound of Colleen's voice.

'No, I thought I'd wait for you to arrive.'

I didn't bother adding, *I wasn't sure you'd show up, so I wanted to be able to cut and run without buying anything.* I was used to

Greggs prices. This place, Colleen's suggestion, was a lot more upmarket.

'What are you having? It's my treat.' Colleen smiled.

'I can't let you do that.' It was eye-wateringly expensive.

'I insist.'

'Can I have a cappuccino, please?'

'Of course. Don't you want something to eat?'

'No, thanks.'

Colleen would need to rob a bank to pay the bill if we had food as well. And besides that, my insides were full of knots, so I wasn't sure I'd be able to stomach anything.

'I'll be back in a minute.'

Colleen pushed her chair out and walked up to the counter. A couple of minutes later, she came back carrying a tray with two cappuccinos and the biggest double chocolate muffins I'd ever seen. They were the size of large oranges.

'Get that down you,' Colleen said as she placed the cup, saucer, and plate in front of me. 'I couldn't resist them. They were calling to me. Everyone would have thought I was a greedy bastard if I got one for myself and left you with nothing. My mum always used to say cake was good for the soul and I'm inclined to agree with her. Comfort food always makes me feel better when I'm upset. How about you?'

'How did you guess? You're a woman after my own heart. Thank you, they do look good.'

I gave Colleen a half-smile and then peeled back the paper surrounding the giant muffin. I was glad I hadn't bottled it now. Even though we hadn't seen each other for years, I already felt comfortable in Colleen's company.

'I know I've been out of the picture for a long time, but if there's anything I can do to help with the funeral arrangements, just let me know,' Colleen said before sipping her coffee.

'Thank you, but to be honest with you, I wouldn't know where to start with any of that, and Mum seems to want to deal with organising everything herself...' I let my sentence trail off, hoping that would put an end to that topic of conversation.

'How's Tara doing?' Colleen fixed me with a look of sympathy.

It was an obvious question, and I should have realised Colleen would ask it. I was tempted to tell her the truth. Mum was behaving like a total bitch. Blaming me for everything. But instead, I took a swig of my cappuccino and composed myself before I delivered the edited version of my thoughts.

'Dad's death's hit her hard. She's inconsolable, and she's struggling to cope with her grief,' I replied.

'I'm not surprised. She's young to be widowed. And how's Lily doing?'

How could I answer that without giving the game away? My twin and I had always fought like cat and dog, even as children, but she'd probably presumed we'd grown out of that. Presumed that the bereavement had brought the family closer together. I didn't want to spend the time we had together talking about family politics. I shifted in my seat. The long pause was making me uncomfortable. I had to say something soon, or my silence would speak volumes.

'She's OK,' I said, deciding the least I said about Lily the better.

'That's good to hear,' Colleen replied, and then we fell silent again as we ate our chocolate muffins.

I'd pretty much forgotten about Colleen Ahearn until I spotted her name in Mum's address book. I doubted I'd be sitting here now if her surname hadn't begun with an A. She was the first entry in the book, but the mention of her had made Mum blow a fuse. Her extreme reaction had got me thinking.

My underdeveloped childhood memory was patchy. Unreliable. I couldn't remember what happened, but it must have been something big. It cost them their friendship.

I had a thirst for answers. But I was relying on Colleen to be willing to fill in the blanks. If she chose to stay tight-lipped, the details would remain a mystery forever. Although, intuition told me that if I nudged her in the right direction, all the dirt would come out. I wasn't sure what I would do with the information if I managed to get hold of it. But having ammunition I could fire back when the need arose wouldn't go amiss.

'I've been wracking my brains trying to remember how long it's been since I last saw you,' I casually dropped in to reopen the communication and steer the conversation in the direction I wanted.

Colleen leaned back in her chair and tilted her head to one side as she considered what I'd just said.

'It must be about fifteen years. You and Lily were around six,' Colleen replied.

'We're twenty-three now. So that makes it seventeen years.'

'Jesus! That's a long time.'

'You can tell me to mind my own business if you don't want to talk about it, but why did you fall out with my parents?' I asked, getting straight to the point.

I needed to get the question out there and see where it led. Awkwardness crawled through me while I waited for her to respond.

Colleen arched an eyebrow. 'So they never talked about what happened?'

I shook my head.

'I suppose I get that. You were just little girls. You wouldn't have understood. But I don't see the point in covering it up now. You and Lily are grown women.'

Her words sent my imagination into overdrive.

'I don't know if you remember, but me and your mum and dad were always together. We were the Three Amigos.' Colleen laughed.

'I remember. I loved spending time with you.'

'Likewise.' Colleen paused.

Her eyes were fixed on mine. I'd thought she was about to spill the beans, but now it looked like she was having second thoughts.

'So you and my parents were great friends,' I said to prompt her before taking a large bite of my cake.

'We were, and there's no point in being too anal about who did what, but your dad and I used to get on like a house on fire. We started getting on a little too well. One minute, we were pals, and the next, we were lovers...'

I didn't know what I'd expected Colleen to say, but it wasn't that! The thought of my dad being anyone's lover made the muffin I'd been devouring get caught in my throat. I thought I was going to die as I practically coughed my lungs up onto the table. I stared at Colleen with wide eyes as I hit myself on the chest with my fist, trying to dislodge the chocolatey crumbs. Colleen looked concerned and leapt out of her chair, ran around behind me and started welting me between the shoulder blades so hard she nearly loosened my teeth.

'Are you OK, Daisy?' she asked, rubbing my back with the flat of her hand once I'd stopped coughing.

'I'm fine, thank you. I don't know what happened there. A piece of the muffin went down the wrong way,' I lied.

'I hate it when that happens,' Colleen replied as she went back to her seat. She knocked back the contents of her cup before she began to speak again. 'So now you know the ugly truth. I hope you don't hate me...'

'Of course not. Does my mum know?'

I was fairly certain I already knew the answer to my question, but I asked it anyway.

'Yes. That's what ended our friendship. But I'm not a home-wrecker. It takes two to tango.'

Wasn't that the truth?

'I'm glad you told me.' I offered Colleen a half-smile.

'You had a right to know.' She tore her deep blue eyes away from mine and glanced at her watch. 'It's been great seeing you again, but I've got to go.'

A wave of panic rushed through me. If Colleen walked away, I might never hear the end of the story.

'Can't you stay a bit longer?' I gazed at her with pleading eyes.

But Colleen was already on her feet. Already shrugging her arms into the sleeves of her coat. She looked at me with a weird expression. Her face was saying she'd rather jump into the back of a serial killer's van than do as I'd asked. I was gutted that I'd fucked this up.

'Sorry, no can do, but we should meet up again soon,' Colleen said before she stooped forward and planted a kiss on my face.

My pulse sped up. I could feel myself going into panic mode. I didn't want to wait for next time. There might not be a next time. I wanted to hear the details of their affair now. This minute. Not their bedroom antics, but the timeline of events so I could piece it together in my mind. I didn't want to frighten Colleen off by being too forceful, so instead of running after her to arrange another catch-up, I stayed where I was and watched her walk away, not knowing if I'd ever see her again. I felt defeated. Deflated. A silent tear rolled down my cheek.

19

LILY

Mum was lost in her own private world. Consumed by grief. It was out of character for her to be so needy. So dependent. I guessed it was understandable, given the circumstances. Dad's passing had been sudden. Unexpected. It would take a while to adjust to.

In the meantime, I was left shouldering the burden. Daisy had selfishly made herself scarce. Big surprise. She always put herself first, no matter the situation. Nasty as it sounded, I found propping Mum up draining. I could have done with some help. I was usually a patient person, but I already had too much on my plate. I didn't want to be at the helm. The captain of the ship. Trying to steer the family into calm waters was an impossible task. I wasn't cut out for the role.

I was beside myself. Worried sick. How could we clear Dad's debt? It had been hanging over him for as long as I could remember. My insomnia had come back in full force and agitation was circulating inside me. My heart was racing. There was no way I'd be able to fall asleep. I'd lain awake last night trying to find a solution. I'd mulled over all the options and come to the conclusion that there weren't any. Not viable ones.

Being face to face with Warren Jenkins had been a hair-raising moment I could have done without. I knew I'd had a lucky escape and swerved a massive threat. *Another* one. I couldn't take much more of this. When would all of this end?

I'd been over the moon when me and Daisy had signed the contract to perform at Eden's. I'd thought it would be the making of us. I'd only met the club owner, Samson, on one occasion, and he'd been singing my praises, falling over himself to flatter me. I'd thought he was our saviour. But it was all an act. And I'd fallen for every word he'd spun me. More fool me. That still didn't explain why he'd kidnapped me. Was it a case of mistaken identity? Maybe? He didn't seem as taken with Daisy.

But bad things happened when you rubbed shoulders with the shadier members of society. If we didn't cooperate with Warren, there would be serious consequences. I'd heard what he'd done to Dad. You didn't need to be a genius to work out what would happen when we didn't come up with the cash he was expecting. But I didn't want to be punished for somebody else's mistake.

20

SAMSON

I always held a grudge against people who wronged me. Harbouring resentment and bitterness long after somebody had done the dirty came naturally to me. Petty was my middle name.

MacKenzie and Bernice had dropped off the face of the earth. There was no sign of them in Dover. They'd obviously gone to ground. I couldn't be arsed to try and flush them out. That was too predictable. And I didn't like to be predictable. I'd leave them to sweat for the time being. Watching and waiting was stressful. It took its toll on a person. Letting them wear themselves out would work to my advantage. They'd crawl out from the woodwork at some point, and I'd be ready to pounce when they did. I'd make my move when they were least expecting it. In the meantime, I'd keep them on my radar, so if they tried something, they'd be mincemeat.

But I hadn't driven all this way for nothing, so I wanted to make good use of my time. Maybe I should swing by the shithole Kyle was guarding to see if there was any news on Carly Andrews.

'Kyle, it's me,' I said when he answered the call. He'd worked for me for years and was a trusted member of my dwindling inner circle.

'What's up, boss?' he replied.

'What's going on with Carly?'

'Not much. There's no sign of any movement. She hasn't ventured out today, but she'll have to come out at some point. The gear won't shift itself,' Kyle said.

Keeping eyes on somebody had to be one of the worst jobs in the world. The boredom would do your nut in, but somehow, Kyle managed to sound upbeat.

'I'm not too far away from you, so I'll drop over in a bit.'

I had no intention of parking myself outside a grotty hostel for hours on end, but seeing the street where I'd executed Roscoe one last time appealed to me. It would be good to walk down memory lane before I headed back to the Big Smoke.

'No worries. What brings you to Kent?' Kyle asked.

'I had a bit of business to attend to. While you're at it, do me a favour. Keep a look out for MacKenzie. The scrawny little scrote's shot through again.'

'Will do, boss,' Kyle said before I ended the call.

Less than ten minutes later, I pulled up in front of Kyle's motor parked across the street from the hostel where Carly was renting a room. I'd barely cut the engine when Kyle appeared at the passenger window. I unlocked the door, and he climbed inside.

'It's good to see you, boss,' Kyle said. He had a genuine smile on his face.

I had a lot of time for him, but I'd never tell him that. I liked to play the power game to keep my staff in line. Being too pally with them gave the wrong impression. My reputation ensured I commanded complete respect and obedience from anyone on my payroll. They knew I could turn vicious at the drop of a hat. It would take more than a close shave with death to change my outlook on life. I had no intention of softening my rough edges. Being cruel and callous made me tick. I had a thirst for spilling other people's blood.

My presence on the scene brought some good fortune to the operation. Five minutes after I'd arrived, the shabby front door opened, and a moment later, a small person dressed in a faded black hooded tracksuit came into view.

'That's her.' Kyle pointed through the front windscreen.

'Are you sure?'

'I'm certain,' Kyle replied.

Carly's hands were stuffed into the kangaroo pouch of her top. She'd pulled the hood up to hide her identity. I wouldn't have picked her out in a line-up, but I trusted Kyle, so I wasn't going to question him. She glanced up and down the street before she stepped away from the doorway. Then she paused for several seconds before she began walking in the direction of the station. She had to be working for somebody. A girl like that wouldn't have had the know-how to pull off nicking my shipment of cocaine.

'What do you want me to do, boss?'

'Bring her over to the car.'

I wanted to have words with the little bitch. I needed to salvage the rest of my gear before the coke disappeared up people's noses never to be seen again.

Kyle stepped out of the car, slipped across the street and closed the gap between him and Carly in the blink of an eye. Judging by her reaction, she hadn't heard the man mountain creeping up on her. Kyle spun her around to face him and then clamped the fingers of his right hand over her mouth. She was tiny, barely up to his shoulder. The element of surprise had done its job. Carly looked like she was going to shit herself as he towed her back to my Range Rover.

As they drew closer, I cast a critical eye over her. Kyle was right; she bore all the hallmarks of a junkie. She was deathly pale; her clothes had seen better days, and they were hanging off her skinny frame. There was something about the sad eyes and hollow cheekbones that rang a bell even though I couldn't put my finger on where I knew her from. I played the name Carly Andrews around in my head to see if I recognised it. It meant nothing to me. But that didn't surprise me. I'd always been better with faces.

Kyle opened the back door and forced her inside before he sat down next to her. She looked terrified, but I wasn't going to go easy on her. Carly was selling coke stolen from me. And to make matters worse, she was undercutting everyone and flooding the market with cheap gear.

I turned around in my seat and glared at her. She looked like a deer caught in the headlights when she came face to face with me. Her fear was palpable, which brought a smile to my face. I was going to enjoy every minute of her suffering.

'Did you really think you'd get away with flogging my cocaine?'

'I'm sorry,' she replied and then burst into tears. She didn't even try to deny her involvement.

I was about to continue my interrogation when she wiped her runny nose on the sleeve of her tracksuit. My eyes fixed on the glistening stripe of slug trail on the dirt-ingrained fabric. It turned my stomach. I couldn't bear to look at her.

'Get her out of here.'

Kyle looked at me with a puzzled expression on his face. 'What do you want me to do with her?'

Carly let out a loud wail.

'Shut the fuck up, or that's the last sound you'll ever make,' I warned, jabbing my finger in her face. 'Bring her back to London. I'll meet you at my house.'·

'Yes, boss,' Kyle said as he grabbed the skanky excuse of a woman by the scruff of her filthy jacket and dragged her out of my expensive motor.

As I watched him manhandle the bag of bones into his own car, I made a mental note to have my car valeted. After she'd been in contact with the leather seats, the whole thing needed fumigating.

21

DAISY

'Daisy, is that you?' Lily asked when I stepped into the hall.

Seriously? Who did she think had just let themselves in to our house? I didn't bother to answer her. I raced up the stairs two at a time, slamming my bedroom door behind me so she'd think twice about coming to investigate. The last thing I wanted to do was get caught up in a meaningless conversation with her about Dad's final days. She was going to analyse my decision until she was old and grey. I'd already explained myself to her. I wasn't about to do it again. I had more important things on my mind.

The conversation I'd had with Colleen was dominating my thoughts. Her coffee shop confession had stirred up a hornets' nest. No wonder Mum had nearly blown a fuse when I'd suggested calling her ex-bestie.

To be honest, I wasn't sure how I felt about Colleen now. What she'd done could have torn our family apart. I was caught in a situation where part of me wanted to know what had happened between her and Dad, but part of me didn't. If she decided to share the details of their affair with me, I would never be able to unhear it. But curiosity was a powerful force, and I had very little willpower. Not knowing would gnaw away at me. I'd torment myself until I heard what she had to say.

I pulled my mobile from my coat pocket and dialled Colleen's number. It rang and rang, and then eventually, it went to voicemail. She obviously didn't want to speak to me, so there was no point in leaving her a message.

Colleen was probably regretting spilling the beans. She'd kept her secret for seventeen long years. It surprised me that she'd blurted it out without much encouragement. My nosiness had opened a can of worms, and now I felt worse than before. Having part of the information had just added to my frustration. I'd been better off when I'd had none at all.

I was lying on my bed beating myself up about sticking my beak in when my phone sprang to life. I answered it on the second ring.

'I'm sorry I missed your call, Daisy...'

The sound of Colleen's voice made my heart skip a beat.

'That's OK. I just wanted to say sorry. I feel bad that I made you rush away...' I decided to take the softly-softly approach. I didn't want to scare her off again.

'Don't be silly. You've got nothing to apologise for. You didn't do anything wrong. I'm the one who made it all weird. I started to panic after I told you about me and your dad. I promised your mum I'd take the secret to the grave. So I needed some space to get my head around what I'd done.'

'I understand,' I replied. Confiding in me was a big deal. She'd been brave to open up.

'Can I ask you something? Have you told your mum we met up?' Colleen sounded uneasy.

'No.'

'So she doesn't know I've let the cat out of the bag?'

'Nope.'

'Thank God for that! I owe you one. Tara already thinks badly enough of me without me adding fuel to the fire.'

Colleen seemed genuinely worried about ruffling Mum's feathers even after all this time. Guilt stabbed at my insides. I couldn't promise I was never going to speak to Mum about Dad's affair.

'I'm really sorry I bailed on our chat so prematurely,' Colleen continued.

'That's OK.' I hoped I sounded more convincing than I felt. I was bitterly disappointed that she'd dropped a bombshell and then made herself scarce.

'There's no problem either way, but I was thinking, if you're not busy, maybe we could go for a drink later.'

'Today?' I quizzed.

'Only if that's convenient.'

That was music to my ears.

'I'd love that! You name the time and the place, and I'll be there.'

'How about The Orange Tree in an hour? Does that give you enough time?'

'That sounds perfect. See you soon.' My tone was upbeat.

I'd been kicking myself for calling Colleen, but now I was glad I had. She might not have bothered contacting me if I hadn't started the ball rolling.

The Orange Tree was only a five-minute walk from my house. It was an olde worlde pub with white-washed walls, crooked beams and concealed booths in various nooks and crannies. It had been a bright, crisp winter's day earlier, but the temperature had dropped considerably since the sun had gone down. A wall of warmth barrelled towards me when I pushed open the door. I could see Colleen at the back of the pub. I was pleased she'd arrived before me. It made me feel like less of a desperado. She got to her feet and waved as I stepped inside.

'Hello, sweetie,' she said as I approached, pulling me into a hug when I was close enough.

A bottle of white wine and two glasses were already on the table.

'I hope you drink vino. Otherwise, I'm going to end up as pissed as a fart. I ordered it without thinking. Force of habit.' Colleen laughed.

'You chose well,' I replied, plonking myself down opposite her.

We sat in silence as she poured the Pinot Grigio. She put the bottle back into the ice bucket and held her glass out in front of her.

'Cheers,' she said.

'Cheers,' I replied.

Then we clinked and took a big swig. We both needed some Dutch courage.

'Did you ever suspect that me and your dad had had an affair?' Colleen asked, getting straight down to business.

I was glad she wasn't beating around the bush.

'Hand on heart, I never had a clue. I always thought my mum and dad were blissfully happy. Dad treated her like his queen. He worshipped the ground she walked on. No offence, but I couldn't imagine him even looking twice at another woman.'

I felt like kicking myself when Colleen cast her eyes to the table. I hadn't intended to make her feel bad. But she shrugged off my comment, and a moment later, she straightened her posture and began her defence.

'Every marriage goes through rocky patches. I'm not making excuses for what we did. It should never have happened, but your mum and dad weren't seeing eye to eye at the time. They were fighting about everything and anything.'

I had no recollection of that at all. I must have been too young to remember.

'Believe it or not, I was acting as the go-between. I was trying to help them through their troubles.' Colleen's blue eyes filled with tears.

'I don't want this to come across the wrong way, but how come you betrayed my mum? You were her friend long before you knew my dad.' The words were out of my mouth before I could stop them. What the fuck was wrong with me? 'I'm not judging you. I'm just trying to understand what was going through your mind,' I added, attempting to soften the blow.

Colleen took a big swig of her wine.

'I honestly hate myself for what I did. I never set out to hurt Tara. I was trying to help her save her marriage. But then I started seeing things from Des's point of view. He couldn't do anything right. Tara used to scream at him whenever she clapped eyes on him. She was hardly ever at home. She reckoned she was working long shifts, but your dad was convinced she was cheating on him. I felt sorry for him...' Colleen let her sentence trail off.

I doubted Dad's suspicions were correct. Even if they were, two wrongs didn't make a right. Why didn't he confront her about his fears rather than start an affair of his own? There was no point in wasting precious time and energy on any of this. Dad wasn't here to give his side of the story.

I'd always known my dad was a weak man. He was selfish to the core. Put himself above anyone and everyone. His needs came first. Fuck the rest of us. Listening to Colleen's account made me feel sorry for my mum. I was amazed she'd stayed with him. It was a pity she had. If she'd left him when this happened, Warren Jenkins wouldn't be looming over us now.

'I'm surprised their marriage survived. It's very difficult to trust somebody once they've cheated on you,' I said, then gulped back half of my wine to catch up with Colleen.

'To be perfectly honest, I'm not sure Tara would have stayed with him if it hadn't been for you and Lily. Being a single parent to six-year-old twins wouldn't have been particularly appealing. From what Des told me, he was in the dog house for years over it.' Colleen downed her wine and then topped up our glasses.

'You stayed in touch with my dad?'

I did my best to hide my surprise, but my face gave everything away.

'Only by text. I never saw him again after it all blew up. He suggested meeting up a few times, but I kept knocking him back, and then his messages dried up,' Colleen replied.

I was shocked to think he'd stayed in contact with the woman who'd almost cost him his marriage. Continuing with the affair would have been a suicidal move. He must have had a death wish. If Mum had found out, she'd have ripped his bollocks off for sure. I always knew my dad was arrogant. Who did he think he was trying to keep his mistress on the go after his wife found out about her? Mum wouldn't be bawling her eyes out now if I let her in on that little nugget of information. At least Colleen had the sense to keep him at arm's length. I had to admire her for that.

'I'm not sure Tara ever fully trusted Des after she found out about us,' Colleen said, draining the wine in her glass.

'I'm not surprised.'

'It's a shame she never felt generous enough to give me a second chance, though. I tried my best to keep our friendship alive, but Tara wasn't having any of it. Nothing could persuade her to forgive me. She blamed me for all of it.'

That sounded familiar. I was also the scapegoat. Colleen and I had so much in common. In my parents' eyes, Lily was a paragon of virtue with no faults or imperfections. Unlike myself. I was the flawed one. The unworthy one. I'd always wanted to be the favourite. Even for a day.

'Tara had double standards where trust was concerned. I'm not trying to make excuses for what I did. I made a mistake. A terrible one, and if I had my time over, I wouldn't go near your dad with a barge pole. No matter how hard I tried, I couldn't convince her I hadn't set out to destroy her marriage. I don't know how your dad managed to win Tara over, but I have a sneaking suspicion that somewhere along the line he threw me under the bus,' Colleen said.

'Same again?' I asked.

'Please,' she replied.

I stepped out of the booth, picked up the bucket containing the empty bottle and walked up to the bar.

'Can I have another one of these, please?'

'Coming right up,' the barman said before shovelling ice into the stainless steel container and replacing the empty with a full bottle of white. 'There you go.'

I tapped my phone on the terminal and then went back to the booth.

'So how did Mum find out?' I casually asked as I poured Pinot Grigio into our glasses.

My question seemed to take Colleen by surprise. She looked horrified and anyone would have thought I'd asked her to give the toothless old guy at the bar a blow job.

'Did she catch you in the act?'

Colleen picked up her glass and downed the contents. Then

she took the bottle out of the ice bucket, gave herself a top-up and glugged that back, too. I sat in silence, studying her. She looked uncomfortable. Fidgety. But I couldn't let her clam up now. My curiosity had reached fever pitch. I had to coax it out of her.

'She walked in on you, didn't she?' I fixed my eyes on Colleen. Saw her swallow down the lump in her throat. 'What's the big deal?'

The question was uncomplicated. But she didn't seem to know how to answer it. My pulse quickened as I waited for her to continue. And when she finally uttered her next words they took my breath away.

'Your mum didn't walk in on us. You did,' Colleen said.

For a moment I thought I'd misheard her, but then the penny dropped. My head felt like it was about to explode.

As the words left Colleen's lips, the colour drained from her face. Her blue eyes grew wide. Then she put her hand over her mouth and scrambled to her feet.

'Are you OK?'

That was a stupid question. Colleen clearly wasn't all right. She was deathly pale.

'I think I'm going to be sick,' she mumbled as she rushed towards the toilets.

I raced after her. By the time I pushed open the ladies' door, Colleen was already retching into the toilet bowl. The sound of her vomiting didn't do me any good. I suddenly didn't feel well myself. We'd downed a lot of wine in a short space of time, and the shock of what she'd just told me made the alcohol start to slosh around inside me. There was a very real chance it was about to make a reappearance. I took several deep breaths and then splashed my face with cold water, hoping the nausea would pass. I was gripping the sink like grim death when Colleen unlocked the toilet door.

'Oh my God, I feel awful. I'm sorry to bail on you again, Daisy, but I need to go home.' She had her arms wrapped around herself, clutching her stomach as she slumped against the door frame.

'That's OK, don't apologise. I feel a bit woozy, too,' I admitted.

'What are we like?' Colleen offered me a half-smile. 'My nerves were getting the better of me, so instead of pacing myself, I kept knocking back my wine. The only thing I've eaten all day was the chocolate muffin we had earlier. I should have known this would happen. I'm a lightweight. I've never been good at drinking on an almost empty stomach. I need at least a kilo of potatoes lining my insides before I go on a session.'

'Do you want me to take you home?' I asked as Colleen staggered out of the ladies' loo and back to the booth.

'I'll be fine. I'm going to call an Uber,' she replied.

'Can we meet up tomorrow?'

'As long as I'm not too hungover,' Colleen said, and then she got to her feet. 'I'd better go.'

I didn't know what I was going to do with myself if Colleen couldn't make it. The suspense would kill me if I had to wait too long to find out what had happened. Mixed emotions swirled around in my mind. The whole thing was such a head-fuck. I didn't remember walking in on Dad and Colleen. How was it possible to have no recollection of something so monumental?

22

MACKENZIE

Bernice wasn't wrong. The farmhouse was in a very secluded spot. I couldn't see it from the road. I'd been driving around and around trying to find it and was on the verge of giving up when I noticed a set of oak double gates poking out from some shrubbery, so I stopped the car. Satnav kept telling me I'd reached my destination every time I passed this spot, but I'd ignored it. I was about five minutes from Elham, a village in the heart of the Kent Downs, which I'd driven through several times while looking for the property. I didn't want to ask for directions in case I inadvertently tipped Samson off to our whereabouts. This had to be worth a try. There wasn't a name outside the entrance, but the gates led somewhere, and they were in the middle of nowhere, surrounded by tall trees and high hedges, so this ticked the right boxes.

I dropped the window and pressed the intercom buzzer, expecting to hear Bernice's voice, but nobody said a word. A moment later, the gates started to part. I hoped for my sake I'd got the right house. The way my luck was going, I was probably about to enter a serial killer's lair. But there was only one way to find out.

My guts started rumbling as I drove along the sweeping gravel driveway, which snaked through formal gardens. When I finally pulled up outside the rambling period property, Bernice was waiting for me. Her face broke into a huge grin when she clapped eyes on me. I was pleased to see her, too. I breathed a sigh of relief, knowing there wasn't an axe-wielding maniac in sight. The horror I'd been anticipating wasn't going to play out.

As I got out of the car, the movement sent waves of agony writhing through my body. I felt myself flinch and I hoped Bernice hadn't noticed. I stood looking up at the red-brick mansion so that I wouldn't have to make eye contact with her and to give the moment time to pass. I'd been numbing the pain with coke and alcohol, but my nads were still throbbing like a bastard.

'So what do you think?' Bernice gestured behind her.

When she'd said she'd meet me at the old farmhouse, I hadn't known what to expect, but this impressive-looking building was nothing like what I'd imagined.

'It's amazing.'

'I wasn't sure you'd be able to find the place,' Bernice said as she walked towards me.

'I nearly didn't. I drove past it a good few times before I spotted the gates.' I smiled.

'I'm not surprised. It's tucked out of the way.'

That was an understatement.

'Come in, and I'll give you the guided tour. Structurally, it's in good shape, which is incredible considering the house dates back to the fifteenth century. But as you can see, it needs a lot of work,' Bernice said, leading the way into the entrance hall.

A warren of rooms ran down either side of it. The exposed

timber beams and wooden floors reminded me of The Castle. When we walked into the library at the back of the house overlooking the extensive gardens, my eyes fixed on a deep red leather winged chair which was the same colour as the walls. It was on the other side of the room, next to the inglenook fireplace. A mahogany side table with a cut glass decanter filled with a dark spirit and a tumbler was within easy reach. I could picture Roscoe sitting there, glass in hand, enjoying the peace and quiet, and a lump formed in my chest. I shook off my sadness as Bernice continued showing me around.

There were six bedrooms on the floor above. The master and the guest bedroom had ensuites. The other four shared two family bathrooms. The place was enormous, and all of it would need renovating in time, but even in its current state, it was far nicer than anywhere I'd lived before. Bernice paused for a moment on the landing after she'd finished the tour.

'Roscoe and I started falling in love with the house the minute we drove through the gates, but when we saw this view over the Elham Valley, it made our minds up. It's easy to see why it's an Area of Outstanding Natural Beauty,' Bernice said, sweeping her arm across the huge window as she beamed with pride.

'Wow!' It was impossible not to be impressed by the patchwork of green fields that stretched out before me.

If we were going to be holed up for the foreseeable future, this would be a great place to be. My time was coming. I was sure of that. Not only had I betrayed Samson's trust, I also knew things that would send him down for a long stretch. That wasn't on his agenda. Samson would kill me to keep me quiet. He wouldn't think twice about it. I wouldn't be wallowing in survivor's guilt if he got his hands on me. I'd be praying for deliverance.

'Would you like a cuppa?' Bernice asked, breaking my train of thought. 'Or maybe you'd prefer something a bit stronger?'

'Now you're talking,' I replied. My pain management needed a serious top-up.

'Coming right up!' Bernice replied.

Then she led the way down the sweeping oak staircase and into the rustic country kitchen, which had 'heart of the home' stamped all over it.

'Take a seat,' Bernice said before lifting two tumblers out of one of the cupboards. She grabbed a bottle of Courvoisier that had been sitting on the work surface and brought everything over to the huge wooden table.

My eyes were glued to her as she unscrewed the bottle and half-filled the glasses.

'Do you want ice, darling?'

'No thanks.'

We clinked crystal, and then I took a huge gulp of the brandy, savouring the smooth taste as it flowed down my throat. It got to work almost immediately, soothing my throbbing parts. Thank God for alcohol. Where would I be without it?

'So tell me what happened when you spotted the car.'

Bernice's blue eyes were wide with curiosity. She put her glass in front of her and wrapped her long fingers around it while she waited for me to reply.

'I couldn't believe my eyes when I saw Samson's Range Rover heading towards me. I don't think he spotted me. Thank God you got out of The Castle before he arrived. You had a lucky escape.'

'Don't jump the gun, darling. It might not have been him behind the wheel.'

I was taken aback by what Bernice had just said. I could tell from her expression that she wasn't buying into my theory. But I knew Samson better than she did, and my gut was telling me that she hadn't killed him.

'I'm not trying to downplay what you're saying. I don't doubt it was Samson's car, but anyone could have been driving it.'

Bernice was in denial, so there was no point in discussing this any further.

'The most sensible thing we can do is err on the side of caution and stay out of the way until we know for certain whether Samson's dead or alive. He'll be on the warpath, and we'll both be in his sights.'

'If it will make you happy, I could ask Fester to see what he can find out.' Bernice held eye contact with me as she took a sip of her drink.

'Now, there's a blast from the past! I haven't seen Roscoe's brother for years. How's he doing?'

'He's good.' Bernice smiled.

'Where's he based these days?'

'He's still in London.' She ran her fingers through the length of her ponytail.

'Is he still running his business?'

Bernice shook her head. 'He's pretty much retired these days. He doesn't need to work any more. He made a fortune cleaning other people's cash. Now, he's busy spending his profits, living the high life.'

Lucky bastard! Whoever said crime doesn't pay?

23

SAMSON

On the drive back to London, I started wracking my brains, trying to remember where I knew Carly from, when a vision of Travis with his tongue down a girl's throat and one hand between her thighs slapped me right between the eyes. I had to speak to him and see if he could shed any light on the matter.

'Hey, mate, how's it hanging?'

'Wouldn't you like to know?' Travis laughed. 'It's good to hear from you, me old mucker. Long time no speak.'

'I've got a question for you.'

'Another one? What is this, *Mastermind*?' Travis quipped.

'Very funny. Do you remember a girl called Carly Andrews?'

'I can't say I do, mate,' Travis replied.

'She's small and skinny. She's got blonde hair and is in her mid-teens...'

'It's not ringing any bells, but she sounds like my cup of tea. You know I like a tight little pussy. Sexy schoolgirls are at the top of my list. But I'm not the only one who fantasises about being spanked with a wooden ruler by one of the Belles of St Trinian's. Most men I know share the same dream!' Travis replied.

I wasn't one of them. He could skip my name from the head count. Travis was his own man and knew no boundaries when it came to age. He liked his bed partners young. I'd go so far as to say the younger, the better.

'Why do you ask?' Travis's tone changed.

'I bumped into her recently and she seemed vaguely familiar, but I'm struggling to place her. I wondered if she was the bird who worked at Eden's a few years ago. You know, the one who lived at the hostel. Turned up looking for a job, pretending to be eighteen when she looked about twelve.'

'I'm not sure, mate.'

'Fair enough. I just thought I'd see if it jogged your memory.'

'My mind's like a sieve, especially where women are concerned. There've been too many for me to keep up with.' Travis chuckled.

Wasn't that the truth? I didn't doubt Travis's multi-million-pound fortune helped him secure a shag. He was a head shorter than most of the leggy women who'd had the pleasure of sharing his bed. I reckoned his stacks of cash made him inches taller in their eyes. Fair play to the man. He was a living legend.

'You're lucky your dick hasn't dropped off, mate!' I smiled.

'You're a fine one to talk!' Travis fired back.

I couldn't argue with that. I had a roving eye and had a serious problem keeping the snake in my trousers. But I'd never liked a woman enough to let her make a claim on me. I couldn't stand all the drama that went with having a relationship.

'Samson, my friend, you're not getting any younger. When are you going to give your mum those grandkids she's so desperate for?' Travis already knew the answer to his question.

'I'm still getting some practice in. But I've pencilled it in my diary for the twelfth of never.' I let out a belly laugh, and Travis joined in.

My mum and dad had set me a good example where wedded bliss was concerned, but I had no intention of following in their footsteps, much to my mum's despair. Travis was right; she was desperate for me to have a tribe of ankle biters. It was never going to happen.

'Married life's not so bad,' Travis said.

'I'll take your word for it. Each to their own, but I can't think of anything worse than being shackled to a wife and kids. Variety's the spice of life, so they say.'

'I couldn't agree more, but having a trouble and strife at home has never stopped me playing the field,' Travis pointed out.

Travis was a 'happily married' man with a rake of kids, but I was a confirmed bachelor. I had no problem leading women on to get what I wanted out of them. But I didn't do commitment. Leaving broken hearts in my wake was all part of the fun.

'It's been good catching up, but I'd better head,' Travis said.

'Why? What are you up to? About to get balls deep in some lucky lady, are we?'

'Nah. I'm on my way to the recording studio. There's a backing track that needs finalising. But once the girls have perfected it, I'm going to shag their brains out,' Travis said.

'Lucky you. Have fun.'

My dick was long overdue some action, but I wasn't in any condition to jump anyone's bones for the time being.

'I fully intend to. Adios, amigo.'

After my call with Travis ended, I started mulling over where to have my showdown with Carly. I considered taking her down to the dungeon but decided against that at this stage. She was already scared of her own shadow, so if I interrogated her in a fully equipped torture chamber, it might be too much for her. Not that I gave a shit about her welfare, but I needed her to open up and spill the beans and she wasn't going to do that if she was chained to the wall.

I was sitting behind my desk sipping a single malt when my mobile started to ring.

'Hi, Samson. I'm just approaching your gates,' Kyle said when I answered the phone.

'I'm in my office. Bring Carly to me.'

A couple of minutes later, there was a knock on the door.

'Come in,' I said, not bothering to get up. I'd finally managed to get comfortable.

Kyle had Carly by the scruff of her hoodie as he towed her into view. I could see her visibly shaking, but I didn't feel an ounce of compassion for the stupid bitch.

'Right, let's get down to the nitty-gritty. How did you intercept my shipment?'

'I, I, d-didn't,' Carly stammered, stating the obvious.

'So who did?'

'I h-have no idea.'

'Well, somebody knows what happened. Either you start talking or...' I let my sentence trail off so Carly's imagination could start running wild.

'I promise you I don't know anything.' Her lips were trembling.

'Amateurs didn't rob me. Who are you working for?' I bellowed.

I was getting bored of this conversation. I wanted her to admit that Roscoe was behind the theft.

'I don't know the guy's name.'

'So how did you get involved in the operation? There's no point in trying to deny it. I know you were in the van. The police found your prints.'

Carly burst into tears. She was wasting her time if she was

looking for a show of sympathy. Watching a woman turn on the waterworks riled me up. It was pathetic. All it did was spike my anger, which was the opposite of what she'd hoped to achieve by opening the floodgates. I was on the verge of losing my shit, so she'd better not wipe her nose on her sleeve again. I couldn't stomach seeing that repulsive behaviour twice in one day.

'Oh my God! Are they going to arrest me? Will I go to prison?' Carly suddenly blurted out. Her green eyes were like saucers.

'That depends...'

A golden opportunity had just presented itself to me. I'd be a fool not to exploit it. I wasn't about to tell her I'd had to practically force DC Boyd, my man on the inside, to investigate the whereabouts of my stolen van. He didn't give a flying fuck about the finer details of the robbery. He was only concerned with how much he could fleece me for this time. My misfortune was his gain. He was a greedy, money-grabbing bastard, always on the take. I'd had to ramp up the pressure to get him to dust for clues. So it was laughable to think the Old Bill would bother pressing charges. I doubted Boyd had even filed a report about the incident. He'd told me Carly was an insignificant petty criminal. I knew she'd been arrested before on a few occasions for selling weed and shoplifting, but she'd never been convicted. She was low down the food chain. A small cog in the machine.

'I have sources inside the force that will look favourably on you if you assist the investigation by telling me everything you know. If you cooperate with me, I'll be able to get your jail term reduced. If you're really lucky, you might just walk away with a suspended sentence and a wrap on the knuckles,' I said, piling the pressure onto her bony shoulders.

Carly buckled under the strain. She buried her head in her hands and started sobbing her heart out.

'What the fuck are you crying about? Nothing's even happened yet!' My patience had worn thin. 'Either you start talking, or Kyle will deposit you at the nearest cop shop. Your prints are on file. The police know your name, and you're the only link to the stolen van. So unless you want to go down for the whole crime, I suggest you think hard about who else was involved. I want names, I want details, and I want them now!' I roared, banging my fist down on my desk.

Carly jumped out of her skin. The jolt seemed to snap her out of her meltdown.

'I'll tell you everything I know, but I'm not sure how much help it'll be.'

'I'll be the judge of that. Did you travel in my van from Rotterdam?'

'No. I joined the driver in Felixstowe and travelled with him to Dover,' Carly replied without hesitation.

My shipment had been intercepted on the ferry, which meant she hadn't been part of the original theft.

'Who told you to join the driver? Who gives the orders?'

'I get my instructions from Zerina.'

The way Carly delivered her response, it was as though the name should have meant something to me. I'd expected a different moniker to spill from her lips.

'Who the fuck's Zerina?'

'She's the cousin of the guy I work for. He never contacts me directly. Zerina organises everything,' Carly replied.

Had I jumped to conclusions and got it wrong? I'd been convinced my old rival, Roscoe Allen, had been responsible for nicking my consignment. But in my defence, what was I supposed to think when my gear started doing the rounds in the middle of his turf?

Zerina held the key to finding out who Carly's boss was. The little scumbag was swearing blind she didn't know who was in command, but her brain had been affected by all the drugs she'd taken, so I wasn't sure I could believe a word that came out of her mouth. Now that I knew Roscoe wasn't responsible, I'd have to work out who the orders were coming from. If he thought I was going to let him take my gear and make a laughing stock of me, he was very much mistaken.

'Zerina's an unusual name. Where's she from?'

I thought my head was going to explode when Carly answered my question.

'Albania.'

A certain person suddenly sprang to mind. Arben Hasani had to be the mysterious cousin. I'd stake my life on the fact that he'd masterminded the stunt. My fury spiked in an instant. There was no controlling my temper. I swiped everything off my desk with my arm. The glass containing my expensive whisky shattered on the floor, and the pile of paperwork sitting next to it floated through the air like confetti.

I was boiling mad and kicking myself for not realising sooner. Roscoe wouldn't have had the balls to pull a stunt like this. I should have guessed Arben was behind the theft. Since MacKenzie had borrowed cocaine from him behind my back, the Albanian had given me no end of grief. He'd been lording it around my manor like he owned the place. Enough was enough. I wasn't going to let him muscle in on my territory. Murderous thoughts started racing through my mind.

'What's happened to my coke?'

'I was told to sell it cheap and flood the market,' Carly said and then cast her tear-filled eyes to the floor.

I could feel my jaw twitching as I clenched and unclenched my fist. What I wouldn't give to ram it in her face right now to drive home the fact that she'd ripped off the wrong person.

While I was considering whether to restrain myself or not, a call came through on Carly's mobile.

'Aren't you going to answer it?' I asked through gritted teeth.

Carly delved into her hoodie's pouch and pulled out her phone.

'Put it on speaker,' I instructed.

'Hello,' Carly said in a tiny voice barely above a whisper.

'Carly, it's Zerina. Where are you?'

The sound of her voice made my blood pressure spike.

Carly looked sideways at me before she answered. 'I'm out and about.'

'I've just spoken to the boss. He said to tell you he'll give you double the amount of coke as agreed as an incentive to shift the rest of the shipment by the end of the week,' Zerina said.

Carly's eyes lit up. The temptation was so great. Kyle was right; she was an out-and-out junkie, a complete waste of space. She was little more than a kid, yet she was already a slave to drugs. She was pathetic. A disgrace to her species. I hated weak women.

'Are you still there, Carly?' Zerina asked.

'Yes,' Carly replied.

'Should I tell the boss you'll do it?'

'Yep,' Carly agreed.

'Over my dead body,' I yelled once she'd ended the call. I leapt to my feet and grabbed Carly by the front of her hoodie. 'You must have a screw loose if you think I'm going to stand by and let you flog the rest of my cocaine. You can forget about selling it on the cheap. I want what's left of it back.'

'My boss will go mental if I don't do as he asked,' Carly replied.

She stared up at me with a puzzled look on her face. She was lost in a cloud of confusion. It seemed to have slipped her mind that I was the rightful owner of the consignment, not Arben.

'You're worried about how your boss will react. What do you think I'm going to do to you? You're not in a position to follow through with his orders, are you?' I got right up in Carly's face.

She slowly shook her head. She looked terrified. So she should. When somebody wronged me, no matter how slightly, they could expect serious repercussions. My fearsome reputation was built on that. I couldn't bear to look at the snivelling wretch, so I shoved her away with the palm of my hand. She staggered backwards but then managed to find her feet.

'Get her out of my fucking sight. The next time I see her, she'd better be delivering my coke on bended knee,' I shouted.

Kyle and I exchanged a glance before he made himself scarce. He knew what was required of him without me having to utter another word. Carly must have been storing my cocaine at the hostel, so Kyle would have to drive her to Dover so that she could retrieve the last of it, then bring her back to London. My warehouse was sitting empty. It was the perfect place to hold Carly until I decided on my next move.

24

DAISY

Sunday 11 January

I'd been awake half of the night. Tossing and turning. Thoughts racing through my head. The anticipation of contacting Colleen was making me feel sick. I kept looking at the time on my phone, but it seemed to be standing still. I was desperate for it to reach a respectable hour so I could text her to see how she was feeling. Once it got to 8 a.m. I typed out a message and hit send. I couldn't wait another minute.

DAISY

> Good morning. Hope you're not feeling too rough. How do you fancy going for breakfast?

I wasn't expecting to hear back for hours, but I'd barely placed my phone on my bedside table when I heard a message come through.

COLLEEN

> I'm feeling a bit delicate, but that sounds good.
> A bacon roll is just what the doctor ordered.

Colleen's reply was music to my ears. I could murder one, too.

DAISY

> Greggs is already open. Unless you'd prefer somewhere more upmarket...

COLLEEN

> Greggs is perfect. Meet you there in half an hour?

Colleen seemed as keen as I was to continue our conversation.

DAISY

> Half an hour it is!

* * *

'Hey, Colleen,' I called.

I could see her ahead of me, pacing along the high street towards Greggs, her long blonde hair splayed out behind her, when I turned the corner. She stopped in her tracks and looked over her shoulder.

'Hi, Daisy.' Colleen's face broke into a huge smile. 'I'm really sorry about yesterday,' she said when I drew level with her.

'There's no need to apologise.'

It was usually me who had too much to drink and made a show of myself, so it made a refreshing change that it was somebody else for once. But I didn't mention that because I didn't want to embarrass her further.

'How are you feeling?'

Colleen looked bright-eyed and bushy-tailed, but carefully applied make-up could work wonders on a death-warmed-up complexion. I knew that only too well.

'Surprisingly good.' Colleen laughed and then opened the door to Greggs. 'What would you like?' she asked.

'It's OK, I'll get this. It was my idea to go for breakfast, so it's only right that I should pay.'

'That's because you got in first with the suggestion. I've been rattling around the house since six this morning, but I didn't want to text you too early in case I woke you up. I need to make up for yesterday's fiasco, so it's my treat. I insist!' Colleen had a determined look on her face.

'I'll have a white coffee and a bacon buttie then, please.'

'You grab a table, and I'll go and order,' she replied.

There were already half a dozen people spread out around the cafe so I had trouble finding somewhere out of the way to sit.

'Breakfast is served. Bon appétit!' Colleen said a few moments later when she joined me.

'Thanks.' I smiled.

We sat in silence while we took a couple of bites from our rolls. I felt a lot more comfortable in Colleen's company than I had yesterday, but my nerves started to pick up as I thought about how best to broach the subject. Addressing the elephant in the room was never an easy thing to do.

'I was shocked when you told me I caught you and my dad out. What happened?'

I threw the question out there to get the ball rolling. There was no point in delaying the inevitable. We both knew we'd come here to discuss this. It seemed to take forever for her to finish chewing her mouthful of food. While I waited, it crossed my mind that she was buying herself some time, trying to work out what to say.

'You don't remember anything?'

Colleen's eyes searched my face. The intense scrutiny made me squirm. Made me feel uncomfortable. It was as though I was on trial.

'No.'

My reply was abrupt but to the point. There didn't seem to be any reason to elaborate.

'I suppose you were very young, but the fallout was so bad, I would have thought the memory would have stayed with you. I wish I could block out the details, but they're ingrained in my mind,' Colleen said, then she stared off into the middle distance.

Maybe the gap in my recollection was my brain's attempt to protect me from something that had caused me a lot of pain.

'I hope you don't mind me dragging all of this up, but I'd love to know what happened...'

My insides were squirming as the tumbleweed moment played out. Then Colleen fixed me in her sight and let out a loud sigh.

'I don't really like talking about it. I lost the best friend I've ever had over my own stupidity.'

Her eyes misted up, and guilt rose up inside me. I felt bad that I was putting her through this, but I needed her help to understand the bigger picture. She was the only person in a position to share the facts. I could confront my mum about it, but I doubted very much she'd be willing to spill the beans. Even if she was prepared to open up, the chances were she'd only have a watered-down version of events. Mum probably didn't know half of it.

'I feel like a bitch pressing you on this. I understand where you're coming from, not wanting to drag it all back up, but Mum said something really spiteful to me the other day, and I was wondering if it had something to do with the affair.'

I hadn't intended to tell anyone what my mum had said, even though her cruel words still dominated my thoughts. They'd speared my skin like poison darts. Cut me deep. Wounded me. Despite my best efforts to silence them, they played over and over in my mind. But Colleen wasn't going to give up the details easily, so if sharing my mum's barbed comment loosened her lips, it would be worth the humiliation.

'Why? What did your mum say?' Colleen fixed me with a look of concern.

'She told me that my dad despised me.' A huge lump had formed in my throat and nearly stopped my voice from coming out.

Colleen's loud gasp silenced the room temporarily. She looked around at the curious faces, then covered her mouth with her hand. Her eyes were wide. I could see she was shocked.

'Oh my God, Daisy. I can't believe Tara said that to you.' She spoke in a hushed tone.

'I know.' I felt my eyes fill with tears.

'How did you respond?'

'I didn't get a chance to. She stormed out of the kitchen with Lily hot on her heels before I could say anything.'

On the surface, I'd kept my composure. But inside, I was dying. Mum's words had been like daggers to my heart, silently tearing me apart.

'You poor thing. What a horrible thing to say.' Colleen reached across the table and touched my arm with her fingertips.

'She's not the only one who's grieving. She had no right to

lash out at me.' A sudden burst of anger pushed my sadness out of the way.

'You're dead right. There's no excuse for the way your mum behaved. I don't know why Tara said that. Your dad didn't despise you. He loved you.'

'Yeah, right.'

'He did,' Colleen insisted.

'Well, he had a funny way of showing it.'

'What do you mean? You girls were the apple of your dad's eye. He was so proud of the two of you.'

It was clear Colleen didn't know that Dad and I had shared a lifetime of tension and butting heads. We'd been sparring partners for as long as I could remember, constantly at each other's throats. But I didn't want to deviate from the topic of conversation to talk about our troubled relationship.

I felt a bit sly playing my trump card to make her feel sorry for me, but it had done the trick. Colleen was opening up to me. I felt confident that if I didn't rush things, she'd eventually tell me what happened when I discovered the affair.

'You and Lily used to get so much attention when you were little. Des never got bored of the fascination people had for the two of you. Every time someone stopped him to ask about his beautiful identical twin girls, he was as pleased as punch.' Colleen smiled as she remembered the past.

So that was how it began. I bet that interest sparked the idea in Dad's head to exploit his daughters to the max. He was a skilled manipulator who spent years honing his craft. Much as I enjoyed listening to Colleen reminiscing, I was desperate to cut to the chase and ask her what happened on that fateful day. But if I steamrolled ahead, she might put the brakes on again.

'Des was a great dad. I always admired that about him.'

I had to stop myself from laughing out loud. Talk about

viewing him through rose-tinted spectacles. I could tell by the way Colleen spoke that she had real feelings for Dad. Whatever it had meant to him, their affair hadn't been a casual fling for her.

'Were you in love with him?' I asked. I knew I probably shouldn't have blurted that out, but I couldn't stop myself.

Colleen's cheeks flushed, which answered my question.

'Is it that obvious?'

'Kind of.' I smiled.

'You don't mind?' Colleen's eyes bore into mine.

I admired Colleen's honesty. It took courage to allow yourself to be vulnerable in front of somebody. Letting down carefully built walls wasn't an easy thing to do.

'Of course not. You can't choose who you fall for.'

'That's so true. I tried to fight it. I *did* fight it. I kept a lid on my feelings for years and never acted on them. But when I realised Des felt the same way about me, I couldn't stop myself.' Colleen's eyes filled with tears, and then she tore her gaze away from mine.

It looked like my patience was about to pay off. I reached across the table and rubbed my fingertips on her forearm, mirroring the show of compassion she'd given me earlier. The action made Colleen take her eyes off her half-eaten bacon roll and fix them on me again.

'What we did and the hurt we caused wasn't worth it. Des and I were selfish. We didn't consider the consequences. Our affair nearly tore your family apart. It ended my friendship with your mum and we'd been besties since our first day at primary school, and I'd thrown it all away for a fling with your dad. I knew he'd never choose me over Tara. I wouldn't have wanted him to.'

Tears ran down Colleen's cheeks. She looked distraught. I

squirmed in my seat. I felt bad for making her relive something that still caused her so much distress.

'Even after all these years, the guilt and shame burn deep within me.'

'I can see that. But you can't keep beating yourself up over something that happened almost twenty years ago.'

My sympathetic manner set Colleen off, and she dissolved into floods of tears. The sound prompted a nosey old bastard on the table in front of us to turn around in his seat and start rubbernecking. I was glad she couldn't see him. He wasn't being a bit subtle. There was no way he was going to look away while Colleen was sobbing her heart out. So I took actions into my own hands. What I was about to say would no doubt piss people off. The youth of today have no respect for their elders. Blah. Blah. Blah. Good. I'd never been one for political correctness.

'What are you gawping at?'

The man didn't answer. I'd been hoping to embarrass him and put the matter to bed, but now everyone else in Greggs was staring at our table.

'You can see my friend's upset. Why don't you all mind your own fucking business.' I glared at each of them in turn, which worked like a charm, giving Colleen the privacy she deserved.

'I'm sorry, I'm making a show of myself. I've really tried to stay strong and put on a brave face, but I've been bottling up my emotions for years. Now that you've loosened the cork, everything's come pouring out,' Colleen admitted.

'There's no need to apologise. You're not making a show of yourself. I'm sure you'll feel better once you get this off your chest.'

She smiled and then wiped away her tears with her hand. 'Has anyone ever told you you're a good listener?'

'I can't say they have.'

I supposed it helped that I was captivated by everything that came out of Colleen's mouth, so I didn't have to feign enthusiasm.

She leant across the table to avoid being overheard, aware that everyone was now eager to hear the ins and outs of our conversation, before she began to speak again.

'I should never have let myself get so close to Des. I remember the day he met your mum. We were in the local pub. We'd both been eyeing him up. Tara and I used to share the same taste in men. We even dated the same bloke once. Not at the same time, I might add, but after he split up with your mum, he started seeing me. He thought he was God's gift to women. Fancied himself as the local stud.' Colleen laughed as she recalled the memory.

The idea of that seemed weird to me. I wouldn't like a guy comparing notes on me and my bestie. I remembered my mum telling Lily and me this story years ago. It had creeped me out then too. I hadn't realised Colleen was the friend she was referring to, though. She'd never mentioned her name.

'There's no excuse for what Des and I did, but we were spending more and more time together. It was like we were the couple. We were the parents...'

Colleen paused. I could see she was struggling. Recalling the events was distressing for her.

'How long were you and Dad together?' I pressed on regardless.

She let out a long breath. 'Too long. Almost a year, which makes the deception so much worse. It wasn't a drunken one-night stand where we'd got up the next morning and regretted what we'd done. We betrayed your poor mum over and over again.'

Colleen was wracked by guilt. My heart went out to her.

'I don't know what happened on that fateful day when you walked in and found the two of us writhing around on the bed. What had we been thinking? We were usually so careful. We'd never usually have sex while you and Lily were in the house. Admittedly, we'd become a bit careless in front of the two of you. A cheeky snog here, a quick grope there, that kind of stuff. Risky moves. We were becoming reckless. It was almost as though we wanted to be found out. The idea of being caught made everything seem exciting. Until we were, and then all hell broke loose.' Colleen's face crumpled.

'Did it all kick off after I walked into the bedroom and found the two of you?' I prompted.

She closed her eyes and shook her head from side to side as though she was trying to banish the memory. Then she inhaled a deep breath and blew it out slowly before her lids opened again.

'I don't know how long you'd been watching us going at it hammer and tongs. You were just an innocent little girl. You couldn't work out why we were both completely naked, moaning and groaning. I can still hear you asking Des what we were doing. We sprang apart as if we'd been shocked by something when we realised you were there. It was the worst moment of my life. Time seemed to stand still. I didn't know what to do, so I dragged the quilt up from the bottom of the bed and clutched it around my chest. Des told you to get out, and you ran from the room in tears.'

Oh my God! The incident must have been hiding in the shadows of my brain. Now that Colleen had given me a nudge in the right direction, some recollection had come back.

'I don't remember the part about the two of you being naked, but I do remember my dad yelling. Mum and Dad's bedroom was out of bounds to me and Lily. I don't know what made me open the door.'

'You must have heard the commotion. We were lost in the moment, so we weren't keeping it down. We'd forgotten you guys were in the house,' Colleen explained.

Ew! What she'd just said gave me the ick. It was too much information. It was horrible picturing my dad pounding away at her. It made me feel weird. Unsettled. But I only had myself to blame. I was the one pushing Colleen to spill the beans.

'We both panicked when we realised we'd been caught out. We decided to try and cover our backs and say I hadn't been feeling well, so I'd gone for a lie down. Des told Tara he was just checking up on me when you walked in on us. We were going for damage limitation.'

How did my mum fall for that load of crap?

'Once we'd been rumbled, I went home. I didn't want to be there when Tara got back from work. I couldn't bear to look her in the eye, and it fitted in with the story perfectly. Your mum was really concerned that I was poorly and phoned me that night to see how I was feeling, which made me feel a hundred times worse.' Colleen let out another sigh.

A frown settled on my face. 'If Mum believed your story, how did she find out about the affair?'

'We thought we'd got away with it, and we had to start with. But Tara isn't stupid – far from it. She noticed that Des was suddenly being snappy with you and that you seemed reluctant to be left alone with him. You were teary, which was out of character. Lily was the cry-baby. You just dusted yourself off and got on with things, took everything in your stride, so it raised Tara's suspicions.'

What Colleen had said came as a complete revelation. My

mum and dad had always professed that I'd been trouble since the day I was born. My memory didn't stretch that far back, so I never disputed what they'd told me. I hadn't realised that Lily and I had started on an even keel before I'd ruined things for myself by being curious. If I could turn back the clock, I wouldn't go anywhere near that closed bedroom. I'd stay in the front room watching CBeebies with Lily like Dad had told us to. Having a rebellious streak had got me into grief more times than I cared to mention, but you couldn't change the way you were wired, could you?

'So how did the truth come out?'

'Tara said when she came home from work a couple of days later there was an envelope with "Mummy" on the front waiting for her. She was expecting to find a drawing one of you had done at school but there was a note telling her you were sorry for being naughty and going into the bedroom but you could hear funny noises. And when you opened the door, Daddy and Auntie Colleen had no clothes on. You were too young to understand what we were doing, but Tara didn't need you to spell it out. She read out your exact words, written in your best handwriting, when she confronted us. They've been etched into my memory for the last seventeen years,' Colleen said with a haunted look on her face.

'I wrote a note?'

She nodded. 'Using different coloured pencils. It must have taken you ages.'

'Why didn't I just tell her?'

Colleen shrugged. 'Maybe you were scared how she was going to react.'

That made sense.

'Did she believe me?'

'She did at first. How could she not? You had no reason to lie. Tara went mental and threatened to throw Des out of the house.

She told me she never wanted to see or speak to me again. But then Des somehow managed to talk her around. He convinced Tara that you'd made it all up because he'd told you off for being naughty, and you wanted to get back at him. He swore blind you were lying. You were only little, so you couldn't fight your corner. You didn't understand what you'd witnessed.' Colleen threw me a sympathetic look.

'Surely Mum didn't fall for that?' I couldn't believe the strong woman who'd raised me would be so gullible.

'Tara didn't want to be a single mum. So she chose to trust Des's version of events and sweep yours under the carpet. I'd put money on the fact she knew which of you was really telling the truth.'

My temples started to throb.

'How could my dad turn his six-year-old daughter into the scapegoat to save his own skin? His affair drove a permanent wedge between me and my parents.'

'I had no idea. I thought once the dust settled, it would all blow over,' Colleen said, looking up at me through her eyelashes.

'It never did. I couldn't do anything right in their eyes.'

I couldn't hide the sadness in my voice as I struggled to hold in the bitter tears that were threatening to fall. I felt lost. Numb. In a state of disassociation.

'I'm so sorry, Daisy. I hope in time you'll be able to forgive me for my part in all of this. I'd give anything to turn back the clock.'

Colleen and I had both borne the brunt of Mum's hurt. Her anger. The only one who'd walked away unscathed was Dad. It was upsetting to think my mum was happy to think badly of me rather than face up to what had happened.

I'd done Mum a favour, telling her about his infidelity. So why did she blame me? Dad was the one in the wrong. He hadn't just deceived Mum. He'd deceived us all. Almost tore our family apart. I suddenly felt lightheaded. It felt like the walls and ceiling were closing in on me. I pushed my chair back and got up from the table.

'Are you OK, Daisy?' Colleen looked concerned.

'I don't feel too good.'

That was an understatement. My stomach was convulsing. Any minute now, the bacon roll was going to reappear.

'I'm not surprised. It's a lot for you to take in.' Guilt was written all over her face.

'I have to get out of here,' I said, picking up my bag and grabbing my coat from the back of the chair.

'I understand, but when you've had time to process it all, I'd love to see you again if you still want to talk. It would be good to stay in touch, but no pressure. Only if you want to,' Colleen said as I rushed for the door.

I wasn't sure how I felt about any of this. My world had been rocked. Knocked off its axis. I could feel myself disappearing down a never-ending rabbit hole. My thoughts were scrambled. Disjointed. None of this seemed real.

25

DAISY

I glanced up at the sky. Shafts of winter sunlight were struggling to break through the thick black clouds. It looked like it was going to start pouring any minute, so I needed to find somewhere safe to shelter before I got drenched. More than that. I needed somewhere safe to stay. There was no way I could go home. If I came face to face with Mum, everything Colleen had told me about her and my dad would come spilling out of my mouth. I wouldn't be able to hold it in. I'd have to confront her about it.

I'd been wandering around aimlessly since Colleen had delivered the earth-shattering news. There was so much to take in, my mind was struggling to process it all. I turned the details over in my head, trying to play catch-up. Bits and pieces were coming back to me, but my recollection was still shadowy and not real enough to be reliable. If Colleen hadn't enlightened me, I don't think I'd ever have remembered the event that sent my childhood on a different course. I knew I couldn't change the past. But I couldn't help myself. It was human nature to wonder *what if?*

Mum might not have had an issue turning a blind eye to Dad's indiscretion, but I did, especially since I'd become the scapegoat. The villain. One of us had been lying. But it hadn't been me. Why had she abandoned me and sided with my dad? Simple. She loved him more than she loved me. That hurt. Tears pricked my eyes. I needed to get a grip. I prided myself on my independence and the fact that I didn't give a shit what anybody thought about me. So why did I care? Why waste my time fretting over something that was out of my control?

Grief does strange things to a person. It normally wouldn't bother me to go it alone; being self-sufficient was an important life skill. I had my mum to thank for that. So I didn't understand why I felt a desperate need to cling to the remaining members of my family like they were life rafts in a stormy sea. They didn't feel the same way. Instead of holding me close, they kept pushing me away. Dad's loss had upset the balance. Three was an awkward number. Mum and Lily didn't want me around. They had each other. Two against one. I needed somebody I could confide in.

As the fat raindrops started to fall, my thoughts turned to MacKenzie. I took my phone out of my bag and dialled his number. It went straight to voicemail. I'd been hoping that he'd let me crash at his place for a while.

I wouldn't usually turn up on somebody's doorstep unannounced, but I was desperate, so I hot-footed it around to his flat. The place was in darkness, but I rang the bell anyway. Maybe he was sleeping. While I waited, it suddenly occurred to me there might be another reason the lights weren't on. If he was lying low, he was hardly likely to open the door to me. I didn't like the thought of being in the spotlight in case somebody had eyes on MacKenzie's property.

The rain wasn't easing off, but I didn't want to wait any

longer for a response I knew wasn't coming. Even though my down jacket was warm and snuggly, I'd catch my death if I stayed out in this. There was a bus shelter around the corner, so I decided to make a run for it. I pulled up the hood on my puffer and raced down the steps outside MacKenzie's flat. As I ran along the pavement, I trod in a huge puddle, which splashed icy cold water up the legs of my jeans. For fuck's sake! Could my day get any worse?

I gritted my teeth, tucked my chin down and carried on pacing down the street. Thank God nobody was waiting for a bus. I couldn't handle having a mind-numbingly boring conversation about how shit the weather was with some random stranger. I plonked myself down on the hard plastic seat and pulled my phone out of my bag. Gusts of wind were whipping around the sides of the shelter, but at least it was dry.

With everything that had been going on, I'd forgotten to phone Bernice to see how she was doing. Crap friend I'd turned out to be. Roscoe hadn't even been laid to rest yet and I should have been in regular contact with her. She'd gone out of her way to help me. She was my protector. My biggest cheerleader. Bernice had looked out for me the way a mother should. Bernice was everything my own mum wasn't. Regret started swirling around me. So much for me being the person she could depend on.

'Hi, it's me,' I said when she answered the call.

'Hello, darling. It's lovely to hear from you. I've been worried about you. How's everything going?'

The sound of her voice sent a wave of relief crashing through my body. Tears pricked my eyes. Bernice had every right to tell me to fuck off. I was overwhelmed by her response; her concern was touching. Her caring nature never failed to bring my emotions to the surface.

'I don't know where to start. So much has happened.' Wasn't that the truth?

'Has it been awkward being under the same roof as your mum and Lily?' Bernice asked, but I'd say she already knew the answer to her question.

'How did you guess?'

'Intuition. Do you want to talk about it?'

Bernice was a great listener, and I was desperate to get everything off my chest. But this wasn't a conversation to have over the phone. I wanted to be face to face with her when I blurted everything out.

'Let's just say it's unbearable. Anyone would think I was the one who'd murdered my dad. Mum and Lily are looking for somebody to take their grief out on, and guess who's found herself in the firing line?' I replied as an opener.

'Oh, for God's sake! You poor thing. You shouldn't have to put up with crap like that. Do you want me to come and get you? You can stay at my place for as long as you like,' Bernice offered.

Tears started rolling down my cheeks. Bernice was such a generous, kind-hearted person. I sniffed them back before I replied. I didn't want her to know she'd made me cry. It would only make her more concerned.

'Now there's an offer I can't refuse, but only if you're sure you don't mind,' I said in as chirpy a voice as I could manage.

'Of course I don't mind. It'll be an absolute pleasure. I hate rattling around the place on my own. You'll be good company. I'll be with you as soon as I can. Do you want me to pick you up from your house?'

I couldn't help noticing the change in Bernice's tone. She'd gone from being upbeat to cautious, which was hardly surprising. The last time she'd come face to face with the woman who'd given birth to me, my mum had torn into her and started screaming like an old fishwife. No wonder she was weary.

'Why don't I get the train? Maybe you could pick me up from the station instead,' I suggested. I'd only have to hang around waiting for her, so it made sense to me.

'I don't want to worry you, but it looks like Samson's still alive...' Bernice trailed off.

Her unexpected words stole my breath and my shoulders slumped. I felt defeated. I should have known it was too good to be true. I wished Bernice had pumped him full of bullets while she'd had the chance. We should never have left without checking him for signs of life.

'Travelling on the train on your own is too dangerous. You need to keep a low profile. If he's still in the land of the living, Samson's going to be gunning for both of us.'

And there was I, thinking the day from hell couldn't possibly get any worse.

'I'll come and pick you up.'

'Are you sure you don't want me to get the train? I'll be careful.'

'No. I'd rather collect you. The traffic's usually pretty good on a Sunday, and I'm staying at the farmhouse, so I'm much closer to London anyway.'

Since Bernice put it like that, I wasn't going to argue with her. I'd be shitting myself if I had to travel alone now that I knew Samson might be on the loose.

'What would I do without you? You're so good to me.'

Bernice had come to the rescue again. I felt so choked up by her kindness, the words almost got stuck in my throat.

'Honestly, it's nothing. Should I come to your house?'

'How about The Orange Tree,' I suggested.

The last thing I wanted was for Bernice to turn up at my

place and for the slanging match to begin again. I could almost guarantee Mum would start on her, and then the curtain-twitching neighbours would be in their element. If World War Three broke out on the doorstep, it would give the gossipmongers enough fuel for months. Witnessing a showdown between the four of us would be essential viewing and I didn't want to deal with the drama. Besides that, I needed a drink after the morning I'd had.

'I don't know what the weather's like in Kent, but it's chucking it down up here.'

'It's not raining yet, but it looks like it could start any minute,' Bernice replied.

'Drive safely,' I said.

Those windy roads through the Kent Downs were treacherous at the best of times, but they'd be even worse if the weather was bad.

'Don't worry. I will.'

'If you give me the heads up when you're five minutes away, I'll come outside and wait for you. It'll save you trying to park.'

'OK, darling. I'll see you soon.'

After we finished our call, I seriously considered slipping home so that I could fling some stuff into a bag. It would be good to have the opportunity to pack for a change rather than having to cut and run with just the clothes on my back, but the thought of bumping into my mum and Lily made my mind up for me. Travelling light it was then. Mum should only ever have had one child. She didn't have the capacity to love two.

26

MACKENZIE

'MacKenzie, can you come down here for a second,' Bernice called from the bottom of the staircase.

I'd been standing on the landing looking out across the valley, checking for signs of suspicious activity and keeping my eyes peeled for unwanted visitors. We couldn't afford to take our eye off the ball. Samson would ambush us when we least expected it if he found out where we were holed up. Thankfully, the farmhouse was surrounded by acres of land, so the only things I could see for miles were green fields and trees.

'Coming,' I called back.

I dragged myself away from the floor-to-ceiling windows and tried to walk down the stairs as casually as possible so that Bernice wouldn't realise every step was causing me agony.

'I'm not disturbing you, am I?' Bernice said as I approached.

'Nah. I was just admiring the view.'

It was the perfect spot to stay out of sight. The isolation and ultra-thick walls made it feel safe. Well, as safe as it could be.

'I've just been talking to Daisy,' Bernice said.

My heart sped up at the mention of her name. Thoughts of Samson vanished into thin air.

'How's she doing?' I asked. Then I bit the inside of my cheeks to stop my lips from stretching into a huge smile.

'She's not good.' The corners of Bernice's lips turned down. She looked sad.

My face slackened. 'I suppose that's to be expected.'

'It sounds like there's a whole load of shit going down.'

'How come?'

'She didn't go into details, but by all accounts, tensions are running high. Tara and Lily are giving her a hard time. She sounded like she needed a sympathetic ear to get it all off her chest. I told her I'd go and get her and bring her back to the farmhouse.'

The contents of my stomach dropped. What was Bernice thinking of? Leaving the house and travelling to London was a huge risk. I opened my mouth to say something but then thought better of it. Daisy was in danger, too. We couldn't just forget she existed.

'Daisy offered to get the train, but I don't want her to travel alone. I wondered if you fancied keeping me company.' Bernice smiled.

'I'd love to.'

I couldn't think of anything worse than being stuck in the car for hours on end, but I couldn't let Bernice go on her own. It was too dangerous with Samson on the prowl.

'Give me a couple of minutes. I just need to have a slash and get my jacket.'

I also needed time to snort a few lines of rocket fuel to dull the throbbing in my nuts.

Bernice was waiting by the front door when I reappeared. She was wearing one of her slinky black outfits and over-the-knee high-heeled boots. God knew how she was going to drive the car in those, but I wasn't going to question her choice of footwear. I didn't need the backlash. The journey was going to be bad enough without us bickering the whole way.

'Are you ready?' Bernice's glossy red lips stretched into a smile.

'Raring to go,' I replied.

It always amazed me how easily shit rolled off my tongue.

27

DAISY

I set off in the direction of the pub, huddled into my jacket with my head bowed, hoping that if Samson had spies in the area, they wouldn't spot me. It was only a short walk, but the icy rain stung my cheeks as it pelted my face. I couldn't get there soon enough for my liking. At least I'd be warm and dry while I killed some time. Even on a good run, it would take Bernice well over an hour and a half to reach me.

Being out in the elements was grim. My hands had turned bright red, and my teeth were chattering. I was definitely a wimp when it came to cold and wet. Every step was torture. I thought I'd never get there, but when I glanced up, the warm glow of the V-shaped string of white lights outside the entrance beckoned me towards it, and my spirits lifted.

I pushed open the door with numb fingers, and a wall of heat barrelled towards me. It felt good to be out of the rain. I paced up to the bar with renewed energy but felt myself inwardly groan when I saw it was the same guy serving as yesterday. I'd tried to be as discreet as possible when I'd bundled

Colleen out of the door, but I was a bit pissed, too, so we must have looked a right state.

'Hi, what can I get you?' he asked with a smile on his face.

Was he trying to stifle a laugh or just being friendly? Embarrassment crept up inside me, but I'd have to brazen it out. There was no point in being paranoid and reading too much into what was more than likely a friendly greeting. The guy worked in a pub. He'd seen it all before. Some people came here specifically to get drunk. For others, unintentionally getting hammered was a by-product of the night out. Colleen and I fell into that category. We hadn't done anything wrong. We hadn't smashed the place up or caused a fight. We just got legless. Simple as that. I wasn't normally an irrationally anxious person, but I was rattled by all the upheaval and uncertainty that was going on around me.

'Do you want me to give you a minute?' the barman asked.

His voice broke into my thoughts and brought me back to reality. I suddenly realised he was waiting for me to order a drink.

'Sorry, I was mesmerised by all the bottles,' I replied to make light of the awkwardness.

'You're not the first person to say that! We're very well stocked, so you're spoilt for choice.' He smiled.

'Absolutely. But I'm a creature of habit. Can I have a large glass of Pinot Grigio, please?' I said.

'No worries.'

Once I'd paid for my drink, I took a seat at a table furthest away from the bar and closest to the roaring open fire so that I could thaw out while drying off. The place was virtually empty, which was a blessing. I needed time to think. Time to process what Colleen had told me. I wouldn't have been able to concentrate if a load of rowdy customers were rabbiting on at the top of their voices.

As I took a sip of my wine, something occurred to me. I wondered if Lily remembered the day I burst into Mum and Dad's bedroom any clearer than I did. Identical twins shared loads of traits. We thought alike and processed information alike, so it would seem reasonable to assume our recollection of an event would be similar. Or had I developed selective amnesia because I'd been trying to block out the bad memory? I'd never know the answer to that question. It wasn't as though I could ever ask Lily. We didn't have that kind of relationship. We didn't have any relationship at all at the moment.

After Bernice and I had freed her from the warehouse, we'd got off to a good start. I'd hoped things were going to be different between us. But then my dad died, and everything went tits up. I'd hoped the tragedy would bring my family closer together. But it was tearing us apart.

I absentmindedly lifted my glass to my lips and realised it was empty. I'd virtually downed the wine. Bollocks. I'd have to get a refill. I couldn't sit at the table for the next hour without buying another drink, but then I'd have to pace myself. I didn't want to be bladdered when Bernice came to collect me. I knew I could follow my teetotal sister's example, but I'd never been a fan of mineral water.

When I returned to my seat, I put my large glass of wine over the other side of the table, almost out of my reach, so I didn't gulp it down. I reasoned that if I had to consciously think about lifting the stem, I wouldn't keep sipping away on automatic pilot like I had with the previous glass.

I didn't know whether it was the effects of the wine or my imagination playing tricks on me, but I could hear my dad's voice stuck on a loop in my head. He was saying the same thing over and over again.

'*Happy now? You couldn't leave things alone, could you? Nothing ever changes. You're always out to cause trouble.*'

I wished it would fuck off and leave me be. I couldn't escape from him. He'd come back from the grave to haunt me. Taunt me. Nagging. Badgering. Looking for a reaction. What the hell was wrong with me? Why did I crave his approval even at this stage when he was no longer around to give it? I was finding it hard to accept that I'd never be able to right the wrongs.

I'd been eyeing the dregs of my glass for what seemed like an eternity. I knew I wouldn't be able to resist polishing it off for much longer when my mobile sprang to life. I scrambled to open my phone and read the text.

BERNICE

I'm five minutes away xxx

DAISY

Perfect. I'll wait outside Xx

I reached for the glass and swallowed the last mouthful before I picked up my bag and jacket. I shrugged my arms into the sleeves as I walked towards the door. I glanced over at the counter, but the barman was busy serving a customer, so I slipped out without saying goodbye.

A gust of cold, wet air hit me in the face when I stepped outside. I felt myself shudder. The sun was still hiding behind the clouds, and the rain continued to pelt. But now the wind had picked up. Mother Nature was flexing her muscles. The bare branches overhead creaked as the elements battered them. Mini cyclones full of litter and fallen leaves whirled on the pavement in front of me. Five minutes was going to seem like a lifetime. It had been lovely and cosy in the pub, so being back outside was horrendous.

I peered down the street, extending my neck to give myself the best view, but there was no sign of Bernice's Jag, so I delved my hand into my bag, pulled out my Marlboros and lighter, and then lit a cigarette to pass the time. I took a long drag and exhaled slowly. The smoke swirled around me, rapidly changing directions as the wind caught it. I couldn't put my finger on it, but something seemed off. There was a strange atmosphere. The busy street seemed unusually quiet. No pedestrians. No cars. No signs of life.

I stubbed my cigarette on the floor, and as I looked up, I noticed a large black car approaching me. I couldn't see whether it was a Range Rover from this distance. Even if it was, it didn't mean it was Samson's car. But that didn't stop terror start to rise within me. The sight of it edging closer like a shark fin in open water filled me with dread. I had to try and stay calm. No good would come from panicking. I breathed a sigh of relief when I realised it was a Lexus. But I couldn't deny it had spooked me. I'd been hoping one of the few customers in The Orange Tree would come out for a smoke so that I wouldn't be alone, but nobody had appeared.

I checked the time on my phone. Bernice should be here any second. Five minutes had been and gone. What was keeping her? Agitation began swirling inside me. I suddenly felt anxious. I couldn't explain why, but I had a bad feeling about this. Being out in the open made me feel vulnerable. Should I stay where I'd agreed to meet her or go back inside the pub? I was still trying to decide what to do for the best when the Lexus pulled up at the kerb. My heart leapt into my mouth when the front passenger door opened. I'd been so worried that Samson was closing in on me that I hadn't considered the other threat.

'Fancy seeing you here,' Warren Jenkins said as he stepped out of the car.

He was wearing the same flat cap and long leather trench coat as the last time I'd been unfortunate enough to cross paths with him. He pulled up the collar to shield himself from the rain as he walked towards me. I glanced up and down the road. There wasn't a soul around, so there was no point in screaming or trying to make a run for it. There was no one close enough to help me.

I'd forgotten how huge he was. Warren was the size of an ogre. I felt like a small child as I craned my neck to look up at him. My breath caught in my throat when he stooped down to my level.

'I'm glad I ran into you. Seeing you standing on the street corner like an old brass looking for business has just given me a brilliant idea. I don't know why I didn't think of it sooner. It'll be a great way for you to pay back the money you owe.' Warren laughed.

His lips were close to my ear as he delivered the threat. His words sent a shiver running down my spine. My mouth dropped open in horror. I was glued to the spot. Paralysed by fear. I felt physically sick as I watched the way his eyes roamed all over me. The contents of my stomach did a double flip. I thought I was going to spew Pinot Grigio all over his shoes. If Warren thought he could pimp me out, he could think again. I wasn't going to be forced to turn tricks for anyone. Warren looked over his shoulder at the two heavies who'd joined him on the pavement.

'Put her in the car, lads,' he said.

It all happened so fast. I didn't have time to come up with an escape plan. Any thoughts of cutting and running vanished into the ether. The human gorilla standing closest to me must have realised what I was planning to do, so he lunged at me and grabbed hold of my upper arm before I had the chance. His hands were so big his fingers almost closed around my limb, and that was over a thick winter puffer jacket. Then the other guy grabbed hold of my other side, and they dragged me towards the car. I bucked and wriggled with all my might to try and break free, but my efforts were in vain. They were holding me too tightly. A vision of Lily being bundled into a car hit me smack between the eyes. I shook the image from my mind. I needed to concentrate all my energy on getting away before the same thing happened to me. I repeatedly kicked out at the two guys. I definitely made contact with both of them, but it wasn't enough to stop them pulling me to the car. I saw a flash of red out of the corner of my eye as they forced me onto the back seat.

Bernice had just turned into the road. If she'd arrived five minutes earlier, I wouldn't have been in this position. What was wrong with me? Why had that thought even entered my head? It wasn't her fault; I'd been in the wrong place at the wrong time. I should have let her collect me from the house like she'd suggested rather than making myself an easy target by waiting for her out in the open. I was kicking myself. But then again, it could have been worse. If she'd arrived five minutes later, I'd have vanished into thin air. Bernice was a badass. I had every faith in her. She'd tail the car and get me out of this mess before I knew it. I'd put money on that.

28

SAMSON

Arben wasn't going to get away with what he'd done. I needed to think carefully about my next move. His outfit was huge. I didn't have the numbers behind me to back me up, so I'd have to formulate a tactical plan. I intentionally kept my inner circle tight, but it was smaller than I'd like it to be these days. My trusted crew were dwindling. I couldn't just pull people off the street to fill the void Gary, Smithy and Tank had left behind. Those guys had worked for me for years and gradually risen up the ranks through their hard work and loyalty. Their shoes weren't easy to fill.

'Hi, boss. I'm at the warehouse,' Kyle said.

'I'll be with you shortly.'

Carly had a drink and drug problem, so the most sensible thing to do was feed her habit. If I let her go into withdrawal, she'd be no use to man nor beast. A rattling junkie was about as helpful as a one-legged man in an arse-kicking competition.

On the way to the warehouse, I stopped my Range Rover outside a scruffy corner shop to pick up some supplies. I'd have to be quick. This was a rough neighbourhood. I didn't want to come back and find some arsehole had taken off in my motor.

The guy behind the counter could have learned a thing or two about treating paying customers with respect. The look of disdain on his face when I pushed open the door instantly got my back up. If I'd had another option, I'd have gone elsewhere. I didn't want to be in his shitty little shop either, but I needed to grab a few bits so that I could get down to business.

Even though I was wearing a handmade suit, the guy eyed me like I was some kind of thief, which made me wonder what type of suspect low-life clientele he was used to serving.

'I'll have a bottle of that vodka,' I said, pointing to the cheapest one he had behind the counter.

The money-grabbing shopkeeper's eyes lit up when he dusted off the clear spirit before scanning it at the till. Judging by the cobwebs clinging to the neck, I couldn't imagine he sold many of them. It was probably like paint stripper, but I didn't give a toss. Carly looked like the kind of girl who'd drink anything. It stuck in my throat to have to pay thirty pounds for a bottle of turps masquerading as the finest Russian vodka, but needs must. I had to keep Carly's vocal cords well-oiled with something.

My eyes searched the shelf for a bottle of single malt, but there was nothing but blended rubbish. I briefly considered buying it anyway but decided not to bother when I took a closer look. I thought the veil of dust on the vodka was thick, but it was nothing compared to the layer that had settled on the whisky. The Scotch had obviously been there for years.

I picked up some cans of Peroni. Then I grabbed an equally overpriced two-litre bottle of Coke to dilute the fire water with. Drinking something like that neat would be out of the question, although Carly would probably give it a go. The guy's smile widened as he rang everything through the till. By the time he'd finished, he was grinning from ear to ear. I tapped the terminal with my card. He didn't bother to thank me for my custom as I went to leave his flea pit, so I walked back up to the counter and headbutted him. The look of horror on his face as blood started pouring from his nostrils went some way to making up for his rudeness. If I hadn't been pressed for time, I'd have gone to town on the bastard. He needed to be taught a lesson.

* * *

Carly and Kyle were sitting side by side at the table in the kitchen area when I arrived at the warehouse. I handed Kyle a Peroni – stuff this ladies first bollocks – before I poured Carly a Samson-sized measure of vodka, then placed the bottle of Coke down in front of her. To my surprise, she filled the rest of the glass with it, which screamed lightweight to me. I'd been expecting her to add a splash, being the hardened drinker she was.

Kyle and I had barely taken two sips out of our cans when she put her empty glass down in front of her. She'd practically downed what I'd given her in one. Carly reached her bony hand across the table and poured herself a top-up without asking if that was OK. Cheeky bitch. I had to stop myself from snatching the bottle out of her grasp. I had a thing about bad manners. I couldn't abide it when people didn't treat me with respect.

I'd been so preoccupied with what she'd just done that her next move took me completely by surprise. I'd intended to interrogate Carly to see if there were any other nuggets of information she was holding on to that might be helpful before brainstorming ideas with Kyle to work out where we went from here, but that wasn't how things panned out. I nearly fell off my chair when she launched into me.

'Do you make a habit of exploiting underage girls?'

Carly fixed me with a menacing look, and I almost laughed out loud. She was about as threatening as an elderly, toothless Chihuahua.

'What the fuck are you talking about?' I sneered. Then I took a gulp of my Peroni.

'I had a feeling you'd say that. I was naive, of course I was; I was fourteen. I didn't have a clue how these things worked. It's not who you know but who you blow that puts you on the ladder to fame and fortune.'

'What are you bleating on about, you stupid bitch?' I was bored of this conversation already.

'My fate was in your hands, and you used me to your advantage. You said you were going to make me a star.' Carly's words were bitter.

So I did know her from Eden's.

'Women use their sex appeal to advance their careers all the time. Spreading their legs for the chance to sign a lucrative deal is a smart move, but I'd stake my life on the fact that I never slept with you. I have high standards, and you don't meet them. You're a bag of bones. I like a bird who's all tits and teeth. I prefer the natural variety, but if they're done well, I'm not opposed to surgical enhancements.' I laughed.

'This isn't a laughing matter,' Carly said as though I was a kid in her class at school. 'I never said that you had. But because of my situation, I was easy prey. Travis used me. He stole my innocence...' Carly was choked up.

If I had a pound for every time I'd heard that old chestnut, I'd be minted. Carly downed her vodka and then reached for the bottle again. I didn't bother to stop her.

'Travis did nothing that you didn't sign up for.'

It didn't matter what he'd done. I'd always have my friend's back.

'I didn't sign up to be sexually assaulted. Travis is a predator, and the fact that I was underage was a huge turn-on to him.' Carly was on the verge of tears.

From what she'd just said, I was sure she was the bird who'd turned up at Eden's looking for a job. I'd suspected she wasn't old enough to work in a club, but I'd turned a blind eye. She wasn't the first schoolgirl I'd had on the books, but I wasn't about to share that information with her.

'Now you listen to me,' I said, getting up from the table and ramming my finger in her face. 'You're nothing but a little slag who drops her knickers for anyone and everyone, and you're trying to tarnish my good friend's name by throwing wild accusations around.'

I stood glaring at her for several seconds before I dropped back into my seat.

'It's true, and you're every bit as bad as he is.' Carly's voice broke.

My temper was threatening to erupt. If it did, it would be hard to restrain. She was moments away from my wrath descending on her.

'You'd better wind your neck in right now. I'm not a nonce. I don't sleep with underage girls!' I roared, and Carly jumped out of her skin.

I hadn't been expecting her to go on the attack. Her confidence was buoyed up with booze. She was goading me. I wasn't going to stand for that. She needed a slap and bringing back down to size.

'I know some really deep, dark secrets, which I'm on the brink of spilling. Dirt has a habit of catching up with a person.

It's only a matter of time until the truth comes out,' Carly said before draining her glass again.

'You're getting right on my tits. Who the fuck do you think you're speaking to? Listen to me, you little bitch, if you open your mouth and start spouting shit like this, you're dead.'

Carly's eyes were locked on mine as I issued the warning. I could hardly believe what I was seeing. She'd changed into a different person with drink in her. She was deluded if she thought she could threaten me. I was the one in the power seat.

Carly had no intention of backing down. She'd managed to turn the focus of our meeting on its head. I didn't usually shy away from an argument, far from it. I could do battle with my own shadow when the mood took me, but this particular conversation was of a delicate nature. I didn't want to discuss the details in front of an audience, even though I knew Kyle was trustworthy. I'd had enough of listening to Carly shouting her mouth off for one day, so I pushed my chair back and got to my feet.

'I'll leave you to sober up. I'm not going to get any sense out of you while you've got that shit sloshing around in your system,' I said, eyeing the almost empty vodka bottle. I grabbed hold of the neck of it and lifted it off the table. 'You've had quite enough of that for one night.'

'Hey. Don't take it away. I was enjoying that,' Carly protested.

'Tough shit! Keep her here until I decide what to do with her.'

My eyes scanned over Kyle's face.

'No worries, boss,' he replied.

Carly was a liability. Having a loose cannon around was bad news for all of us.

I stomped out of the warehouse, got behind the wheel of my

Range Rover, and tore out of the industrial estate at a rate of knots. I was absolutely boiling mad.

I needed to get Travis up to speed on the latest development with Carly. He'd told me her name wasn't ringing any bells with him, but she remembered him extremely well. Too well. Her encounter with Travis had scarred her for life. I had to warn him that trouble was on the horizon if we didn't put a stop to it. I dialled his number, but it went straight to voicemail, so I slammed the palm of my hand down on the steering wheel and let out a roar of frustration. Did he never think of anything else other than his dick?

'Call me back as soon as you get this message. I need to speak to you urgently.' The tone of my voice said it all. I didn't need to spell out what was wrong.

I'd put money on the fact that Travis was busy banging the backing singers' brains out at this precise moment, so he wouldn't give a flying fuck about anything that was going on around him. If Carly was telling the truth, and I had no reason not to believe her story, Travis was in crap up to his neck. If she blabbed, he could go down for years. And we all knew what happened to child molesters while they were residing at His Majesty's pleasure, didn't we?

I wasn't sure Travis would slip easily into the role of being somebody's bitch. Finding himself violated whenever or wherever they chose wouldn't be his cup of tea, but other lags didn't take kindly to kiddie fiddlers. I had first-hand knowledge of how these things worked. My dad served five years for cheating the tax man. That was the least of his crimes. He'd have gone down for a hell of a lot longer if he'd got done for smuggling drugs. His time inside taught my family a valuable lesson. If you wanted the Old Bill to stay out of your hair, you had to keep the pen pushers at the Inland Revenue happy. It wasn't as though Dad couldn't afford to pay what was due. He just liked to feel he was getting one over on the state. Half the country was on the scrounge, claiming benefits. Dad took umbrage to keeping strangers on the dole, so he'd been making a stand.

I was thrown into the deep end, but while he was banged up, the business thrived so much that he decided to retire and hand over the reins to me. His heart wasn't really in it after he'd done bird. He wanted to make up for lost time and thank my mum for sticking by him. I couldn't keep up with the pair of them. They were always flitting off to one luxury resort or another like a couple of love-struck newlyweds. I very much doubted Travis's young wife would stand by him if the shit hit the fan. And the last thing I needed was to be charged as an accessory.

29

MACKENZIE

The twenty-mile-an-hour zones in London were a pain in the arse. It took an age to get anywhere these days. This particular stretch of road had traffic enforcement cameras all along its length, so there was no way Bernice could chance going any faster, or she'd end up with a hefty fine and three points on her licence. Or worse still, she'd have to attend a speed awareness course.

'These bloody restrictions are doing my head in,' Bernice said as she fixed her eyes on her speedometer.

'You could walk faster.' I laughed.

The frustration in the car was palpable as we inched our way along Denmark Road, then turned onto Coldharbour Lane. I could see a woman in the distance who looked very much like Daisy talking to a group of guys. I sensed something bad was about to happen even before they started dragging her towards the open back door of the black car parked at the kerb.

'Is that Daisy?' Bernice's eyes were like saucers as she leaned towards the windscreen to get a better look.

'I think so.'

I couldn't be certain. The rain was lashing against the windscreen, so the visibility was poor. We were viewing the scene through a haze.

'Jesus, is that Warren Jenkins?' Bernice peered at the huge guy in the long coat and flat cap as we drew closer. 'I haven't set eyes on him in years, but that's his trademark outfit.'

I couldn't say either way. I'd never seen the bloke in the flesh. I just knew him by name. My heart nearly leapt out of my chest when the two other guys suddenly dragged the girl across the pavement and forced her onto the back seat. We were too far away to help, and the car sped off.

'Oh my God, what should I do?' Bernice turned her eyes away from the road and glanced at me.

'Follow them, but stay back. We don't want whoever's driving to know we're tailing them.'

Bernice put her foot down to try and close the gap, but whoever was behind the wheel of the black Lexus was on a mission. They were driving like a lunatic, jumping red lights and going around corners practically on two wheels. The streets were deserted, so Bernice had trouble keeping up. We only managed to follow for a short while before it left us for dust and disappeared out of sight.

'For fuck's sake! Give me a break!' I shouted through the windscreen.

'I'm sorry, darling, I tried not to lose it, but I can't drive like Lewis Hamilton.'

I could see she was angry with herself, which made me feel like a prize dick. My outburst wasn't directed at her.

'Take no notice of me. I'm not pissed off with you. I was just venting my frustration. Nobody would have been able to keep up with that maniac. Let's hope he doesn't end up wrapping the car around a lamppost.'

'Don't tempt fate by saying things like that.'

Bernice threw me a look. But she wasn't the only one who was worried. If anything happened to Daisy, I'd never forgive myself.

'Something's just occurred to me. Maybe that wasn't Daisy in the Lexus. I'm going to go back to The Orange Tree in case we missed her. She might have decided to stay inside the pub to shelter from the rain,' Bernice said, her voice full of hope.

I felt she was clutching at straws, but I couldn't think of a better alternative, so I went along with her plan.

'I suppose it's got to be worth a try.'

When Bernice pulled up outside the pub, the street was eerily empty.

'Why don't you check if she's still in there? She might have got talking to somebody...' Bernice suggested.

I thought that was highly unlikely, but I kept that to myself. I didn't want Bernice to think I was being defeatist.

'No worries.'

I pulled up my hood and dashed for the door. Once I was inside, I did a quick scout of the pub before heading up to the counter. I might as well have a quick drink while I checked things out. It would help to take the edge off my pain.

'Hi, mate, what can I get you?' the barman asked.

'I'll have a double rum and a small splash of Coke, please.'

As the guy prepared my drink, I picked his brain. 'I was meant to meet a friend of mine in here, but I'm running a bit late. I don't suppose you saw her? Early twenties, blonde, really pretty girl...'

The barman nodded. 'She was in here earlier, sitting at the table closest to the fire, but I'm fairly certain she's gone.'

'No worries.'

I hovered my phone above the terminal so I could pay for my drink, and then I downed it in one.

'Somebody's thirsty.' The barman laughed as I placed the empty glass in front of him.

'I'm plucking up the courage to go back outside.' I gestured to the door with a flick of my head.

'Rather you than me.' He laughed.

A gust of wind grabbed the door and almost ripped it off its hinges as I forced it open. I tucked my chin down and headed for the car, battling against the gale threatening to knock me off my feet.

'Any luck?' Bernice asked when I pulled the door closed on the Jag.

Her eyes fixed on mine, but she knew what I was going to say before I replied.

'No. But the guy behind the bar said she'd been in earlier...'

We didn't need to say it out loud to know our worst fears were confirmed. Daisy was the girl in the Lexus.

'What a desperate situation.' Bernice was close to tears. Her blue eyes were glistening.

'Try not to worry. We'll think of something.'

'I know it's a long shot, but I'm going to try phoning her mobile and see if she picks up.'

Bernice held her phone to her ear until Daisy's voicemail connected. She didn't leave a message. What was the point? Daisy wasn't going to be able to return her call.

'Back to the drawing board,' Bernice said. 'How about I drive around and see if we spot anything?'

'Why not?' I replied, but I could think of a million reasons why we shouldn't bother.

I didn't waste my breath. Bernice wouldn't want to hear

them. I had to admire her steely determination. She was definitely the sort of person you'd want in your corner. Her never-give-up attitude was inspirational.

I didn't want to rain on her parade, but we both knew we weren't going to find the car that had spirited Daisy away.

30

DAISY

My heart beat like a drum as the Lexus drove off into the night. I had no idea where Warren was taking me. I was kicking myself for being so stupid. I should have just gone back to my house and waited there for Bernice. What was the worst that could have happened? Mum and Bernice might have had words. Big deal. That was nothing compared to what I'd got myself involved in now. I felt like bursting into tears, but I wouldn't give Warren the satisfaction of seeing me cry.

Putting on a brave face was easier said than done. I was shitting myself, absolutely terrified of what he was going to do to me. I knew what he was capable of. I'd seen the way he'd butchered my dad in the middle of our living room. He was bloodthirsty. Deranged. He wouldn't think twice about doing the same to me if I didn't do what he wanted. He was a maniac.

I could see my legs trembling as I sat wedged between the two heavies. I dug my feet into the floor to try and stop the tremors, but it didn't help. My knees kept knocking together. We were going way over the speed limit and the driver had shot through every red light we'd come to. Where was a patrol car when you needed one?

As we sped along, my mind kept going to dark, scary places. The thought of being forced into prostitution against my will turned my stomach. Was Warren just threatening me with that to scare me into being compliant or was he really planning to go through with it?

I clung to the hope that Bernice would intervene before he got the opportunity. So often, people didn't have the energy to do the right thing. They didn't want the hassle of getting involved. Thank God Bernice wasn't one of them. I couldn't see whether she was tailing us. I'd give the game away if I looked over my shoulder, so I stared straight ahead and prayed she was following behind.

We hadn't been driving long when the car pulled into the car park of a pub called The Beehive. As we cruised to the back of the building, I peered out of the windows, hoping to catch the eye of a passerby now that we'd slowed down, but there was no one around. I wasn't familiar with this neck of the woods even though, judging by the distance we'd travelled, it wasn't far from where I lived.

The driver pulled up close to a set of wooden doors. He picked up a bunch of keys from the compartment next to the handbrake and got out of the car. Walking over to the double doors, he opened the padlock, pulled the chain back through the handles, and folded the doors outwards. I squinted through the windscreen, but it was too dark to see what was inside. The structure was attached to the side of the pub, so I assumed it was some kind of outhouse.

After the driver got back behind the wheel, Warren and the henchman on my right stepped out of the car. Then the driver nudged the huge Lexus through the small opening. The car barely fit inside. There wasn't even enough room to fully open the car doors. The heavy sitting on my left had to practically bend himself in two to squeeze out of the tight space. Once he was on his feet, he yanked me out by the sleeve of my jacket. I wondered why we hadn't got out before we drove inside the lock-up. But I supposed there was more chance of somebody spotting me then.

After we squeezed past the car, the other guy grabbed my free arm. Now that I was outside, I made one last-ditch attempt to break free, but the more I struggled, the tighter the men gripped onto me. They dragged me towards a metal staircase at the side of the garage. I could see the driver out of the corner of my eye, padlocking the doors closed to conceal the Lexus.

Warren's men pulled me along, but I wasn't going willingly. I was digging my heels in. The fact that they were leading me underground spiked my fear and made my blood pressure soar. I didn't know why I was so scared. Lots of pubs had working basements they used for storage, didn't they?

The glow of an antique-looking brass lantern drew closer, so I sucked in a breath in case it was the last one I'd take. I felt like I was being led to a tomb. To a coffin. To my death. My blood ran cold. Shivers shot up and down my spine. I'd fought so hard to keep my tears under control, but I'd lost the battle. I was powerless to stop the floodgates from opening. I started screaming at the top of my lungs, which made Warren roar with laughter.

'You can fight and struggle all you like, no one can hear you, and even if they could, they wouldn't give a shit about what happens to the likes of you. You're the spawn of scum. You might have been blessed with good looks, but you'll never amount to anything. People like you never do.' Warren looked down his nose at me.

His comments halted my cries for help and sent tingles of

irritation coursing through my body. But I didn't react. For once, I had the sense to let it go. What a fucking cheek? That was rich coming from him. He was a criminal, and a violent one at that. He hadn't exactly reached dizzying heights on the achievement ladder himself. But I was in no position to point that out to him unless I had a death wish. If I told him what I thought about him right now, there'd be no taking it back.

Warren held open the fire exit door, and the two heavies roughly manhandled me through it. The area was dimly lit by more of the brass lanterns. I cast my eyes around. I'd been expecting to see barrels of beer and boxes of wine and spirits stacked up in the space at the bottom of the flight of stairs, but the exposed brick area was empty apart from a life-size portrait of Warren encased in an old-fashioned gilt frame which took up half of the back wall.

I jumped out of my skin when one of the henchmen clanged the fire exit shut behind me. Warren's face broke into a huge grin. I was still trying to figure out why they'd brought me down here when Warren tucked two of his enormous fingers into the frame's ornate edging and pulled it towards him. My mouth dropped open when the picture started to move. I couldn't believe what I was seeing. There was another room, a foyer, on the other side of the frame. I hadn't been expecting that. Plush, bottle green velvet sofas lay along both sides. The walls were dark. The lighting was low.

Warren led the way into the secret room. I had no choice but to follow. A middle-aged woman with brassy blonde bouffant hair and large gold hoop earrings stood behind what looked like a concierge's desk. She should have laid off the orange tan she'd smothered herself in; it clashed terribly with her combed-over hair and made her bear more than a passing resemblance to a certain American politician who was never out of the news. Her pouty plumped-up lips were coated in a thick layer of pearly pale pink lip gloss that looked sticky enough to glue stamps onto a letter.

'Hello, Mr Jenkins,' she said, pushing her cleavage up so much I thought it was going to spill out of her shocking pink, satin low-cut top.

She flashed him a wide smile which exposed gappy, nicotine-stained teeth, giving away the fact that she was a smoker. I made a mental note to quit before mine ended up in the same condition.

'Hello, Raquel. How's business?'

Raquel's smile slid from her lips. 'Fairly quiet to be honest, but a few of the regulars are here.'

Warren didn't reply before he stepped through a door, above which a sign read 'Members Only'. I could only imagine what was waiting for me on the other side. I was bundled into the room a split-second later, and then, to my surprise, the heavies released their grip on me. As my eyes scanned the space, my legs started to tremble even though both of my feet were planted firmly on the ground. I was struggling to control my fight-or-flight response. The temptation to run was overwhelming. But I knew I wouldn't get very far before the two bear-sized men caught up with me. I entwined my fingers to stop my hands from shaking and hoped Warren wouldn't notice. He'd take great pleasure from knowing I was terrified.

The room was set up like a gentlemen's club. The lower half of the walls were lined with dark wood panelling, and paintings of hunting scenes hung above it. Gold-coloured frames leapt out from olive green paint. Chesterfield sofas, winged chairs, and polished mahogany tables were dotted around the black-and-white chequerboard tiles. An impressive-looking semicircular bar sat in the far corner of the room. Two old boys were perched in front of it on high stools, surrounded by a fug of cigar smoke, halfway down pints of what looked like Guinness. They turned around and eyed me up and down like I was a piece of meat. It repulsed me to see the way they were leering at me.

'So, what do you think of my latest recruit, fellas?' Warren asked, and then he started cackling.

My knees buckled in response. He couldn't be serious. I'd rather die than have sex with either of them. They had to be in their seventies. Old enough to be my grandad. Both of them had huge beer guts, thinning hairlines, pudgy fingers and jowly cheeks. I doubted they were related, but they were carbon copies of each other.

'I wouldn't say no,' the pensioner on the left said.

Over my dead body, I thought. But I wasn't stupid enough to say that out loud in case it gave Warren ideas.

'There you go, you've only been here five minutes and you've got your first client lined up.' Warren's eyes were shining.

My heart started hammering against my ribs. How the hell was I going to get out of this? I couldn't believe an old git like him would still have it in him. Surely, once men got over a certain age, their tackle stopped working without the help of Viagra. Or was that just wishful thinking on my part? I had no intention of finding out. I didn't care what Warren did to me. There was no way I was letting that old bastard's wrinkly ball sack anywhere near me.

'Before I let you get down to business, I want to have a little chat with you. We need to go over a few of the ground rules. Then I'll give you a quick tour and allocate you one of the rooms.' Warren grinned.

He was loving every minute of this. I wanted to protest, but I knew from experience he wasn't the kind of man you could reason with.

'Don't look so worried. You'll soon get the hang of things.' Warren smiled as he walked over to one of the closed doors running along the edge of the room.

I wished I wasn't so easy to read. Wished I could choose whether I revealed my innermost thoughts. But I found it impossible to hide what I was thinking. My face made announcements without my permission. There was nothing I could do about that.

Panicked thoughts circled in my mind. My imagination had gone into overdrive. Fear of the unknown was often worse than the actual situation. Trying to second-guess what was in store for me was messing with my head.

As I was towed along behind Warren, my nerves started getting the better of me. My heartbeat sped up when I got my first glimpse inside the small room dominated by a huge bed. The red and gold theme was opulent. Luxurious. No expense had been spared. I wasn't sure what I'd expected, but this was far from it.

'Take a seat,' Warren said, gesturing with a nod to the king-size.

When I hesitated, he raised his massive fist, which made me flinch. Feeling vulnerable wasn't in the least bit helpful. It was a hindrance. Debilitating.

'You already know Des's debt has become yours. It was good of him to leave you a present in his will, wasn't it? Who's a lucky girl, then? I suggest you get straight to work if you're going to start chipping away at what you owe.' Warren cackled.

'You said we could have until Friday to come up with the first instalment,' I blurted out, and then instantly regretted speaking up.

Warren's eyes blazed before he lunged at me. He clasped his strong fingers around my neck and squeezed my windpipe. I clawed at his hand as blood rushed to my head. My eardrums felt like they were going to explode from the pressure. A few terrifying seconds of pulsating silence passed before he loosened his grip, and I gasped for air.

What the hell had I been dragged into? I'd never experienced violence like it. Warren had a split personality. He was unpredictable. Flipped from hot to cold in the blink of an eye. He was on another level. He scared the shit out of me. Backing down didn't come easily to me, but I couldn't afford to put a foot wrong.

'Well, I've changed my mind, so shut the fuck up and do as you're told.'

I wouldn't usually go down without a fight. As much as I wanted to kick back, this wasn't the time to resist. I had no choice but to do what he asked.

'I'm fed up of waiting for my money, so I'm putting you on the game. Like it or lump it.' Warren got up in my face.

My brain was scrambling to decode the situation. I'd been hoping Warren was bluffing. Hoping he was going to suggest I replace Raquel as the front-of-house meet-and-greet hostess. She was a bit long in the tooth. I couldn't imagine she enticed many customers over the threshold. To my horror, that wasn't what happened, and when the reality finally registered, I couldn't stop myself from having another outburst.

'There's no way I'm agreeing to that!' I shouted, voicing my displeasure.

My ears started ringing when Warren's fist connected with the side of my head. Pain shot through the left side of my face. When would I ever learn? My mouth always got me into trouble, but if I didn't wind my neck in quickly, Warren was going to beat me to a pulp.

'I thought I told you to shut the fuck up. You brazen bitch.

You're just like that mother of yours. Either you toe the line or she gets it. I've got no qualms about sending her off to meet Desmond. You too for that matter, but not before you pay off what I'm due.'

I swallowed the lump in my throat as I battled to hold back my tears. Warren had no boundaries. Nothing was off-limits. I was seriously concerned for my mum's safety. For my safety. I didn't want to work for Warren, but he'd made it clear I didn't have another option. I'd have to put up and shut up. This didn't just involve me. He was going to make my mum suffer, too. I didn't want her blood on my hands or her death on my conscience. Warren meant what he said. I took heed of the warning.

Years of locking horns with Dad had taught me how to be stubborn. I was a formidable opponent in the digging-my-heels-in category. I'd stand my ground to the bitter end. But this wasn't the time to show dogged determination. Knowing there was a death threat hanging over Mum was petrifying.

'If you've finished throwing your toys out of the pram, we'll get down to the nitty-gritty.'

Warren flashed me a look and the hairs on the back of my neck stood to attention.

'I'm bringing you on board to complement my team so that all tastes are accounted for. Give the punters what they want: lap dances, blow jobs, full sex, anal. Whatever they ask for. Nothing's off-limits. It's your job to service their needs.'

I followed Warren's eyes over to the bedside cabinet. The pile of sex toys littering the counter made the contents of my stomach rise. I could feel myself start to panic and had to gulp down my fear.

'Raquel will sort you out with some clobber, and then you can start earning your fucking keep,' Warren sneered.

I stared at him with dead eyes. Blinked back my tears. Then he walked out of the room, shadowed by his two bodyguards. My emotions started to flow when I heard the key turn in the lock. As I sobbed my heart out, my thoughts turned to Lily and what she'd been through. I understood exactly how she'd felt. A wave of hopelessness washed over me. But that wasn't going to get me anywhere.

31

MACKENZIE

Bernice and I cruised the side streets for the next couple of hours, looking for the car, but there was no sign of it.

'There's no point in driving around in circles. We might as well head back to the farmhouse,' I said, glancing sideways at Bernice.

I felt bad throwing the towel in, but the rocket fuel I'd taken earlier had worn off long ago. I needed an urgent top-up to help me cope with the pain, and we were miles away from Kent. The sooner we started travelling back, the better.

'What about Daisy? We can't just abandon her...' Bernice tore her eyes away from the road and glared at me.

The weight of her stare was heavy. Accusatory. I had to look away. Guilt flowed through me. I felt like the biggest prick on the planet. Talk about being cut down to size.

'What do you propose we do? We've given it our best shot, but she's disappeared into thin air. I'm not suggesting we abandon her, but there's nothing more we can do for the time being. We've drawn a blank. We're going to need help. Why don't you give Fester a call and get him to put the feelers out? Tell him to spread the word to all his contacts. Somebody's bound to hear something.'

Bernice's features softened. 'That's a good idea.'

'I'm glad you think so. I want to find Daisy as much as you do, but we've exhausted every conceivable possibility. There's no point in hanging around here. It's not getting us anywhere. We might as well get back on the road.'

Bernice flashed me another filthy look. 'I'm not driving all the way back to Kent. It makes more sense to stay local so that we're on hand to help.'

I bit down on my bottom lip to stop a stream of obscenities from coming out as irritation started clawing away at me.

'I get what you're saying, but if we stay in London, we're right in the middle of Samson's territory.'

'Fester doesn't live far from here. His place is like Fort Knox. When I phoned him to tell him Roscoe was dead, he begged me to come and stay with him for as long as I wanted. I'm sure he wouldn't mind if we crashed there for a few days. Then I could ask him in person to help us find Daisy rather than phoning out of the blue.' Bernice gave me her brightest smile as she tried to win me over.

'For fuck's sake,' I said to myself.

Beads of sweat broke out on my upper lip. I couldn't go long without another hit. This was turning into a nightmare. In desperation, I patted down the pockets of my jacket. Both sides felt empty, so I slipped my unbandaged hand into the zip-up compartment on the inside and rooted around in it. I let out a sigh of relief when my fingers landed on a stash of baggies. I hadn't put them in my jacket recently. They must have been sitting there for ages. Don't you just love it when that happens?

'Is everything all right? Have you lost something?' Bernice said, giving me a sideways glance.

'I must have left my fags and wallet back at the farmhouse,' I replied, having to think on my feet and come up with a feasible explanation in a split second.

'Don't worry, darling, I've got my purse with me, and Fester will have ciggies and everything else your heart desires. His place is always fully stocked. It's like the duty-free at Heathrow Airport.' Bernice laughed.

That was good to know. Maybe staying with Fester wouldn't be so bad after all. I'd never met the guy before. I only knew him through my association with Roscoe, but he sounded like a top bloke.

'Just out of curiosity, why's he called Fester?'

'I'm not entirely sure. It's not the sort of thing you can ask, is it? But I think it's because he's bald, and he often wears a long velvet coat like the guy from *The Addams Family*,' Bernice replied.

* * *

Fester had just got out of the back seat of his Bentley when Bernice pulled her Jag up next to his car. I had to stop my lips from stretching into a smile when I clapped eyes on him. Bernice was right. He was a dead ringer for Uncle Fester with his shiny marble head, ping-pong ball eyes and full-length coat.

'What a lovely surprise! Long time no see. May I say, you're looking as radiant as ever. You've remained untouched by the passing of time. You look half your age. You're incredibly well-preserved,' Fester said, showering Bernice with compliments.

He didn't seem bothered that we'd turned up on his doorstep unannounced.

'I can't take the credit for any of it. My youthful appearance is down to Botox and fillers. I'll have you know, this costs a fortune to upkeep.' Bernice laughed as she pointed to her line-free face. 'This is MacKenzie, by the way. He was Roscoe's right-hand man.'

A lump formed in my chest as I digested what Bernice had just said. It was an honour and privilege to work for Roscoe. I was chuffed to hear he held me in high esteem, too.

'Nice to meet you, son,' Fester said, extending his hand towards me.

'Likewise,' I replied, giving him a firm handshake.

'How are you bearing up?'

Fester turned his attention back to Bernice and fixed his eyes on her. They were intense. Dare I say creepy?

'So-so. It's going to take a long time to come to terms with things.'

Bernice was doing her best to put on a brave face, but I saw her discreetly blink back tears.

'Of course it will. Everyone grieves in their own way. As I said to you at the time, don't be afraid to lean on those around you. I'm so glad you took me up on my offer to stay.' Fester beamed.

'Is that OK? I'm sorry to turn up without running it past you first.'

'Don't be silly. I'm delighted to see you. It must be very painful living in the house you shared with my little brother.'

'It is, but it's also a great comfort. I'm surrounded by so many wonderful memories. I can feel Roscoe's presence woven into the structure.' The corners of Bernice's lips turned up a fraction.

As I watched their interaction, it was clear that Fester and Bernice shared a strong connection.

'Let's go inside before we all freeze to death,' Fester said, linking his sister-in-law's arm.

I trailed along behind them while casting my eyes around. Fester's white-washed, double-fronted house screamed money.

There was nothing understated about the three-storey monster. The planters and flowerbeds were overflowing with colour, which took some doing in the middle of winter, and there wasn't a leaf out of place in the generous front garden. I did a double take when I spotted a pair of golden lions standing on either side of the arched front door, guarding their master's domain. Fester was a character. I'd give him that!

'So, what do you think of my pad?' he asked, beaming with pride.

'It's great.' I didn't want to burst his bubble and tell him what I really thought.

'You'd never guess this used to be two semis, would you?'

I shook my head.

'If you get the right architect, they can achieve miracles. My plans didn't go down well with the Neighbourhood Watch cronies or the planning board, but I took on board their objections and resubmitted the drawings excluding the moat.'

My eyes sprang open at the mention of a moat. I wasn't surprised the locals had kicked up about that!

'I was gutted to have to shelve the idea. Ever since I was a little kid, I'd dreamed about living in a property with a drawbridge. Roscoe and I were given plastic knights' helmets, swords and shields one Christmas. They were the best presents ever. We were obsessed with them, fighting each other and slaying dragons at every opportunity, much to our mum's horror.' Fester smiled as he recounted the memory. 'But I'm not an unreasonable man. I didn't want to alienate myself from everyone in the street, even though I could have pushed through with the original idea if I'd wanted to. Money talks when you know the right person's palm to grease.'

It made sense that somebody had taken a backhander. I was amazed the council had given him planning permission for the monstrosity. It wasn't a bit in keeping with the other properties in the street which were all carbon copies. The only variations were the front door colours and the gardens.

Fester had added a huge red and yellow mural of the Allen coat of arms to the front of his house, along with turrets and battlements. It looked ridiculous, but each to their own. If it gave us a safe place to stay for a few days, I wasn't really in a position to turn my nose up.

When Bernice had said his place was like Fort Knox, I was expecting somewhere more private, more out of the way, not a couple of converted semis on a busy residential street. But it wouldn't be the first time I'd had to hide in plain sight. Beggars couldn't be choosers. Sometimes, being obvious was good.

'An Englishman's home is his castle. Welcome to mine,' Fester said as he ushered us through the Gothic, chapel-style wooden front door.

The hallway was surprisingly spacious. A huge tapestry lined the wall on the right, and a massive crystal chandelier hung in the centre. Fester was lucky the houses he'd converted were Victorian. He wouldn't have had the ceiling height to hang a light as enormous as that in a modern-day property.

'There you are, Buster. Come and meet our guests,' Fester said, dropping down on one knee to stroke a stocky bulldog that had waddled into the room with its stump waggling.

'Hello, mate,' I said as he hurled himself against my calf.

'Follow me.' Fester led the way into the second door on the left. 'I asked the designer to remodel the interior like a medieval fortress.'

They'd done a good job recreating his vision. I could picture Henry VIII sitting in the wooden throne chair at the head of the dining table. Two gold candelabras and an overflowing fruit bowl made up the centrepiece. A suit of armour stood in the corner of the room. It was an obvious addition given Fester's interest in the Middle Ages. There was an open fire at the back of the room, kicking out a massive amount of heat. A huge oil painting of Fester sporting a monocle with his slobbery-chopped bulldog Buster standing by his side hung over the mantlepiece.

Fester shrugged off his velvet coat. He was immaculately dressed in a checked three-piece suit. The chain from his pocket watch hung down the outside of his jacket, and gold cufflinks fastened his white shirt.

'How about I get us a nice drop of brandy to help us warm up?'

That was music to my ears. Fester didn't wait for us to reply. He bounded over to an antique sideboard and poured generous measures into three cognac glasses.

'This Rémy Martin XO should hit the spot,' Fester said, handing it to us. 'Take a seat and make yourself at home.'

Fester flopped down on the sofa closest to the fire. Bernice and I sat on the one opposite. We fell into a comfortable silence as we sipped our drinks.

'I'm sorry for bringing trouble to your door, but I could really do with your help,' Bernice said, jolting us back to reality.

Fester looked alarmed. I wondered when she was going to get around to asking him, but she probably didn't want to bombard him the minute she stepped inside the front door.

'You know I've always got your back. Whatever you need. Just name it. What's wrong, Bernice?' Fester shifted to the edge of the sofa and perched there while he waited for her to reply.

'I was on my way to collect my friend Daisy from outside The Orange Tree and was almost there when I spotted three guys talking to a young woman. They suddenly bundled her into a car and drove off. I was too far away to be certain, but I'm sure it was Daisy. She wasn't where we'd agreed to meet, and she's not answering her phone. I have a horrible feeling Warren Jenkins snatched her. The guy looked exactly like him.' Bernice's words caught in her chest.

It made perfect sense that he was the culprit.

'Now don't go upsetting yourself, doll. Everything will be all right. Leave it to me. I'll sort this mess out.'

If I hadn't known better, I would have thought Roscoe was in the room with us. The tone of Fester's voice and his choice of words made him sound exactly like his younger brother. I glanced sideways at Bernice. She looked startled. I knew she was thinking the same thing. I wasn't sure if that would reassure her or freak her out. It was difficult to tell from the expression on her face.

'Thank you, darling. I knew you wouldn't let me down.' Bernice looked adoringly at Fester while giving him a half-smile.

'Warren Jenkins is a nasty piece of work. If you don't mind me asking, what's Daisy done to catch his attention?'

It was a fair question. If Fester was going to put his head on the block, it was only right to bring him up to speed on what had been going on.

'To cut a long story short, her dad owed Warren a shit ton of money. Warren was fed up of waiting for Des to pay it back, so he attacked him to scare him into action, but he went too far... Des died from his injuries,' Bernice explained.

'I see.' Fester fixed Bernice with a sombre look.

'We all know how these things work. Des couldn't take the debt to the grave with him. The bill passes to the next of kin. There's no way Warren will write the money off. He's expecting the family to become responsible for it.'

Fester blew out of breath as he shook his head from side to side. 'How much are we talking?'

'I have no idea. I don't think Daisy knows how much either, so that leaves Warren open to milk the situation,' Bernice replied.

'Now, I don't want you to freak out when I tell you this, but rumour has it Warren has set up a knocking shop in the basement of The Beehive. He's using the boozer as a front for sex services,' Fester said.

'The Beehive in East Dulwich?' Bernice questioned as a frown tried to settle on her Botoxed forehead.

Fester nodded, eyeing her cautiously.

'I used to manage that pub before I married Roscoe,' Bernice announced. 'It was his local when he lived in the area.'

'I remember, and I'm not trying to offend you or speak out of turn when I say this, but it's always had a reputation for being a bit of a dive.'

I felt myself cringe. Talk about telling it like it is. Fester hadn't minced his words. He'd delivered them with the subtlety of a sledgehammer, but there was no harm done. Bernice swallowed the home truth without turning a hair.

'No offence taken. I know exactly what you mean. It was a man's boozer through and through. The only women brave enough to cross the threshold were the ones on the game.' Bernice laughed.

'It's just crossed my mind that maybe Warren took Daisy there.' Fester fixed his ping-pong ball eyes on Bernice.

She looked worried as she mulled over what he'd said. My head felt like it was going to explode. This didn't sound good for Daisy.

'I suppose it's possible. We'd only been behind the car for a couple of minutes when we lost it, and they *were* heading in the direction of the pub.'

'I've heard he's opened a private members' club. Don't be

fooled by the name. By all accounts, it's nothing more glamorous than an after-hours drinking den with "hostesses for hire". I'd say it's a pretty safe bet he's planning to pimp Daisy out,' Fester said.

I wished Fester would filter what came out of his mouth. It was clear he was a no-nonsense kind of guy who spoke the truth and had no time for bullshit, but it would have been great if he could have toned down his thoughts for our sake. Bernice and I both had a soft spot for Daisy, so his frank observations were distressing. He hadn't sugar-coated the fact that he feared Warren might be about to turn her into a prostitute.

Bernice gasped. 'Oh my God! We've got to get Daisy out of there before anything awful happens to her.'

She was white-faced with shock and on the verge of tears. I couldn't see what I looked like, but I'd felt the colour drain from my face, so I was guessing I was wearing a matching death-warmed-up skin tone.

Fester got up and walked over to where Bernice was sitting. He flopped down next to her and took one of her hands in his.

'Don't you worry your pretty little head about a thing. I told you I'm going to sort everything out. And I mean that.'

Bernice sniffed back her sadness and attempted to paste a smile on her face.

'Oh, Fester, you're such a sweetie. What would I do without you? You're the best brother-in-law in the whole world.'

Bernice leaned forward and placed a tender kiss on Fester's cheek, which made him beam from ear to ear. Then, a moment later, she started grilling him about the logistics.

'What are you going to do? How are you going to get Daisy out of there?' Concern flooded Bernice's face.

But she wasn't the only one who was worried. Warren was as callous as they came, which meant Daisy was in real danger.

'I'm not sure, but when I say I'm going to do something, I never go back on my word.'

Fester gave Bernice a reassuring smile. He might not have been much in the looks department, but he had a heart of gold. There was no denying that. My temples were throbbing. I had to get off the subject. I couldn't bear to think about Daisy being forced into prostitution. I'd never had the pleasure of meeting the bloke, but I'd heard enough about Warren Jenkins by now to form my own opinion. He was a nasty piece of work. What he was doing was depraved. Deranged. He was taking things to another level, trying to turn a beautiful girl like Daisy into a brass.

I'd gone from being terrified to livid in the blink of an eye. My blood was boiling. It wasn't even Daisy's debt, but she was the one paying the price. Des was still haunting her from beyond the grave. When was she going to get a break? Once I got her away from Warren, I'd make sure nothing bad ever happened to her again. I hadn't known her very long, but I knew I was falling in love with her.

'I don't suppose you have Lily's number, do you?' I said, turning to face Bernice. I had to do something to change the subject.

'I do, as a matter of fact,' Bernice replied.

'I know there's some beef going on between the two of them again, but I think we should let her know what's happened to Daisy.'

'I agree. It will only make matters worse if we keep quiet. With any luck, it might smooth the situation over.'

'You reckon?'

Bernice shrugged. 'I have to say, I was shocked when Daisy told me that Tara and Lily had got stuck into her. I just don't get why they're so hard on her. She's a lovely girl. I think the world of her. She's the daughter I never had.'

Bernice broke down, so I threw my arms around her. She'd been through so much. We all had. There had to be something better around the corner. Bernice sobbed into my shoulder, which pulled at my heartstrings. I struggled not to join in. The hopelessness of the situation weighed heavily on me. But I somehow managed to stay strong, and a moment later, Bernice drew away from me. She straightened her posture and wiped away her smudged mascara on the back of her hand.

'D'you know what, when the going gets tough, families should stick together. Be there for each other. All of them are grieving, so emotions are running high. It's not the time to start airing your differences or pointing the finger of blame. Daisy did her best, but she's only human. She couldn't be in two places at once, could she?'

What Bernice had said was true, but I knew enough about Daisy's family to realise she was damned if she did. Damned if she didn't.

32

SAMSON

I hadn't been near the club for days, not since Tuesday when that bogus Southwark Council inspector had shown up out of the blue and started sniffing around. I'd thought there was something fishy about it at the time. The council did carry out spot checks without warning from time to time, but I hadn't been convinced he was the real deal, even though he had what looked like genuine ID. I'd been convinced somebody was trying to stitch me up. Now, it made sense. The swarthy bastard must have been working for Arben. If the Albanian knew what was good for him, he'd stop trying to flex his muscles and meddle in my affairs. I'd sort him out at some point, but I had more pressing things to deal with.

In light of the allegations Carly had made about my good friend Travis, I'd made it my business to go to Eden's so that I could destroy any potentially damming evidence. The main CCTV captured outside and within the club was wiped at regular intervals, but I always kept the recordings from my private suite of rooms. Why wouldn't I? They made entertaining viewing.

'Good evening, Samson,' Igor said when I approached the foyer.

His white-blond eyebrows settled into a frown. He seemed confused by my presence. It was clear he hadn't been expecting to see me, but I never heralded my arrival. I turned up if and when it suited me. That was a perk of being the boss. I had nobody to answer to.

Igor was the head doorman, but since MacKenzie had shot through, he'd fallen into the vacant role of Eden's manager, too. Taking the reins was an unenviable task, but somebody had to do it. I couldn't be arsed with the day-to-day running of the club. The only thing I was interested in was how much money was in the tills at the end of the night.

'How's everything going?'

'It's been a bit slow, but it's Sunday, so hopefully things will pick up later,' Igor replied in his strong Polish accent.

I scowled at him. Since when had Sunday been a big night out for people? His attempts to put a positive spin on the situation didn't alter the fact that the club was virtually empty. Eden's was haemorrhaging money, and its future was hanging in the balance. But I hadn't come here to depress myself. I had a job to do, so I was taking myself out of the equation before I got sucked into trivialities.

'I'm going to my office, but I don't want to be disturbed. If anyone asks, you haven't seen me. Understand?'

'Yes, boss,' Igor replied.

I spent the next couple of hours sifting through all the footage. I'd collected some cracking stuff over the years. I'd forgotten half of the gorgeous-looking birds who'd been lucky enough to join me in some bedroom gymnastics. Watching the antics I'd got up to was making me horny. My balls would be blue by the time the gunshot wounds healed enough for me to get my end away.

By my own admission, I'd been a wideboy in my younger days. I'd seen a lot of action. I was into flash cars and flash women. My teenage years were spent falling out of clubs in the early hours of the morning with a different girl on my arm every time. I had no shortage of admirers. But I never wanted to settle down. I couldn't understand the mentality of men prepared to stick with one woman for the rest of their lives. Why would you do that when you could change the scenery as often as you wanted to?

I was still a good-looking guy, but I wasn't stupid. I knew the kind of women I attracted were impressed by the wads of cash I kept in my wallet. I liked to spread my wealth around, not just to be generous but to show everyone I was the top dog. Money talked, and if you had a lot of it, you naturally found yourself high up on the social ladder without even trying. Birds threw themselves at me, so I took full advantage of that. Use them and lose them.

I had enough clips in my private collection to make my own porn movie. What an absolutely brilliant idea! I was a genius! I fancied turning my hand to a spot of directing to plug the hole in my rapidly depleting finances. This explicit material could make a fortune on the dark web. I didn't give a toss that I didn't have the women's consent to use the pictures the multi-angled set-up had captured, which left nothing to the imagination. I didn't need to ask their permission. It was my club. My equipment. My cock.

They'd agreed to share my bed. I'd made no secret of the fact that I was going to film the sessions. They hadn't had a problem or voiced any objections at the time, so as far as I was concerned, they didn't have a leg to stand on. It was too late now to be highly offended if the footage was leaked.

It was probably common courtesy to ask them first, but I didn't know most of them by name, so even if I'd been prepared to go down that path, it would have been a waste of time. It wasn't a big deal, anyway. Everybody made sex tapes these days. If you allowed yourself to be filmed, you knew at the back of your mind there was a chance that one day it might end up doing the rounds. Putting together a porno film was a blinding idea. I couldn't believe I hadn't thought of it sooner.

I thought I'd watched all the footage and was just about to put an end to the private viewing when I stumbled across a bonus feature on one of the tapes. I didn't have the starring role in this clip. It was of Carly and Travis. No wonder she'd got the hump about him riding her. He looked old enough to be her grandad as he hammered away at her. She'd said she was four-teen. But she was so small and petite she could have passed for an eleven-year-old. Nobody would have questioned her.

Travis was a randy old goat. She'd done her best to bat off his advances when he'd led her into my private suite of rooms. He was as crafty as they come. He'd let her think she'd won, and he'd vowed to be the perfect gentleman, but minutes later, he started plying her with drink. I fast-forwarded the footage. I didn't want to listen to Travis promising her the moon and telling her she could be counting a pot of gold in no time. The standard spiel for wannabes bored me rigid.

She might have been an impressionable teenage girl, but Travis Steele had a reputation for exploiting his position to gain sexual satisfaction, consensual or otherwise. No surprise there. We all did it. And Carly had gone to meet Travis willingly. Nobody had forced her into it.

A few seconds into the clip, I pressed the play button and let the video run. By the looks of it, Carly's desire to become a star overrode her gut instinct to run. She looked nervous as she sat as far away from Travis as possible. He was sticking to his side of the bargain by keeping his wandering hands to himself. I knew that wouldn't last. It was only a matter of time before temptation got the better of him. He couldn't resist the female species. And judging by the footage, once upon a time Carly was an attractive girl. Now she was a skeleton in clothes.

Travis continued being the perfect host up until the point where Carly passed out. He sidled over to where she was slumped on the sofa, uncurled her fingers from the stem of the cocktail glass and placed it down on the side table. Then he scooped her into his arms. Her head lolled backwards when he carried her through my office and into the bedroom. She was out for the count. She didn't stir when he laid her down and pushed her skirt up. He watched her for a couple of seconds before he dropped his trousers. Travis was rock-hard. His dick was sticking out in front of him like a broom handle. Carly's head flopped to one side when he eased her knickers off and then spread her legs. He didn't waste time with foreplay. He got straight to work.

Travis wasn't a bad-looking bloke. Admittedly, he wasn't in my league, but I'd seen worse. Even if he wasn't Carly's cup of tea, all she had to do was endure a short amount of unpleasant-ness. It didn't take him long to shoot his load. The look of horror on her face when she came around and found him naked from the waist down, pumping away between her thighs, was price-less. I nearly split my sides laughing. Stupid bitch. She got what she deserved.

I didn't feel sorry for her. It was a business transaction. This kind of thing had been happening since the beginning of time. Ask anyone in the industry. If you were dumb or gullible enough to think record deals were ten a penny, then you deserved what was coming to you. Never underestimate the power of greed. Women handed themselves to Travis on a plate for the chance to hit the big time. What was the man supposed to do? Turn them down? Yeah right!

Carly never reported Travis to the police at the time. She'd kept it to herself for the last three years. It made me wonder what had happened for her to suddenly start playing the victim. The world was full of underage girls who were sexually active, but she was making a song and dance out of the fact that she was fourteen and hadn't said 'yes' before Travis climbed on board. But that was a technicality. She hadn't said 'no' either. The minute Carly agreed to go into my private suite of rooms with Travis, she'd given him the green light to do whatever he wanted. That was the way things worked with powerful men. It was an unwritten rule. More fool her if she didn't know that. Common sense told me to destroy the tape in case it fell into the wrong hands, but if I did that it would take away my opportunity to blackmail Carly with it or use the other footage.

I'd done what I needed to do, and Travis hadn't called me back yet. I had better things to do than sit here all night waiting for him to put in an appearance. I wanted to get out of Eden's before I got caught up in the drama that seemed to breed in this place. Don't get me wrong, I got it. When people were drinking and taking drugs, explosive situations weren't far away. Especially if you added a crowd into the equation. That could spell disaster for an evening.

Eden's was a legal front that conveniently provided a market for my illegal activities. But the days when the club drew in the hordes were long gone and we were barely managing to stay afloat.

I peered into the bar on my way past. There were only a

handful of people inside. No surprise there. It was January. No fucker had any money. The desperate few who'd ventured out in search of a good time wouldn't spend enough to cover the staff bill for the day. I was stuck in a rut. The same thing happened every year. Truth be told, I'd lost interest in the place. It was causing me no end of grief.

'I'm heading home,' I said to Igor as I walked through the foyer.

'No worries,' he replied without engaging any further.

It suited me fine that our exchange was short and sweet. Igor was a man of few words. I liked that about him. I couldn't abide listening to bollocks or anyone with verbal diarrhoea. I clocked the other door staff milling about, but I didn't speak to them. I couldn't afford to get caught up in a conversation while I was moving the X-rated material out of the building.

'Good night, all,' I called as I headed for the door.

'Night, Samson,' chorused the bouncers.

I'm sure they all wondered what I was carrying in the black holdall, but they knew better than to ask. Their eyes were trained on me as I swanned out of my club and got into my Range Rover parked directly outside the front entrance.

I only had a short distance to go, but I was glad when I'd made it to the car without being apprehended by a member of the filth. They were always hanging around the area making a nuisance of themselves, ruining people's nights by confiscating their drugs. It would have been just my luck to bump into the Old Bill while in possession of some very questionable videos. If the clips fell into the wrong hands, Travis would be in shit up to his liver-spotted neck and I'd have lost a prime business opportunity.

Moving the tapes was risky but unavoidable. I'd been keeping them in my office safe, but it was better for all concerned if I locked the footage away at my house, where random police inspections couldn't be carried out without a search warrant. The last thing I needed was the council or cops raiding the club, looking for drugs and stumbling across the illicit material. That was a disaster I could do without.

33

LILY

Mum and I had been sitting across the table from each other, trying to plan a decent send-off for Dad on a non-existent budget, when my mobile started to ring. I didn't recognise the number but thought it was probably the funeral director, so I answered the call. I nearly dropped the phone in shock when MacKenzie started to speak. Although nothing had been confirmed, we'd all presumed he was dead.

I pushed my chair back and stepped out into the hall, closing the kitchen door behind me. MacKenzie wasn't Mum's favourite person, so she wouldn't be impressed that he was phoning the house, but my gut instinct told me something was wrong, so I needed to hear him out whether Mum liked it or not.

'I know you and Daisy aren't exactly seeing eye to eye at the moment...' MacKenzie began.

The mention of my sister's name ignited the embers of anger still smouldering in my belly. Daisy must have felt bad about the situation she'd caused, so she'd roped MacKenzie in to smooth things over for her. Daisy wasn't usually slow in coming forward.

She normally had plenty to say for herself, and some. She was losing her touch.

'That's an understatement. You can tell Daisy from me that what she did was unforgivable. Mum wants her to stay away from the funeral, so if she knows what's good for her, she'll keep her distance. And tell her not to bother coming back here for the foreseeable future. Mum doesn't want her here; nor do I, for that matter.'

I was surprised at myself for speaking up like that, but I was desperate to voice my opinion. It felt good to vent and get things off my chest.

'In my experience, siblings fall into two categories: supporters or rivals. It's easy to see which camp you're in. I thought Bernice was exaggerating, but you guys really are gunning for Daisy, aren't you? Talk about conducting a witch hunt. Who needs enemies when you've got a family like yours.' Sarcasm dripped from MacKenzie's words.

'It's not your place to get involved. This doesn't concern you,' I fired back.

'Look, I didn't phone up to get into an argument with you, but I thought you might like to know that Warren Jenkins has taken Daisy...'

I felt my mouth drop open.

'Are you sure?'

'Yes, I'm sure. Bernice and I saw him bundling her into his car.' MacKenzie's tone was abrupt.

Visions of the night Samson's guys dragged me from the dressing room in Eden's came barrelling towards me. The memory hit me with such force it almost knocked me off my feet. There was so much power behind it.

'It's ironic. Daisy wouldn't rest until she found you. She

started looking for you the minute Samson's guys took you, but now the tables are turned, it's clear you're still holding on to your resentment.' Bitterness was radiating off MacKenzie as he delivered some home truths.

There'd been such a horrible atmosphere in the house. I was glad when Daisy left. But that was before I realised she was in danger. While I'd been in the warehouse, I'd been relying on her to help me. Left to my own devices, I wasn't sure I'd ever escape from Samson's guys. They'd held me captive for days, and if Daisy and Bernice hadn't freed me, I might still have been chained to the wall in the bedroom. Daisy must have been scared, but she hadn't let me down. Of course she hadn't. We were twins. We were meant to share an unbreakable bond. So why didn't I instinctively want to help her? What was wrong with me? I was disgusted with myself. It was time to dig deep and do the right thing. I was stronger than I gave myself credit for.

'Oh my God, poor Daisy. If there's anything I can do, just ask.' The offer flew out of my mouth before I could stop it.

'You've changed your tune,' MacKenzie pointed out.

My cheeks flushed as embarrassment flowed through me like a red-hot current. I felt awkward. Uncomfortable. I was relieved we weren't face to face as the agonising silence stretched out between us. It was pointless trying to defend myself. His observation was correct. I'd done a complete one-eighty.

'Now that I know she's in trouble, I've had a change of heart. Is that a crime?'

MacKenzie didn't answer. Instead, he steered the conversation onto a different path.

'Bernice and I have been looking for her. We spent hours driving around trying to spot Warren's car. We had no joy. But we think we may have a lead on where he's holding her.'

What MacKenzie had just said gave me a small glimmer of hope. Having been in Daisy's position, I was worried for her safety. I owed it to my sister to repay the favour.

'Like I said, I'll do whatever I can to help. Just name it.'

'Thanks. I appreciate that. Anyway, I'd better go. I'll keep you posted.' MacKenzie's frostiness had thawed.

'Please do.'

My heart was beating like a drum. What had I just done? The idea of getting involved scared the shit out of me.

'I'll know more once I've had a chance to check out the gentlemen's club…'

My knees buckled. I knew first hand what it was like to have a man force himself on you. I couldn't let that happen to my twin. I had to do something. In my heart of hearts, I knew I'd be too scared to get involved. Too selfish to put myself forward in case I ended up in the same boat. I couldn't go through it again. I massaged my temples with the heels of my hands to try and derail the memory. But every detail of the attack was tattooed on my brain.

I knew it wasn't good to bottle things up. But I wasn't ready to share the details of my kidnap. I couldn't bring myself to talk about what happened when I'd tried to escape from the warehouse. I felt myself shudder as I recalled Tank assaulting me. I'd done my best not to dwell on it and push it to the back of my mind, but it tortured me day and night. Haunted me. His weight. His smell. His roughness. I'd fought him with all my might, but the attack was frenzied. Devastating. I wasn't sure I'd ever get over it.

I only allowed myself to think about what I'd been through in the darkest hours of the middle of the night when Mum was asleep in her bed. For the rest of the time, I tried to erase the memory. But it was too vivid to block out completely. It sprang into the forefront of my mind when I was least expecting it to. Random things seemed to trigger it. I'd have to find a way to put it behind me. Bury it deep and throw away the key. Otherwise, I'd end up being ruled by fear. And I wasn't going to let it define me.

34

DAISY

I'd cried myself dry, waiting for Raquel to arrive. Not that I was in any hurry to see her, but I'd been locked in the bedroom for hours now. I was beginning to wonder if she'd gone home for the evening and had forgotten about me when I heard movement on the other side of the door.

I scrambled to my feet. I didn't want to be sitting on the red satin sheets in case it wasn't her. Warren thought he owned me, so I didn't want to give him ideas if he'd popped back to check on me.

'Oh, there you are,' Raquel said as though she was surprised to see me when she poked her head around the door.

I spotted her blonde bouffant before she came into view. Dopey cow! Did she think I'd dug an escape tunnel under the building with my bare hands while I'd been unattended?

'You look like you've been crying,' Raquel said after her crepey eyes scanned my face.

'Do I?' I snapped.

I couldn't help being abrupt. Talk about stating the obvious.

'There's no point in upsetting yourself. Being on the game's not so bad. I turned tricks for thirty years before I hung up my suspenders.'

Raquel looked proud of herself. I was appalled. I felt my swollen eyes widen. Hideous thoughts started circulating in my brain. I wasn't sure which was more horrific: being on the game for three decades or Raquel in suspenders. Both were equally unappealing.

'Chin up, love. You'll come around. You just need a bit of time to get used to the idea.' Raquel paused to flash me her discoloured smile. 'Look on the bright side. It could be a lot worse.'

'Could it? I don't see how.'

My tone was blunt. I knew I was being a bitch to her, but I couldn't help myself. I'd been moments away from being in Bernice's Jag heading for the Kent countryside when Warren had stumbled upon me.

'Warren might look big and mean, but trust me, his bark is worse than his bite.'

If Raquel thought that, she hadn't witnessed what he was capable of. I'd seen him in action. I knew what kind of depraved lunatic we were working for.

'As long as you don't try to step out of line, you won't have any problems with Warren. Believe me, there are a lot worse pimps out there. I should know. I've worked for some nasty bastards in the past.'

I didn't recognise the man Raquel was referring to. She painted such a glowing picture of Warren that it shocked me how different our opinions were.

'Warren wants me to tell you how things work around here and show you the ropes. Not literally. He's not expecting me to stay in the room and give you a running commentary on your performance.' Raquel cackled, highly amused by her own joke.

But I couldn't see the funny side. My intestines were tying themselves in knots.

'You'll be fed and watered three times a day.'

Raquel sounded upbeat, as though I should be happy about that, but I felt like I'd become Warren's pet.

'There are no set hours, but the club's open from midday until late. You'll be on duty any time there are clients on the premises. Some days will be quiet, and you'll have no takers at all.' Raquel laughed. 'Other days, your fanny will be red raw, and you'll be begging for mercy. I can vividly remember times when I've sworn there was something in the beer they were serving that was making the men so horny!'

Raquel was doing her best to be friendly and make me feel welcome, but her horror stories of life as a hooker weren't settling my nerves one bit. They were doing the opposite.

'I appreciate you're trying to let me know what I'm in for, and I don't mean any disrespect by this, but you chose to go into this profession. I'm being forced into it.'

I realised I'd overstepped the mark when I saw a flash of anger spread across her face. I was my own worst enemy. When something came into my head, I blurted it out even though I knew I should shut up. My runaway mouth always got me into trouble.

'Listen to me, love, nobody chooses this profession. Some of us don't have any other options, so don't bother looking down your snotty little nose at me.' Raquel put her hands on her generous hips and glared at me.

'I'm sorry. I shouldn't have spoken to you like that.'

Alienating myself and making an enemy out of Raquel was a stupid move. I needed to keep her sweet. Keep her on side.

'Warren likes his girls to look sexy.' Raquel gave me a coy smile.

Fuck! I didn't know what was worse, being called Warren's girl or the thought of having to wear a porn star's outfit to entice the old men at the bar. Panic began snaking its way around me as Raquel waddled over to a mirrored bedside cabinet in her skyscraper heels. Her massive boobs nearly fell out of her top when she bent over and pulled open the top drawer.

'All the private areas have a theme. As you're in the red room, this is your uniform.'

The red lacey underwear and black patent stilettos were a far cry from the staff clothes I wore at Nando's. I felt like I was going to burst into tears when she brought the stuff over to me. My eyes fixed on the matching bra, crotchless pants and suspender belt as she placed them in my hands.

'I'm sure you already know there's a bathroom in there.' Raquel gestured with a flick of her head to the closed door behind where she was standing.

I hadn't felt the urge to look around my new home. I'd been too busy feeling sorry for myself. Too distraught to think straight. Too busy trying to formulate a plan. How was I going to get out of this mess? There was no point in bleating on about any of this to Raquel. She wasn't in a position to help me or do anything to change my circumstances, so I kept my fears to myself.

'Punters pay in advance for an allotted amount of time, which the bouncers police, so you don't have to worry. They can't overstay their welcome, much as they'd like to, without coughing up more cash.'

Raquel laughed, and I felt myself shudder.

'Don't look so worried. You should be thankful for small mercies. At least you're not on the street corner like I was when I first started out. Trust me, being in a club is a far safer option than shagging some bloke in a dingy alleyway or car. The club has security staff and people milling around in case a punter turns nasty.'

I knew Raquel was trying to be reassuring, but all sorts of horrors started shuttering through my mind.

'Do you have any questions?' Raquel asked.

A million of them rattled around in my brain, but I didn't ask any.

'Well, if you think of something, you can always ask me at a later stage.'

The way Raquel was talking, I was in here for the long haul. I couldn't bear to think about being stuck in this shithole for the foreseeable future. The only way I'd be able to cope was to take each day as it came. Minute by minute. Hour by hour.

'Right, I'll leave you to get changed into your gear,' Raquel said, eyeing the underwear in my hand.

'What, now?' I felt panic rise within me. Talk about throwing me in at the deep end. 'Why do I need to put this on?' I forced myself to ask, even though I was dreading her response.

'You have to be ready and waiting for clients. If Warren comes in to check up on you and you're still in your coat and jeans, he'll go ballistic. And you don't want to get off on the wrong foot, do you?' Raquel flashed me a look.

'No,' I replied without hesitation. I knew what he was capable of.

Raquel leaned towards me and dropped her voice to a barely audible whisper. No doubt cameras were recording the goings on in the room, which added another level of discomfort to the way I was feeling.

'Look, I'm not supposed to do this, so don't throw me under the bus with Warren, but I know how hard it is the first few times. If you take one of these, it'll help you to feel more relaxed.'

Raquel discreetly handed me a small bag of pills. I didn't do drugs apart from weed, but I took them all the same. Beggars couldn't be choosers, and if it meant I could block out the experience, I'd swallow the whole bag.

'Don't take more than one. They're pretty lethal,' Raquel warned as though she'd just read my mind. 'Chin up, girl. You never know, you might even enjoy yourself. Some of the punters bring a bit of comic relief. They don't always want sex. I've had regulars who pay me just to listen to them talk. Although, there was one guy a few years back who could talk a glass eye to sleep. I used to dread it when he came in. It was a shame really. He was just a lonely old man who craved female company.'

And that little story was supposed to make me feel better, was it? I stared at Raquel in disbelief. What planet was she living on? The woman was insane if she thought I was going to get any pleasure out of this.

'It's been lovely chatting to you, but I'd better get back to work. Good luck! Not that you'll need it,' Raquel said in an upbeat voice before she left me alone in the room.

Tears started rolling down my cheeks again as I heard her turn the key in the lock. My head was spinning. There was a lot to take in. I felt suffocated by the situation. I'd never felt so helpless waiting for the cavalry to arrive or the inevitable to happen.

I'd never seen eye to eye with my dad, but witnessing him being butchered and left for dead had initially changed the way I'd felt about him. I'd been so gutted that I hadn't had a chance to put things right between us. I'd wished I could turn back the clock. Not any more. Not now I was having to work off his debts with my body and spread my legs for all and sundry.

I was glad I hadn't wasted precious time at his bedside. I hated him with a renewed passion. Every fibre of my being despised him. I wasn't a religious person, but I hoped he was rotting in hell, if such a place existed. I couldn't let this situation break me, or Dad would have won. My loathing for him would keep me strong.

I stared down at the pills in the bag. It was tempting to swallow the lot. As I traced their outline through the plastic, I wondered if it would please my dad to know my life had reached an all-time low because of him. His final gift to me would be a lasting legacy. He'd put me on the conveyor belt for sexual exploitation.

35

MACKENZIE

Since Bernice had enlisted Fester to help find Daisy, we'd all fallen silent. None of us had spoken or moved for what seemed like an eternity. It was like we were frozen in time. Lost in our own thoughts. I glanced over at Bernice. Her eyes were filled with fear. She looked like she was losing hope by the second.

'I'll be back in a minute. I'm going to get us a nice bottle of plonk. I'm sure we could all do with a drink,' Fester said as though he'd just read my mind before he darted out of the formal dining room.

'Fester keeps his extensive wine collection in the basement.' Bernice smiled. 'You wouldn't think he'd be a connoisseur, would you?'

'I'd never have guessed.'

'He hides it well! I had him down as a real ale man when I first met him, but he's an out-and-out wine buff who lives and breathes the stuff. He spends a fortune on it. Don't get me wrong, I'm partial to a nice red myself, but I wouldn't know the difference between a Malbec or a Merlot,' Bernice said.

'Neither would I!' One or both of them would hit the spot right now, though.

'I've been saving this lovely bottle of Beaujolais for a special occasion, and I can't think of a better time to crack it open than now.' Fester beamed when he reappeared a few moments later.

I started salivating at the sight of it.

'I'll show you how the experts drink wine to allow all the aromas to shine through.'

He had to be joking, right? If Fester started sniffing, swishing and sipping, there was a good chance I'd lose the will to live. I wanted the booze circulating in my bloodstream as soon as possible. I had no interest in savouring the flavour of the vintage. As Bernice had just pointed out, they all tasted the same anyway.

'We'll just leave them to breathe for a bit, and then I'll talk you through the next stage,' Fester said as his googly eyes bounced between Bernice and me.

I felt beads of sweat break out on my upper lip as I eyed the thimble full of red liquid in the bottom of the huge, long-stemmed glass. There was barely enough to wet my lips. I was struggling to resist grabbing the bottle by the neck and tipping it down my throat. I had to tear my eyes away from the temptation. I couldn't trust myself not to act on my urges. We were still waiting for the vino to come up to room temperature and hadn't tasted a drop of Fester's French import when he sprung to his feet.

'I've just had a brilliant idea. I could get one of my friends to pretend he's interested in joining the gentlemen's club. Then he could have a good scout around inside the venue and see if he can spot Daisy or, at the very least, find out if she's working there and how the land lies.'

I had to admit, what he'd said sounded good on paper, but I

wasn't convinced tracking Daisy down would be as simple as that.

'Well done, you!' Bernice clapped her hands together. 'That could work! How soon do you think you can arrange everything?'

She looked excited, but I couldn't help feeling she was jumping the gun.

Fester glanced at his Breitling watch. 'Soon. I have just the person in mind. His dick's as limp as a wet lettuce leaf these days, so he'll be no threat to Daisy, but he had a reputation as a top shagger when he was young, and he knows Warren well, so the bastard won't suspect a thing.'

The contents of my stomach dropped. I got what Fester was saying, but Daisy would be terrified even if the guy was no threat to her. I could see so many flaws in my plan while I hurriedly formed it. It seemed brilliant one second and idiotic the next. But I was running out of time. Fester was on his feet, phone in hand. The words gushed out of my mouth like water from a tap before I could give my suggestion another thought.

'I've got a different solution.' Bernice and Fester fixed their eyes on me. 'Why don't I go to the club instead? Warren doesn't know me, and Daisy will be reassured if she sees me, rather than a stranger…'

I paid no attention to Bernice's dubious expression and chose to ignore her scepticism. Doubting Thomas! I knew my worth. Never underestimate the underdog! It was as good a plan as any.

'Look, darling, I don't want to speak out of turn,' Bernice began.

Then she paused as though she was trying to find the best way to deliver what she had to say without offending me. I could sense she was about to reject my proposal. She scooted forward and perched on the edge of her seat before she continued to speak.

'Warren might not know you, but what if somebody else recognises you? You're not exactly a stranger around these parts, are you?'

Before I had a chance to fight my corner, Bernice's mobile started to ring.

'It's Carly,' she said, staring at me with a puzzled look on her face. 'What the hell does she want?'

'Why don't you find out,' I suggested, willing Bernice to pick up the call before it rang off.

Carly knew she wasn't in the good books with Bernice since she'd helped herself to the takings from The Castle's till, so she wouldn't be phoning her unless she was desperate.

'Hello,' Bernice eventually said, hitting the speaker button on her phone so that we could eavesdrop on the conversation.

'I'm sorry to call you out of the blue, but I'm in real trouble. I've tried MacKenzie's number over and over again, but he's not picking up. I didn't know who else to phone...'

Carly wouldn't have known that Samson had taken my mobile. She probably thought I was ignoring her. After the wave of guilt washed over me, my heart started hammering in my chest. She sounded petrified.

'What's going on?' Bernice asked with a sense of urgency in her voice. Her earlier hostility had disappeared into thin air.

'Samson was holding me in a warehouse, but I managed to escape. I pretended to be drunk and completely out of it so that Kyle wouldn't bother to handcuff me or tie me up. So I legged it when he went for a slash,' Carly said.

So Samson *was* still alive.

Bernice inhaled sharply, then put her hand on her chest. 'Where are you now?'

'I'm hiding on the industrial estate, but I don't know where I am, and it won't be long before it starts to get dark.' Panic started rising in Carly's voice.

'I know where the warehouse is. I'll come and get you. Stay out of sight, but try and get as far away from Samson's lock-up as possible if you can,' Bernice said.

'I'm shitting myself. Please hurry.' I could tell Carly was on the verge of tears.

'I'll be with you in ten minutes.'

I was on my feet before Bernice ended the call. Much as I wanted to help Daisy, Carly was in immediate danger, so she had to take priority. When she'd started flogging the gear, she'd thought she was onto a good thing, but Carly was too young and naive to see what a dangerous situation she'd got herself into. Being the last link in the chain wasn't an enviable position. It was risky.

'Will you come with me?' Bernice asked.

'Of course.'

'I'll come, too,' Fester said.

Bernice didn't argue. Safety in numbers and all that. She picked her bag up from the floor, sat it on the table, then delved her hand inside and started rummaging around. I did a double take when she pulled out a micro gun and shoved it inside the waistband of her trousers. I'd never seen this side of Bernice before, but it was clear she knew how to handle herself.

Once we were in the Jag, Bernice put her foot to the floor. A short time later, we pulled into the trading estate. She leaned towards her mobile, nestled in the hands-free device on the dashboard, brought up Carly's name, and hit dial.

'I'm here now. Where are you?' Bernice said when the call connected.

Carly didn't reply, and my heart started hammering in my

chest. Tension hung in the air as the car inched its way along. I nearly shit myself when Carly shot out in front of us. She was dressed head to toe in black, so she wasn't easily spotted and almost ended up on the bonnet. Bernice slammed the brakes on, and we all jolted forward.

'Jesus! She frightened the life out of me,' Bernice said, clutching her heart with her hand. 'She must have moved like the wind since she called me. Samson's lock-up is at the other end of the trading estate, and she's almost made it to the main road.'

Carly ran around the Jag with a black rucksack slung over her right shoulder. She wrenched open the back door and flung herself into the footwell so she wasn't visible to passers-by. Bernice didn't mess around. She spun the car around and sped off in the direction of Fester's house.

I peered over the front passenger seat. Carly was curled into a ball with her arms wrapped around herself. I knew she was crying from the rise and fall of her shoulders even though she wasn't making a sound.

'What the hell happened? How did you end up at Samson's warehouse?' Bernice asked.

I glanced over in her direction and saw her craning her neck to peer in the rear-view mirror. Sudden movement behind my chair caught my attention. Then Carly emerged from her hiding spot and settled herself on the back seat next to Fester. She wiped her tears away on the back of her hand before she began to speak.

'He found out that I'd been shifting his cocaine, and as you can imagine, he wasn't best pleased. He was absolutely livid! I didn't know it belonged to him. I didn't nick the gear, I was just selling it. He spent ages grilling me about who I was working for. I told him I didn't know. That I get my orders from Zerina. But

Samson wanted to know where she was from. When I said she was Albanian, he reckons he's worked out who the Head Honcho is, a guy called Arben. But the name means nothing to me,' Carly said.

'That makes sense,' I said. I'd had my suspicions that Arben was the mystery man Carly was working for.

'Zerina phoned me while Samson was interrogating me and said the boss was offering me double the amount of cocaine if I shifted the rest of the gear by the end of the week. Samson went ballistic and made Kyle drive me back to Dover so I could get what was left of his gear before he lost it for good.'

My ears pricked up at the mention of the shipment. I could seriously do with a top-up. I was desperate to know the whereabouts of the missing coke, but it was hard to get a word in. Carly was blabbing fifteen to the dozen.

'Did you give Samson the last dregs of his gear then?' I dropped in as casually as I could as Bernice pulled into Fester's drive.

'Nah. It's safely stashed in my bag,' Carly said.

I instantly felt more relaxed, knowing that more coke was within easy reach and that an opportunity to use it would present itself very soon.

Fester ushered us back to the fire, where our vino was patiently waiting. He picked up another glass and poured a decent measure into it before emptying the rest of the bottle into the other three. I was glad to see all thoughts of wine tasting had gone out the window. Fester handed the drinks around and then settled onto the sofa next to Bernice. We'd swapped positions as Carly was sticking to me like snot on a jumper cuff.

I thought Fester's eyeballs were going to hit the coffee table when Carly knocked back half of her expensive vintage in one swallow. But then he took a large glug himself to calm his frazzled nerves.

'Do you feel up to talking about what happened?' Bernice's voice was soothing.

Carly nodded. 'When we got back from Dover, Kyle took me to the warehouse and not long after, Samson came over. He started plying me with vodka. Little did he know I can drink like a fish.' Carly laughed and polished off the rest of the booze in her glass.

Fester's googly eyes ping-ponged around the room. He looked worried. He was probably terrified that his extensive wine collection would be wiped out during Carly's visit. I moved my lips around to stop them from settling into a smile.

'I let him think I was bladdered because I thought it might work to my advantage.'

I nodded. 'That was a good move.'

Carly turned towards me. There was genuine warmth in her smile, so we grinned at each other for several seconds. No wonder she looked pleased with herself. She'd done well to outsmart Samson and Kyle. She was streetwise, a survivor. More fool them for not giving her credit for any of that.

'I'd never have been brave enough to speak up if I hadn't drunk half a bottle of vodka, and I wanted to confront him over something that happened to me a few years ago...' Carly said when she began talking again.

We exchanged confused looks before our eyes fixed on Carly. You could have heard a pin drop as we waited patiently to hear what she was going to say. I felt the hairs on the back of my neck stand up. I knew before she'd even told us what happened that something serious had gone down.

'It was a gamble. I didn't know how Samson was going to react, but I had nothing to lose. I was valuable to him because he wanted to find out about Zerina's operation, so I figured now was as good a time as any to put the pressure on him.'

The suspense was killing me. I was glad I had some booze floating around in my system now. Otherwise, I'd have been climbing the walls. Carly stared into space while gripping the stem of her glass. We were all desperate for her to continue. I turned to look at her when I felt vibrations radiating through the sofa cushions. She'd started shaking like a junkie badly in need of a fix.

'Are you OK?'

When I touched her arm, she jumped out of her skin. She was clearly terrified.

Carly nodded, sniffed back tears and then the words spilt out of her mouth.

'Once we were alone, the energy shifted. I felt uncomfortable. The first time I met him, he told me he'd take me under his wing and treat me like his daughter. Be the father figure I never had. I looked up to him. I believed him. I trusted him. I was an idiot. He was a pervert. Dads don't touch up their children. Suggest inappropriate things. I was underage. He was the worst kind of sex pest...'

'What the fuck did Samson do to you?' I was raging by the time she'd finished speaking.

'It wasn't Samson. It was Travis. But Samson was instrumental in setting it up.'

36

DAISY

I leapt up from the bed and tried to back myself into the wall when I heard the key turn in the lock. Something told me Raquel wasn't on the other side, and I was right. Warren stood in the doorway, glaring at me. The intensity of his stare made my pulse speed up. He scared the shit out of me. I felt self-conscious as his eyes roamed over my body. Dread started welling up inside me as he walked towards me. I started shaking my head as fear raced around my body at a rate of knots.

Warren towered over me, grinning from ear to ear. When he traced his massive finger down the length of my neck and between my boobs, I started to panic before the urge to fight back got the better of me. I lashed out at him, intending to make a run for it as the door was slightly ajar. But that plan failed before it even got off the ground.

'You're a feisty little bitch, just like your mother, aren't you?' Warren yelled in my face as he grabbed a clump of my blonde hair and wound it around his hand.

I yelled out in pain. My scalp was on fire as he lifted me onto my toes. The more I tried to wriggle free, the tighter he held on to me. I started screaming blue murder, hoping somebody in the club would hear. That was when I spotted the huge guy blocking the other side of the doorway.

'She's a proper handful, this one.' Warren laughed, clamping his hand over my mouth to smother my cries for help. Then his demeanour changed in an instant, and he got right up in my face. 'Shut the fuck up, or I'll beat the shit out of you. Understand?'

My lips trembled under his suffocating hold, but I had to push my fear aside. I didn't want to show any weakness by breaking down in front of him. He dropped his hand to his side and curled his fingers into a fist.

'Answer me, you stupid bitch,' Warren bellowed, his face inches from mine.

I jumped when his spit landed on my chin. His eyes were wild and he was practically frothing at the mouth. I could see he was moments away from losing it. This wasn't the time to make a stand by being defiant. I should have been bending over backwards to try and please him. Begging for his forgiveness, but I couldn't do it. My voice had deserted me.

Pain ripped through the side of my face when Warren's hand connected with it. My cheek burned. Throbbed. My knees buckled. Much as I wanted to stand up to him, he was going to beat me to a pulp if I didn't back down.

'I'm sorry,' I sobbed when I saw him pull back his arm, preparing to take another swing at me. I was embarrassed that I'd had to grovel, but I was desperate.

'I bet you are. I warned you, didn't I? But you think you're so fucking clever, don't you? Just so we're clear, I don't tolerate rudeness of any kind.'

If I was going to survive this, I'd have to slip into the unnatural role of people-pleaser. That had always been Lily's job and I didn't remember applying for the position. Being subservient didn't suit me. Maybe I should have told Warren he'd got the wrong sister. Much as I despised Lily right now, I wouldn't do that to her. I could imagine a double act would be hugely appealing to the type of pervy customers who frequented Warren's club.

Warren suddenly released his grip on me and I staggered backwards.

'How the mighty have fallen. It just goes to show how quickly a person's fortune can change,' he sneered.

I didn't know how to respond. I couldn't trust myself to speak. I was worried I might say the wrong thing, so I opted to keep my mouth shut and faced him with a wall of silence while fixing my eyes on his to show I was giving him my full attention. Anger began to rumble inside me and hatred crept through my veins. I didn't take kindly to somebody trying to railroad me into something. The pressure to keep a lid on my temper was overwhelming. But I had to force myself to stay in control. Stay focused. Stay strong.

'I expect you to look sexy at all times. Lose the attitude and be complimentary to your clients. The more services you give them, the more they'll get charged, and if you ply them with expensive booze while you're entertaining them, the quicker the debt will be paid off,' Warren instructed.

I had a feeling I'd never be out of Warren's clutches.

'Clients get what they're willing to pay for. Very little is off the table. As far as I'm concerned, they can do whatever they like as long as they cough up, so you'd better not go upsetting any of my regulars. I take customer satisfaction very seriously.'

Resentment was seeping out of every pore in my body. Becoming a hooker was going to be humiliating. Degrading. The thought of catering to a stranger's sexual demands or having their grubby hands copping a feel at my expense turned my stomach.

'I'll be watching you like a hawk, so you'd better not step out of line or your mum's going to get it. Nothing would give me greater pleasure than silencing that mouthy bitch once and for all. Do I make myself clear?'

'Yes.' I forced myself to look him in the eye as I spoke.

The minute he left the room, I fell to pieces. I threw myself face down on the bed and started sobbing my heart out. I wasn't sure I'd be able to go through with this, but if I didn't do what Warren wanted, he was going to kill my mum. The only way I could protect her was to sell my soul and make a deal with the devil.

37

LILY

MacKenzie had given me the information, but I didn't know what to do with it. Should I tell Mum or stay quiet? I couldn't decide what to do for the best. Mum was already struggling. I didn't think she'd be able to handle more bad news.

Part of me wished MacKenzie had never told me. If he'd kept me in the dark, I wouldn't have had to make the agonising decision. I'd been furious with Daisy when I found out she hadn't told me that Dad was fighting for his life. Now that I was in a similar position, I finally understood why she'd clamped her mouth shut. She was worried I wouldn't be able to cope. I'd been in a fragile state of mind. I was still in a fragile state of mind.

I'd blamed Daisy for robbing me of the opportunity to spend Dad's final days by his bedside. Mum was livid about that, too. A pang of guilt stabbed me in the stomach as the realisation hit me. Daisy hadn't stayed quiet out of malice, she'd been trying to protect me, and I'd turned on her after everything she'd done for me.

Even though my mum and sister weren't on good terms at the moment, Mum had a right to know what was going on. If I left her out of the equation, Mum might turn on me like she had Daisy. I couldn't bear the thought of being ostracised from the family.

Knowing Daisy was in dire straits was messing with my head. The roles had been reversed, but now that it was my turn to stand up to the plate, I wasn't sure I could do it. We were identical to look at, but our personalities couldn't be more different. Daisy was the leader; I was the follower. I wished I had her fire, her fight. Now more than ever. It was strange because I had an unshakable determination when it came to performing. But that was where my drive started and ended. I'd have to try to channel my inner diva, but it wouldn't be easy away from the stage.

Beads of sweat broke out on my upper lip. I'd promised MacKenzie I'd be there to help, so I couldn't go back on that, no matter how uncomfortable it made me feel. I'd never forgive myself if something happened to Daisy, even though things between us were as strained as ever. For as long as I could remember, we barely tolerated each other.

Daisy was my twin, but we didn't have a bond. It was fractured. Broken. I hadn't been pining for her since she'd been gone. Truth be told, I was glad to see the back of her. The thought of that sent a wave of regret racing towards my heart. I wanted things to be different between us. I wanted us to be close. I wanted my sister to love me the way I loved her. But it wasn't as easy as that. Our relationship was complicated. Complex. At this moment in time, it lay in tatters.

Ever since I'd been a kid, I'd always tried to blend into the background, say the right things, smile and agree, even when I didn't. I shied away from confrontation and never shared my opinions for fear of being judged. No matter what happened next, I knew I was about to learn a lot about myself. I needed to change my mindset and let go of the restrictions holding me back.

I had so much to be thankful for. I was lucky to be alive. Lucky Daisy and Bernice found me when they did. Lucky Tank hadn't given me an overdose. Lucky he didn't manage to rape me. Lucky I'd been given the chance to put all of this behind me and get on with my life, so why did I feel like the unluckiest girl in the world? Who knew being in the wrong place at the wrong time would have such tragic consequences? Would leave me permanently scarred. Would leave me wishing I hadn't survived. Wishing I was dead.

Daisy was a glass-half-full kind of girl. I was the opposite. But maybe it wasn't that my glass was half-empty, it just wasn't big enough to satisfy me. If that was true, what did that say about me? I was ungrateful. A spoiled brat!

The more I mulled over my conversation with MacKenzie, the more anxious I became. I didn't want to look like a complete arsehole by backing out. I'd hoped the experience in the warehouse would have changed me for the better. Made me stronger. Made me resilient. But I'd never be a fighter. I was pathetic. I hated myself for being such a coward, but that was me all over. I'd never been brave like Daisy. I'd never had her spirit. Her edginess. I was dull and bland in comparison. Weak.

I was desperately trying to keep a level head, but I couldn't seem to shake off the anxiety that had plagued me for most of my life. I'd promised I'd help find Daisy, but now I'd changed my mind, so instead of doing something constructive, I was pouring my efforts into coming up with a good excuse.

I picked up my phone and texted MacKenzie. There was no point in putting it off.

I'm really sorry to do this, but I'm going to have to pull out. I won't be able to help you find Daisy after all. There's no way I can leave Mum on her own. She's too unstable to be alone right now. Sorry, L xx

But I knew there were people I could ask to take my place. Mum had friends and family who would gladly offer their services so that I could be there for Daisy the way she'd been for me. What had got into me? Why was I being so selfish? I was ashamed of myself, but even though the guilt weighed heavy on my conscience, it wasn't enough to force me into action. I'd rather let it suffocate me than push myself out of my comfort zone. Tears started streaming down my face, but crying wasn't going to help Daisy. Sobbing my heart out wasn't going to bring her home.

38

MACKENZIE

Carly had gone to pieces after she'd dropped the bombshell and told us that Travis had molested her. Bernice had taken her out of the room to try and calm her down. While we waited for them to reappear, Fester and I sat in silence, lost in our own thoughts.

I had a lot on my mind. Arben was expecting me to cough up one hundred grand by Tuesday, which was only a couple of days away. The original debt had been sixty grand, so that was some interest rate on something I didn't even owe. He reckoned I'd paid him for the cocaine with fake notes. What a crock of shit! But I was powerless to dispute it.

There'd been so much going on that I'd pushed the problem to the back of my mind, but the clock was ticking, and I was nowhere near finding a solution. I didn't have a hope in hell of coming up with the dosh in time. I was tempted to ask Fester for a loan. If he had as much money as Bernice claimed, it would be chicken feed to him. But the Albanians were ruthless fuckers, so I didn't want to get Roscoe's brother involved in case everything went tits up.

An idea suddenly popped into my head. It was a last resort,

but I was fresh out of options. Maybe I could offer to work for Arben until I paid off the debt. How bad could it be? I'd worked for some dodgy people in my time, but no other boss demanded the level of commitment that Samson had. Being on Arben's payroll couldn't be worse than that, could it?

My guts started to rumble. That always happened when I was in a stressful situation. I could have done with some more rocket fuel to help me think straight. Its effects had long since worn off, so it was becoming hard to focus on anything. I was stuck in the middle of a no-win situation. Even though I'd have treated him with the utmost respect, I didn't want to be involved with Arben. I was petrified of him. He'd been brutal to me in the past, so I knew what he was capable of, but I'd weathered that particular storm and lived to tell the tale. And from what I'd seen, he hadn't mistreated Carly while she'd been selling cocaine on Roscoe's patch. At the time, I couldn't understand why Arben had wanted her to flog the gear in Dover instead of London. But now it made sense; Samson thought Roscoe was the culprit, so it kept the heat off the Albanian.

I was snapped out of my thoughts when I heard Bernice and Carly coming back into the room. They were deep in conversation, but I couldn't make out what they were saying because their voices were low. Carly sat down next to me and gave me a half-smile before she bowed her head. I could see she was nervous; she was wringing her hands in her lap.

'I was just telling Bernice. I'm really worried Zerina's cousin will hang me out to dry if I don't follow his orders.' Carly turned towards me. She looked troubled.

Carly had every right to feel nervous. Her boss was a big player. She'd be a fool to cross him. And much as I wanted to help her, if I started interfering, I could end up with a bounty on my head. I was already in shit up to my neck with him.

'If Zerina's operation cut me adrift, I'll have no protection from Samson.' Carly's shoulders slumped.

I could see she was bricking it, so I needed to choose my words carefully. I didn't want to worry her further. I decided the best approach was to keep things light.

'I'll look after you. You can count on me to have your back.' I grinned but immediately regretted offering my services.

Who was I trying to kid? I was a talker, not a fighter. Over the years, I'd learnt to express myself without using my fists. Carly wasn't impressed by my show of bravado anyway. She looked at me dubiously.

'I haven't spoken about what happened to me to anyone apart from when I confronted Samson. I was terrified of the repercussions, so I buried it for three years. But when I came face to face with him, it all came pouring out. My life's a mess because of what they did to me. I thought Samson and Travis would take care of me. They promised to put me on the path to fame and fortune. Travis said he'd turn me into a star. He turned me into a victim,' Carly blurted out, desperate to get things off her chest.

My heart bled for her. Travis Steele was a predator. Somebody you'd want to keep a million miles away from your loved ones. He'd exploited her. Groomed her. Carly was skin and bone and had a washed-out complexion and dark circles all around her eyes like a panda, which made her look permanently tired. Her brown hair hung limply over her shoulders, dull and lifeless. She looked so fragile, vulnerable. How could anybody take advantage of her?

'I was desperate for money. One of the girls staying at the hostel told me about where she was working. Eden's in Denmark Hill,' Carly announced.

I felt myself shudder. 'When was that?'

'About three years ago,' Carly replied.

'You must have been on the scene just before I started working there. I was the manager up until quite recently. Sorry, I didn't mean to interrupt you. What were you saying?'

'The girl I was living with was gushing about the place. She'd said it was the easiest money she'd ever made. She told me to come and see for myself. It sounded too good to be true. It was. They were looking for dancers, and she managed to get me an audition. I wasn't expecting to get the job, so I was blown away when Samson asked me if I could start straight away.'

Alarm bells were ringing.

'It sounded like a great deal. The money was good. Cash in hand, and I could keep all of my tips on top. Costumes were provided, and as staff, we had access to free booze and drugs. I'd only ever drunk cider before. I'd never smoked weed, snorted coke or taken pills. So this was all new to me.' Carly shook her head.

'I wouldn't have expected you to. Not many fourteen-year-old school kids would have sampled all of those illegal substances. No offence, but surely Samson must have realised you were underage when he offered you the job.'

Carly could have passed for a preteen now. She had that skinny, child-like quality, which made her look years younger than she was.

'I'm sure he did, but he didn't question me about it. I told him I was eighteen, and he didn't ask to see any proof.'

'Oh, Jesus.' I shook my head. What the hell had she been thinking of?

Carly bowed her head. She looked embarrassed that she'd been so naive.

'I know I did a stupid thing, but please don't judge me. I was desperate. I had to support myself. It was either work as an exotic dancer or turn tricks. Dancing seemed the lesser of two evils.'

Carly's green eyes filled with tears. She looked haunted by the experience. We'd all done things we weren't proud of, myself included. I reached for her hand and gave it a squeeze.

'Honestly, babe, I'd never judge you. I feel sorry for you. You've been through so much.'

'Thank you. That means a lot,' Carly replied, then she pushed her shoulders back and continued speaking. 'I'd only done a couple of shifts when Samson introduced me to his friend Travis Steele...'

Samson had hardly ever showed his face at the club when I was the manager, but it sounded like he was a permanent fixture while Carly worked there. No prizes for guessing why that was.

'I can't begin to tell you how awful it was...' Carly said, and the colour drained from her face.

I'd always thought the guy was a perv, but I'd never had him down as a paedophile. The thought of what he'd done to an innocent girl made my stomach turn.

I didn't think I could detest Samson more than I already did, but he was just as bad as Travis. He might not have jumped her bones, but he facilitated the abuse by introducing Carly to him in the first place. He would have known what was in store for her, yet he turned a blind eye to it.

'You can tell me to mind my own business, but why didn't you report him?'

'I was a runaway, so I couldn't exactly make myself known to the police or social services, could I? I was worried nobody would believe me. Travis made me swear to keep what happened to myself, and I have until now. But it's been eating away at me.'

'Couldn't you have told your mum?' Bernice asked.

'No. She didn't give a shit about me. *Doesn't* give a shit about me. All she cares about is that dickhead of a boyfriend she's shacked up with. He's the reason I left home. They didn't want me around and must have been delighted when I cleared off. My mum didn't even bother to try and find me.' Carly's green eyes misted over.

It made me sad to think that Carly felt she had nobody she could turn to.

'Oh, you poor thing. You've been through the mill, haven't you?' Bernice gave Carly a sympathetic smile.

My heart bled for her. Once you went down that route it was hard to turn back. No wonder she'd ended up going off the straight and narrow. She'd lurched from one disaster to another since she'd run away from home. She'd escaped from Samson and Travis's clutches but landed in the path of Arben Hasani. I didn't get how men could treat women like this, but then again, I was a sucker for a damsel in distress.

Carly's arms were stick thin and covered in scars and needle marks. She looked like she hadn't had a square meal in ages. Her pathetic excuse of a mother needed locking up. How could she allow her fourteen-year-old daughter to move out and do nothing about it? It blew my mind that something like this could happen without anybody turning a hair. Surely the school had noticed her absence. What about her friends? Her neighbours? Somebody must have cared about her welfare. I barely knew her, but I was still concerned about her safety. So were Bernice and Fester, for that matter.

'I got the coach to London and spent the first couple of nights sleeping rough before I found out about Springfield Lodge, the Salvation Army place on Grove Hill Road,' Carly said, brushing away her tears with the cuff of her hoodie.

'I know the place you mean,' I replied.

'I only stayed there for a short while. After everything that happened with Samson and Travis, I wanted to get away from Camberwell. I was scared of what people would think if it ever came out. I didn't want my name associated with a scandal that would permanently follow me around.' Carly cast her eyes to the floor.

She had nothing to be ashamed of.

'I didn't understand the consequences of my decision when I agreed to let Travis hear me sing. I should have realised something was up when my so-called audition took place in Samson's private suite of rooms. There were cameras everywhere. I presumed they were filming my performance. Now I know that's not the case. They must have filmed the abuse.' Tears started to roll down Carly's cheeks.

Travis and Samson were as thick as thieves. It sounded to me like they'd had it all planned.

'I'd warmed my voice up and had my version of Ed Sheeran's "Thinking Out Loud" polished and ready to go, but just when I was expecting to start, Travis told me to take my clothes off. I was terrified. I turned on my heel and ran for the door, but it was locked. I panicked. I didn't know what to do. Travis started laughing and told me to calm down. He said he was only joking. He told me to take a seat. Then he poured me a drink and asked me to tell him about myself and why I wanted the opportunity to work for him.' Carly couldn't hide her anguish.

I was appalled by what Carly had just said. How could Travis do that to an innocent young girl?

'Jesus, you must have been scared to death,' I said.

'I was, so I made a point of telling him how old I was. I wanted him to know I was underage. I thought that would put him off. I think it had the opposite effect and turned him on. I knew I was taking a risk. I'd lied to them and I thought Travis might take the auditioning opportunity away from me, or Samson might terminate my employment, but what I told him seemed irrelevant.'

I glanced over at Bernice. She had a look of horror on her face while Fester kept shaking his head from side to side. It was clear that none of us could believe what we were hearing.

'Travis kept refilling my glass, and because I was so nervous, I didn't have the sense not to drink it. I must have passed out at some point. When I woke up, I was in the bedroom in Samson's suite,' Carly said.

'There's a bedroom?' I'd been in Samson's private space loads of times, but I'd never seen it.

Carly nodded. 'He keeps the door locked for obvious reasons. You have to go through his office to access it. There are mirrors on the ceiling and on every wall. Video cameras set up on tripods. Black satin sheets...' Carly's voice trailed off as she shuddered at the unpleasant memory.

I was dumbstruck. I couldn't think of anything to say.

'When I came to and found Travis hammering away at me, I was powerless to stop him from stealing my innocence.'

'Oh, Carly, that's so awful.' Bernice clamped her hands onto her chest. I could see the tears glistening in her eyes. She looked heartbroken.

'What I don't understand is why he did that to me. Plenty of women would sleep with a powerful man like Travis. He didn't need to rape me. He seemed to get off on my fear.'

'I'm sure he did. I can guarantee you're not the only one who's suffered at his hands. My guess is he's a serial sex offender,' Bernice said.

I was inclined to agree with her. It was common knowledge that Travis had trouble keeping his dick in his pants, but it was news to me that he was a paedophile. He was no oil painting, yet he'd worked his way through a long list of stunners. I used to think he had charisma. Yeah right!

'Travis tried to normalise the fact that I was underage. But he knew exactly what he was doing. He kept repeating that I'd been given the opportunity of a lifetime, but if I didn't want it, there were plenty of other wannabes waiting in line. It was a case of play the game or somebody will fill your shoes. Little sluts like you are disposable. I needed to learn to put up and shut up. Do as I was told, or I was out.' Carly stared into my eyes as she swallowed the lump in her throat.

I was disgusted that Travis had used his position to assault Carly.

'I'd thought things were bad before, but after what happened at Eden's, I felt like I had no purpose in life. I didn't know how to process it, so I started self-harming and taking gear as a release. I tried to resist the temptation, but there were drugs everywhere and they helped me cope. Samson and Travis used to joke that they were leg spreaders. Those bastards have sailed through life while I've been left with severe depression, anxiety and a massive drug problem.' Carly looked down at the scars on her thin arms.

I had a drug problem too, but mine was of my own making.

'Travis and Samson need to be brought to justice. Carly can't be the only one this has happened to. How hasn't it come out before?' Bernice questioned.

I knew she'd be at the front of the queue to bring Samson down.

'How can I report them? They might be arrested and released without charge. If that happened, they'd come after me,' Carly replied.

'Justice comes in many forms. I wasn't planning on reporting them.' Bernice's voice was cold. She had murder on her mind.

Carly straightened her posture. 'I'd love nothing more than getting revenge for everything Travis and Samson have put me through.'

'You've been so brave confiding in us, darling. I promise I'll help you get even with those bastards,' Bernice said.

Travis and Samson were high rollers. Head of their establishments. I knew they were both sexual predators, but Carly's ordeal had shocked me to the core. She was hell-bent on settling the score and I didn't blame her. Bernice and I were determined to stand alongside her and show her that somebody cared. Samson and Travis had destroyed her life.

39

SAMSON

Monday 12 January

'Bonjour,' Travis slurred when I picked up the phone.

I glanced down at my Cartier watch. It was two o'clock in the morning.

'For fuck's sake, Travis. What time do you call this? I've been trying to get hold of you for hours.' A vein in my temple started to throb.

'Have you? That's news to me.'

'If you bothered to check your voicemail, you'd realise I'd left you an urgent message ages ago.' My tone was far from pleasant.

'All right, all right, calm down, mate. Don't get your knickers in a twist. You certainly know how to put a dampener on a guy's evening, don't you?' Travis laughed.

'You won't be laughing when I tell you what's been going on, you arsehole!'

'Fuck me! What's all the drama about?'

Even though I couldn't see him, I knew that had wiped the smile off Travis's face.

'I can't tell you over the phone. Come over to my house.'

'What, now?'

'Yes, now!' Travis was making my blood boil.

'No can do, I'm afraid. I can't just drop everything the minute you click your fingers. I'll pop by tomorrow afternoon.'

Who the fuck did Travis think he was? I had a good mind to let his tape fall into DC Boyd's hands to teach the randy old git a lesson he wouldn't forget in a hurry, but I'd be spiting myself if I did that and dragging Eden's into the mix, too. If his indiscretion hadn't happened on my premises, I'd be sorely tempted to throw him under the bus.

'This isn't up for negotiation. Trust me. I'm doing you a favour. The sooner this shit gets sorted, the better. Now if you know what's good for you, you'll get your arse over here pronto and stop acting like a clown.'

'Jesus, Samson, do you know what time it is?'

Travis was still bitterly resisting doing what I'd asked. I was only trying to look out for the wanker, and he was giving me grief. Much more of this, and I'd wash my hands of him.

'I don't give a fuck! Listen to me, you ungrateful bastard. I've stuck my neck out for you, so have the decency to come and see what the issue is before I change my mind and screw you over,' I raged into the phone.

The fucker was very lucky I wasn't within striking distance right now, or I'd have grabbed him by the throat and squeezed the life out of him.

'I'm not going to say this again. Get yourself over to my house right now!' I bellowed, then cut off the call.

* * *

The unmistakable sound of Travis stumbling along the corridor towards my office, bouncing off the walls with every couple of drunken steps, filled the air around me.

'So what's all the fuss about?' Travis asked.

He stared at me with a sheepish look on his face when I opened my office door. I didn't bother to reply. I glanced over his head and spoke directly to my housekeeper.

'You can knock off for the evening. I won't be needing you again.'

The poor woman had stayed on well past her clocking-off time. She'd remained on duty while we'd waited for Travis to finally put in an appearance. He was a selfish bastard through and through. I supposed I could have relieved her and opened the door to Travis myself, but that wasn't the way things worked in my household.

'Thank you, Mr Fox. Good night,' she replied, seemingly unconcerned by the inconvenience Travis had caused her.

Travis had stepped into my office and was busy pouring himself a drink by the time I closed the door.

'Make yourself at home, why don't you?' My tone was hostile. The way Travis was behaving was doing my nut in.

'I fully intend to, mate,' Travis replied with a stupid grin on his face.

He was well able to hold his drink, but I could see he was swaying as he stood facing me with a large tumbler of expensive single malt gripped in his liver-spotted, perma-tanned hand.

'Don't you think you've had enough?' I asked through gritted teeth.

'You can never have too much of a good thing,' Travis quipped before holding the glass to his lips.

He might not feel quite so chirpy when he heard what I had to say. There was no point in going over old ground. When I'd questioned him about Carly, he'd said he didn't remember her. That was before he'd spent the entire afternoon and evening boozing. I could smell the alcohol fumes even from this distance, so I dreaded to think how much he'd already poured down his neck without topping up his units.

'Sit down, you big tart. I've got something to show you.'

For once, Travis did as he was told. He'd known me long enough to realise I was ready to blow my top. He didn't need help deciphering the angry vibes radiating off me.

When I projected the image of him nestled between fourteen-year-old Carly's milky-white thighs onto the blank wall, his eyes doubled in size. If you caught somebody off guard, their face always revealed more than they'd like. I could see Carly wasn't any old shag. He remembered the encounter the video had captured in glorious technicolour. The zoom feature left nothing to the imagination. He'd have some explaining to do if the footage fell into the wrong hands. It was a shame he wasn't an enemy of mine. Stuff like this was a powerful tool in the social-media-crazed world we lived in.

'Are you still going to tell me the name Carly Andrews means nothing to you?'

'Now that I've seen her face, she does look vaguely familiar. But you know as well as I do, there've been hundreds of wannabes flat on their back on that bed,' Travis replied, attempting to brush the incident under the carpet.

But his response wasn't much of a defence. I couldn't see it standing up in court.

'Listen, mate, your secret's safe with me, but I'm not the one you need to worry about. Carly's suddenly found her voice. She needs silencing before she gets a chance to blab,' I warned.

'So the little slut's back on the scene. What's she planning to do? Shop me to the cops?'

'I'd say there's a fair chance of that, or maybe she's hoping to blackmail you for money.'

Travis let out a belly laugh. 'As if I'd part with hard-earned cash to shut her up. There are easier ways to do away with trash like her.'

'You don't look bothered by any of this.'

I was shocked by his reaction. I thought Travis would be shitting himself when I showed him the tape. But he wasn't the least bit ruffled.

'That's because I've heard it all before, mate. If she was that worried about what happened, why didn't she report it at the time? She wouldn't be the first whore to try and stir up trouble for me, and I dare say she won't be the last.'

Travis's super-confident exterior was either a well-practised front, or he was buoyed up from the booze floating around in his system. He wasn't thinking straight and would start making mistakes that could land him in hot water if he didn't deal with the situation correctly.

'Once upon a time, cops viewed allegations made years after they happened with suspicion. But things have changed. These days, historical sex offences aren't glossed over like they used to be. The minute one of the slags opens her mouth, the others will come crawling out from the woodwork. I hate to say it, but you've got a lot of skeletons lurking in your cupboard,' I pointed out.

'I can't for the life of me work out why the Old Bill take these slappers seriously. If they'd felt that bad about the situation, why didn't they speak up when it happened? It's an absolute disgrace when wealthy pensioners, who aren't used to roughing it, get locked up for crimes they committed thirty years ago. If you ask me, there should be a cut-off point for these things. If you manage to evade being nicked for five years after you commit a crime, the filth shouldn't be able to make a case out of what you'd done,' Travis said.

I was inclined to agree with him, but unfortunately, that wasn't the way things worked.

'Maybe you should drop Sir Keir an email and get him to ask the House of Commons to vote on your suggestion. There are so many dodgy politicians in the government, I can't imagine a change in the law would meet much resistance.' I laughed.

'Does the bitch know about the tape?' Travis's expression darkened.

'No. She was just mouthing off that you'd sexually assaulted her and stolen her innocence.'

Travis shook his head. 'Yeah, right! I bet she's used the same line on half the blokes in London. Well, you can tell her from me the police never take matters like this seriously because there are no witnesses, so it's going to be her word against mine.'

The camera never lies. I hoped for Travis's sake the footage never fell into the public domain.

'I hear what you're saying, but this needs to come from you.' Since when had I become Travis's bitch?

'Give me the video. I need to destroy the evidence.'

Travis held his hand out towards me. It got my back up that he hadn't tagged 'please' onto his request. If he wasn't careful, he'd be on the receiving end of my temper quicker than he knew it.

'I can't let you have it. I'm going to make a film out of the footage. There are some cracking clips on the tape crying out to be shared. It would be rude not to.'

'Are you mad? You can't do that!' Travis shouted, bitterly objecting to my brilliant idea.

If we were about to have a dick-swinging competition, he

should have known I had the upper hand. Mine was bigger and better, so naturally, I was going to win.

'Jesus, Samson. What's got into you? I thought we were friends.' Travis's face had turned purple as he stood eyeballing me.

I wouldn't usually tolerate behaviour like that in my own home, but I'd cut him some slack because he was drunk and didn't have the sense to keep his trap shut. Despite what he thought, I didn't need to justify my actions.

'I'm not sure why you're flipping your tits. I'm not going to use the clips with you and Carly.'

Travis scowled at me.

'Drop the attitude, or I'll reconsider my decision. We both know there'd be a market for the stuff. There are plenty of pervs out there who'd pay good money to watch you writhing around between Carly's legs.'

I wasn't stupid. I had no intention of ending up in the slammer if the video fell into the wrong hands.

'Really? I can't believe cash is more important to you than my friendship.' Travis pouted.

'Stop being a fag. You know I'm winding you up. But honestly, you need to put the frighteners on Carly asap. I'm holding her at my warehouse if you feel like paying her a visit. She'll shit a brick when she comes face to face with you. She's making a lot of noise. But if you scare her enough, I doubt she'll talk. I'd renew the threat just to be on the safe side, though. Something must have happened to make her suddenly want to speak out. If the cops take her seriously, and they start digging around, you could end up going down for a long stretch,' I said.

'So what are we waiting for?' Travis asked before draining the contents of his glass.

40

DAISY

I jolted awake from a fretful sleep, relieved to find I was alone. There was no sign of the faceless men from my nightmare. I'd pictured myself being sold from punter to punter like stolen gear, the recipients not wanting to keep me in their possession for too long before passing me on to the next perv in the chain. Being a hostess in Warren's gentlemen's club was going to be the pits.

My long blonde hair was stuck to my face and the back of my neck. Clutching the covers to my chest, I glanced around the room. My eyes were drawn to a sliver of light at the bottom of the locked door. The club must still have been open, which meant a client might still cross the threshold. An involuntary shiver ran down my spine. I swallowed hard. Tried to chase the thought from my head. But fear had taken control, and it would send me into a tailspin if I didn't get a grip. I could already feel myself shaking.

Where was Bernice? I'd been expecting her to show up hours ago. I hadn't banked on her failing to arrive. I wondered for a fleeting second if Warren had done something to her before I banished the idea from my head. There was already too much going on inside my brain to compute another possibility. It was exhausting focusing on things that were out of my control.

I had to stop second-guessing, pull myself together and front it out. My mum's safety was riding on this. Warren was going to kill her if I didn't keep my part of the deal. He'd more than likely finish me off too if I tried to double-cross him. I didn't have a death wish. I had to stay strong. Stay focused. It was hard having to take one for the team. I was still pissed off with Mum for blaming me for not doing enough to find Lily when she was missing. We'd fallen out over it. Now, the shoe was on the other foot. What would they do to help me? Nothing. They'd turned their backs on me. They probably didn't even know that Warren had snatched me.

It was a hopeless situation, but I wasn't going to give up. I was determined to see my family again. I wanted to confront my mum about the business with Colleen. About her marriage being in trouble. About my role in all of this. I'd been an innocent child. How could any of this have been my fault? I wouldn't let myself fall to pieces. Not before I heard Mum's side of the story. The thought of making her face the music, making her squirm while answering awkward questions, would give me the courage to face whatever Warren had in store for me.

41

SAMSON

A feeling of déjà vu came over me when I pulled up outside the warehouse and realised Kyle's motor was missing. I sensed something was wrong before I even got out of the car. All the lights were on, but that did nothing to put my mind at rest.

'Something's not right,' I said once we were outside the Range Rover.

I threw Travis a look, and we both pulled our weapons out of the waistbands of our suit trousers. I stood rooted to the spot surveying the scene before I led the way inside.

'Kyle. Kyle!' I shouted into the double-height, echoey space.

I didn't get a response, but I wasn't going to take chances after the last time. Smithy and Tank had paid the ultimate price when they'd been guarding Lily. I hoped Kyle hadn't met the same fate. I paced around, trying to suss out the lay of the land, Glock switch in hand, primed and ready to obliterate trouble. The weapon was small but deadly. It could go from semi-automatic to fully automatic in the blink of an eye and could pump out bullets like a machine gun, but it was a fraction of the size. For each pull of the trigger, my Glock could fire twelve hundred rounds per minute. It wasn't the most accurate gun. It sometimes took out innocent bystanders. But hey, that was life!

Much to my disappointment, my trigger finger didn't see any action. The place was deserted. I breathed a sigh of relief that there was no collateral damage, though. My team was getting smaller by the minute, and I needed all hands on deck. The Albanians were big-time gangsters with numbers behind them.

I pulled my mobile out of my pocket and dialled Kyle's number. 'What the fuck's going on?' I yelled when my call connected.

'I'm sorry, boss. Carly's done a runner,' Kyle replied.

'She's done what?' I bellowed down the phone, hoping to burst his eardrum for letting me down.

For fuck's sake! You couldn't make this shit up! I reached for the almost empty bottle of Russian vodka that Carly had been drinking, poured what was left of it into the glass on the table and knocked back the stiff measure to calm my nerves. As the neat alcohol burned a trail down my throat, my thoughts turned to the runaway. How did that skinny bitch manage to polish off so much booze and still escape? She should have been out for the count, not doing laps around London like Paula Radcliffe.

'How the fuck did she get away?'

'I thought she was bladdered, so I went for a slash. I was only out of the room for thirty seconds. When I came back, she'd legged it,' Kyle admitted.

He was trying to fob me off with a load of old flannel. I wasn't buying the lame excuse. My tolerance for listening to crap had reached an all-time low. I was bored of the bullshit spilling from his mouth. It didn't take much to make me blow.

'I can't believe you let a fucking kid outwit you. You're about as useful as a set of tits on a bull. When are you going to grow a pair? I wish I was close enough to pummel my fists into your thick skull!' I roared.

This was a massive ball ache I could happily do without. I wasn't sure why I was getting so irate. It wasn't good for my blood pressure. This fiasco didn't involve me for once, so I should have stepped back from the situation. It wasn't my fault Lady Luck wasn't on Travis's side. He needed to tread carefully. It didn't take a lot to put the rumour mill into overdrive. Thanks to Arben, I had enough to deal with without attracting unwanted attention. I hated to say it, but Travis was fucked with a capital F. He'd have to take it on the chin. Sometimes life dealt you a huge pile of steaming shit.

'You do realise it's the middle of the night. What the fuck's going on?' Travis asked, squaring up to me.

Was he having a laugh? He should have known better than to question me. I was one step away from unleashing my fury on the useless fucker and spouting a tirade of abuse in his direction.

'Why the fuck did you drag me here?'

Travis threw his arms out in front of him, and I saw red. I started to rain punches down on him, giving him digs to the body and head. He was staggering around like a newborn calf, but I didn't stop. I couldn't stop. My temper had got the better of me. I only came up for air when Travis dropped to the floor, curled into a ball like a hedgehog and groaned in pain. I stood over him, nostrils flaring. I didn't feel a bit sorry for him. He'd pushed me to the edge, so he deserved everything he'd got.

42

DAISY

The sound of the key in the lock startled me. It was barely midday. Too early for customers, surely? My blood ran cold. Warren flung open the door, and my breath caught in my chest. He was an intimidating character. But my excitement built as he stepped to one side, and I saw MacKenzie approach. I couldn't believe he was alive. I'd almost given up hope of ever seeing him again. He was a sight for sore eyes, dressed in a black dinner suit and bow tie. My lips stretched into a smile. He stared at me blankly, so I threw him a toxic glare laced with poison.

MacKenzie and I shared an indescribable connection. We'd been drawn together since the moment we'd first laid eyes on each other. But what the fuck was going on? A million thoughts rushed around in my head. I was doing my best to process them while trying to act normal. I was obviously failing miserably. Warren eyed me with suspicion. MacKenzie silently signalled to me to stay calm, so I put my trust in him. Relief swept over me when Warren closed the door and left us alone.

'Why were you ignoring me?'

'I didn't want Warren to realise we knew each other. He

thinks I'm just a punter who wants to join his club. This was the only way we could find out for sure if you were here,' MacKenzie replied. 'How have you been?'

'Don't ask! It's been a fucking nightmare.'

'Well, don't worry. I'll have you out of here in a jiffy.'

MacKenzie fixed me with his greeny-hazel eyes, and my heart skipped a beat. I didn't ask how he planned to spring me from Warren's lair. I had every faith in him.

'But first, you'll need to get changed into this.'

MacKenzie handed me a holdall. I pulled out a black sequined floor-length dress and strappy sandals. I suddenly felt self-conscious that I was standing in front of him in the slutty red lacy underwear Raquel had given me, so I held the dress to my chest and attempted to hide behind it.

'I don't understand.'

'I paid Warren extra to take you out of the club. He thinks we're attending an event. I wasn't sure he'd fall for that, but the bloke couldn't help himself. His greed got the better of him. All he could see were pound signs.' MacKenzie smiled.

So that was why he was dressed up like a dog's dinner. I thought he'd gone to all that trouble to impress me.

'I won't be a minute,' I said, turning my back on MacKenzie.

'No worries. But try to be as quick as you can. Roscoe's brother is waiting outside,' he replied. He paused for a moment and then continued speaking. 'You've got to promise to keep this to yourself because she told me in confidence...'

'Who told you? What's going on?' I glanced over my shoulder at MacKenzie. He wasn't making any sense.

'Carly. She confided in me about something terrible that happened to her when she was fourteen. Do you promise not to tell anyone?'

'Of course,' I replied, turning to face him as I wriggled into the bodycon dress.

'Travis Steele got her drunk. Then raped her while she was out of it.'

'Oh my God! That's so awful.'

What the hell was wrong with these men? A vision of Samson came barrelling towards me.

'I've kept this to myself until now, but something similar happened to me at Eden's Christmas party...'

'I'm gonna fucking kill Travis!' MacKenzie shouted, and a flash of anger spread across his face.

'Shush. Keep your voice down. We don't want Warren to come bursting in on us, do we?'

'Sorry, but that guy needs sorting out.'

'I know he does, but it wasn't Travis who attacked me. It was Samson. I'd had too much to drink, and he followed me into the toilets. I could barely stand, but he still took advantage of me.'

I was surprised at how easily the words flowed from my lips.

MacKenzie shook his head. 'Jesus Christ! What's the matter with the two of them? Why didn't you say anything? You should have reported the bastard. That's why the pair of them keep getting away with doing this.'

When it came to sex, women couldn't win. Men had double standards.

'Don't blame me. It's not my fault they're a couple of pervs. I'm the victim here. It's not as simple as shopping your attacker. Ask any woman who's been in this position and I guarantee they'll tell you the same thing. It's hard to prove. There weren't any witnesses, so it'd be my word against his. I'd been drinking. I was drunk. Smashed out of my skull. Who do you think people would believe?'

MacKenzie sank his teeth into the side of his lip as he mulled over what I'd just said. I tore my eyes away from him and cast them to the floor when I felt tears start to well up.

'For fuck's sake! Me and my big mouth. I'm sorry, babe. I feel like the biggest arsehole on the planet. You look distraught. I didn't mean to upset you.'

I glanced up at MacKenzie. He looked gutted. I'd hoped he wouldn't notice I was on the verge of tears. I'd intended to brush away his concern, but I could feel myself wobble and didn't trust myself to speak. I was scared I'd break down in front of him. I wanted to come out of this retaining a small shred of dignity. But my emotions had other ideas. When he reached for my hand, I started sobbing my heart out. MacKenzie pulled me towards him and wrapped his arms around me.

'Aww, Daisy. Don't cry.' MacKenzie planted a kiss on the side of my head before releasing his grip on me and holding me at arm's length. 'Come on then. Do your worst. I'll have to suck it up and take the earbashing like a man. It's the least I can do. You can call me every name under the sun. I honestly don't mind. I deserve it for being an insensitive bastard.' MacKenzie smiled.

I grinned back at him. 'I know you weren't trying to be nasty. Your comments were harsh but well-intentioned, so I'm not going to give you a kicking. Especially not before you break me out of jail,' I said to lighten the mood.

'You look amazing, by the way.' MacKenzie's eyes roamed over me.

'Thanks.'

'Are you ready to make a move?' he asked.

'Yes. I just need to grab my stuff,' I replied, running around to the mirrored bedside cabinet where my clothes were stored. 'Is it OK if I put my things in your bag?'

MacKenzie nodded, then walked over to the door and knocked loudly on it. A moment later, Warren appeared on the other side. I immediately wiped the smile off my face. I couldn't afford to make him suspicious in case he went back on the agreement.

'I want her back by midnight at the latest,' Warren said.

'No worries,' MacKenzie replied as he steered me towards the foyer.

My heart hammered in my chest every step of the way. I kept expecting Warren to come after me and stop me from leaving. It seemed to take an eternity to make it to the safety of the car. MacKenzie and I had barely closed the doors when the driver sped off in the Bentley. I was close to tears again. My emotions were all over the place. After what I'd been through, I'd never take my freedom for granted.

43

MACKENZIE

'So what happens when midnight comes and goes, and Warren realises I'm not back? I'm scared of what he'll do if he catches up with me. I watched him butcher my dad with a screwdriver in the middle of our living room. And he's threatened to kill my mum if I don't toe the line. He said he'll kill me too, but not before I clear the debt. Lily won't be safe either. The man's deranged.'

Daisy's face was full of fear. I could feel her body trembling as she cuddled up next to me in Fester's grand hallway.

'Warren's a callous bastard, but that was extreme even by his standards. Don't fret, sweetheart, I'm going to warn him off. You'll be safe here. He won't be troubling you again,' Fester replied before I had a chance to offer her any reassurance.

Although Fester was retired, he still seemed to have his finger on the pulse. I'd initially had my reservations, but I was glad Bernice had brought us to his house now. Fester seemed pleased with the company, too. Rattling around this huge place on his own must have been lonely.

'Am I going to be staying with you?'

I read the look of horror on her face. Daisy was shocked. I'd go so far as to say petrified.

Fester nodded. 'I've got plenty of space for you, Bernice, Carly and MacKenzie. I don't have a wife or family. Take it from me – when you've got a face like this, nobody ever fancies you.'

I understood what he was saying. I was no oil painting either, but at least he was rich. I was surprised he'd been unlucky in love. Plenty of women would ignore how high a man scored on the handsome scale if he had wads of money and offered them a lavish lifestyle.

I glanced at Daisy. She was more relaxed now that she knew she wasn't the only one staying at Fester's. I smiled at her, but her expression remained neutral.

'How come Carly's here?' Daisy eyed me with suspicion.

'She was in a spot of bother, so I offered her a roof over her head,' Fester said.

Fester was an eccentric character, but like Roscoe, he had a heart of gold. Daisy fell silent. She didn't question what he'd said.

'Speaking of Carly, we should see how she's doing.'

Fester led the way. Carly was in a world of her own when we walked into the room. She was rocking backwards and forwards as she perched on the edge of the sofa, staring into the open fire. As soon as she saw me, she rushed over, threw her arms around my waist and buried her face into my neck.

I didn't need to see it with my own eyes to feel the weight of Daisy's stare. It was burning a hole in the back of my head. Her jealousy was boring into me.

'Give me a break,' I muttered under my breath.

Fuck me. Why did shit always land on my doorstep? The last thing I needed was the two of them falling out over Daisy's imaginary love triangle. She had nothing to worry about; I wasn't remotely attracted to Carly. I felt sorry for her. That was all.

I drank, smoked and dabbled in drugs, but my habit didn't have such a hold on me that I couldn't go without. The same couldn't be said for Carly. She was a mess. It was heartbreaking to see a young girl so heavily addicted to gear that she'd pretty much given up eating. The only food she needed were lines of cocaine, pills or spice. I couldn't turn my back on her especially now that I understood what had forced her down the rabbit hole in the first place. There was no place in society for men like Samson and Travis. Taking advantage of grown women was one thing, but abusing an innocent child was a completely different ball game. I was disgusted at the pair of them.

'It's good to see you, darling. Are you OK?' Bernice asked, which momentarily took the heat off me.

Daisy nodded. 'I'm just glad to be out of there.'

'I bet you are,' Bernice replied.

Daisy rushed over to where Bernice was sitting. She dropped down on the sofa next to her. The two women threw their arms around each other and lost themselves in the longest hug. Once they'd peeled themselves away from each other, Daisy glared at me in silent protest. I stared into space as I weighed up how to respond. Carly was wrapped around me like a Russian vine. I wasn't sure why I felt so guilty. It wasn't even a big deal. Nothing was going on between us. But once Daisy got me alone, I knew I'd have some explaining to do. I sensed she wasn't going to believe me.

'You're a singer, aren't you?' Carly asked, breaking the silence.

Daisy seemed startled that Carly had spoken to her. It took her a moment to respond with her one-word answer.

'Yes.'

Daisy didn't try to hide the frostiness in her tone, but that didn't put Carly off her stride.

'Let me give you some advice. If a pervy record producer invites you to a private audition anywhere other than a studio, don't do what I did and step over the threshold. But they're not going to get away with it. I'm going to bring Travis and Samson down,' Carly blurted out.

Daisy's eyes were on stalks. She looked uncomfortable. But her secret was safe with me.

'Travis sucked the life out of me like a vampire. He broke me. Now I want to break him.' Carly's voice was cold.

'And nothing would give me greater pleasure than destroying Samson.' Bernice had an evil glint in her eye.

'I'll be right behind you in the queue,' Fester added.

Samson was after my blood, so it was in my best interest to help Bernice bring him down before he got to me first. And if Carly got revenge on the men who'd wronged her, maybe she'd find some closure. With the right help, she might be able to sort herself out and get back on her feet. She had her whole life ahead of her. It was heartbreaking to think she'd see out the rest of her days looking for her next fix. I couldn't help thinking Carly wasn't the only child Travis had abused. There were likely to be more victims out there who, just like Carly, were too scared to come forward. If I had to hazard a guess, I'd say none of them were brave enough to be the whistleblower, but if she started the ball rolling, who knew what would come to light?

I'd have to enjoy the peace while it lasted. Something told me the situation was going to change on a knife edge.

44

DAISY

I felt jealousy stab me in the gut when we walked into the room and Carly launched herself at MacKenzie, which was ridiculous: I had no right to be a green-eyed monster. He was a free agent. What he chose to get up to in his spare time was none of my business.

MacKenzie flashed me a sheepish smile as I headed to bed, and I threw him a filthy look in response.

'Play nicely, Daisy,' MacKenzie warned, which riled me up even more.

I knew he was prompting me to say something, but unless he wanted me to rip his head off, it was better for all concerned if I stayed quiet. Fester had been good enough to put us all up, so I didn't want to be responsible for World War Three breaking out.

'What? I'm not doing anything. I'm just minding my own business.'

'Yeah, right! I saw the evils you were throwing Carly earlier.' MacKenzie fixed me with his greeny-hazel eyes, and I felt my cheeks flush.

I was trying my best to be civil, but MacKenzie was getting

my back up. Why was he being so protective of Carly? Maybe they were an item. They'd certainly looked very cosy when they were wrapped around each other on the sofa. Interwoven.

'I don't know why you've got the hump with her.'

It felt like MacKenzie was deliberately goading me.

'I haven't,' I replied, rolling my eyes.

MacKenzie laughed. 'You've got nothing to be jealous about.'

'I'm not jealous,' I snapped.

By the look on MacKenzie's face, he'd seen straight through the lie.

'I see Carly as the little sister I never had. I swear to you. Nothing's going on between us...'

'Whatever,' I replied as I began to walk up the stairs.

I'd tried to brush off my awkwardness by appearing unbothered. But I could feel myself glaring at him the further away I got, so I knew my actions didn't match my words. I wanted to believe what MacKenzie had just said. I liked him more than ever. My feelings for him ran deep.

'Don't be like this, Daisy. Don't ruin things between us over nothing.' MacKenzie stared up at me with a hurt look on his face.

I stopped in my tracks and pushed my stubbornness to one side. Why was I doubting him? MacKenzie had proved he cared about me. He'd rescued me from Warren's clutches, so I was confident he had my back.

'It's been a long day and I'm tired and grumpy. I'm sorry. I shouldn't have taken it out on you,' I said as I walked back down the stairs.

'No worries,' MacKenzie replied.

When I reached the bottom step, he grabbed hold of my hand and towed me back to where the others were gathered.

Initially, I'd felt jealous of Carly. But the more I watched

MacKenzie interacting with her, the more I realised it was in a brotherly-sisterly way, which was really endearing and only made me like him more.

Now that I was thinking more clearly, I got where MacKenzie was coming from. I was beginning to feel protective of Carly, too. If luck hadn't been on my side, I could have ended up in her shoes so easily. Carly and I had a lot in common. We'd both been treated terribly, but we'd come out the other side. Survivors.

I'd never had a relationship with Lily, so it would be lovely to form a bond with Carly. Take her under my wing. I'd always wanted a younger sibling. I'd heard it said that sisters made the best friends and supporters, but I had no idea if that was true. Mum and Lily had closed ranks on me, so a surrogate addition to the family couldn't have come at a better time.

45

MACKENZIE

Tuesday 13 January

'Yo, Mac, long time no see,' Leroy said when I walked into the foyer.

Igor, Caleb and Jermaine stared at me in astonishment. I couldn't really blame them. I'd disappeared off the face of the earth.

'I'm about to have a showdown with Samson. Do me a favour, fellas. If you hear a commotion, turn a blind eye, will you?'

Igor nodded, so I knew I wouldn't be disturbed. The team would follow his lead.

I walked down the hallway, past the first door on the left, which led to the bar. The next room along the corridor was my former office. It separated the bar from the live-acts venue where Lily and Daisy used to sing on a Tuesday night. I paused outside it briefly, feeling nostalgic, then shook the memory from my thoughts and headed to the stairs leading to the basement. I bounded down the steps to let the others in through the fire exit. I couldn't resist sticking my head through the dressing room door. I could picture Daisy sitting at the dressing table, applying her red lipstick. What a vision that was. She was a great looking girl. A real stunner.

I dragged myself away. The living, breathing version was freezing her bits off in the alleyway. She wouldn't be impressed if I kept her waiting too long. Bernice, Carly, Fester and Daisy filed through the door, one behind the other.

When we invaded his private suite, Samson was wearing his trademark handmade grey suit, black shirt combo and an air of superiority. He never wore a tie. He reckoned he didn't like the tight feeling around his neck. It made him feel claustrophobic. If he had an issue with being hemmed in, five uninvited guests in his personal space would likely raise his blood pressure.

Samson's mouth dropped open when he clocked us. He hadn't uttered a word and was still staring at us in disbelief when his sidekick suddenly appeared in the other doorway. Travis did a double take, but he wasn't the only one who was shocked. I couldn't believe my eyes. He had a black eye, a split lip and angry grazes on his left cheek. He looked like he'd been in the wars. It was clear somebody had beaten the shit out of him. I was dying to ask what had happened, but I didn't want to deviate from the purpose of our visit.

'I suppose you think you're clever, barging into my premises unannounced. There seems to be a pattern emerging here. You're making a habit of trespassing,' Samson said to Bernice. Then he turned his attention to me. 'You need a rocket up your arse for bringing trouble to my door again. I should have known you'd be harbouring that skank.' Samson looked down his nose at Carly.

Even though there were five against two, Samson acted as though he had the upper hand. He probably thought he could count on his door staff for backup. But he treated his staff like shit, whereas I'd always had a good relationship with the guys. We were a team, and they'd chosen which side they were on. Samson's day was about to go from bad to worse. Thirteen had a reputation as being unlucky for some.

'I wondered when you two would come crawling out of the woodwork. You're certainly stupid enough to think you can get one over on me. You've got shit for brains. I'd admire your ability to get out of deadly situations if you weren't such an annoying fucker. You always manage to rub me up the wrong way. I despise you with a passion,' Samson said.

'You'll be glad to know the feeling's mutual.'

We stood eyeballing each other. Waves of hatred radiating off the pair of us.

'What's the world coming to, Travis? I don't recall inviting a bunch of misfits into my private space. I haven't seen Fester in years. He hasn't improved with age, has he?' Samson directed his question to Travis. But instead of agreeing with his buddy, he stayed tight-lipped. So Samson continued insulting Fester single-handedly. 'You weren't at the front of the queue when looks were handed out, were you? You've got the kind of face only a mother could love. The ugly gene ran in the family, though. Roscoe wasn't a looker either,' Samson said, then roared with laughter.

Bernice didn't take kindly to Samson insulting her husband's memory. She pulled her micro gun from the waistband of her leather trousers and pointed it at him.

'This day has been a long time coming. I'm not going to kill you quickly. I'm going to make you really suffer before I let you take your last breath. And I'm going to enjoy every torturous minute,' Bernice said.

Her voice sounded weird. It was as though she'd become possessed by something demonic.

'It's laughable to think you're the brains of the operation. You don't have the imagination to look past the end of your nose, let alone conjure up fanciful ideas of bringing me down. You're a terrible shot. Remember what happened last time you took a pop at me,' Samson taunted.

'Shooting you would be too quick. Too easy. Would you like to hear the torturous deeds I've got on my wish list?' Bernice replied without missing a beat.

It was plain to see there was no love lost between them. But I didn't want to get caught in the crossfire if it all kicked off.

'You should know, I don't do double standards. I want to kill you, too. If you have the front to go up against me, I'll treat you the same way I'd treat a man,' Samson snarled while glaring at Bernice.

My eyes darted between the two of them as panic inched its way up inside me. I could see Fester hovering close by, ready to protect Bernice if things got too much for her to handle. But she wasn't showing any signs of backing down.

I suddenly noticed some movement in the corner of my eye. We'd all been so preoccupied watching the showdown between Samson and Bernice unfold that none of us had noticed Travis trying to make a run for it. I legged it after him and managed to stop him in his tracks before he made it out of Samson's suite.

'You fucking coward. You're not going anywhere,' I said, twisting his arm behind his back.

I frogmarched him back to the entertaining space. Fester had plastic restraints ready and waiting when we walked into the room. He gestured to me to bring Travis over to a chair before he shackled his wrists and ankles so he couldn't escape, securing him to it with rope to be on the safe side. Samson was furious that Travis had tried to leave him in the lurch. He marched over to his friend, nostrils flaring, ready to give him what for. Fester intercepted Samson mid-lunge, slapping on the same wrist and ankle ties before he had a chance to kick off. I helped bundle him onto the chair next to Travis. It was just as well he was restrained, or he'd be swinging his fists around, taking his anger out on the first person he came into contact with, usually me. It was good to have the upper hand for once. I reached into his suit jacket and took his Glock from the inside pocket. He couldn't get to it, but I felt safer knowing I had control of the weapon. I knew Samson had installed it with a switch, a tiny device that turned the pistol into a machine gun.

Carly suddenly faced her fears and went to stand in front of the men who'd left her life in tatters.

'Do you remember me?' Carly asked.

'I can't say that I do,' Travis replied.

She didn't look impressed. I didn't blame her. Travis had an inflated opinion of himself. He fancied himself as a ladies' man. The only reason he saw any action was because he exploited his position of power. I'd seen how he'd operated when I'd worked at Eden's. Women who wanted to be famous were willing to do whatever he asked for the opportunity to work for him.

'You and Samson took advantage of the vulnerable position I was in. I had no idea what I was walking into. You promised me the world, but it was all lies...' Carly was close to tears, but then she somehow managed to drag herself back from the brink. 'You don't remember pinning me down on the bed in Samson's room, then?' Carly glared at Travis with hatred in her eyes.

Travis shook his head, and his bleached-blonde jaw-length hair swung from side to side.

'You poured booze down my neck until I wasn't coherent. Then you forced me to do things against my will.'

'You were begging for it,' Travis leered.

'I was fourteen.' Carly's voice cracked as she spoke.

'So you were a bit of a goer, were you?' Travis laughed.

Carly looked outraged. Her eyes were blazing.

'I was no such thing. I was a virgin when you raped me, you bastard.'

'Hold on a minute. That's a pretty serious allegation.' Carly's words wiped the smile from Travis's face, and his demeanour changed.

'I never had you down for a rapist,' I threw in for good measure. The words tasted bitter, so I spat them out of my mouth.

'I bet the pair of them have been abusing underage girls for decades. I'd say their operation is well-established,' Bernice suddenly chimed up. 'Travis is the child molester, but Samson is the master puppeteer pulling the strings.'

'Don't fucking drag my name into this. This is between Travis and Carly, and I've got footage to prove that,' Samson said, throwing his best friend under the bus.

Carly's mouth dropped open, and her eyes filled with tears.

'I saw the cameras, so I thought they'd more than likely taken videos of me. I was worried they'd sell them if I told anyone. By the time I managed to break away from their clutches, I didn't recognise myself,' Carly said, glancing between me and Bernice.

'Boo hoo! Carly's not the only one who had to grow up overnight. I had to step up to the plate when my dad was sent down for tax evasion. I'd never had to work so hard before in my life. I'd pretty much been paid for breathing before. Then, out of nowhere, I had to keep things afloat.' Samson was lost in his own world.

He knew what was coming. He knew his time was up, so his

life must have been flashing before him. I bet it shocked him to the core to find himself in this position with Bernice in the driving seat.

'What the hell are you rambling on about? Is this your death row confession? Well, I've heard enough. It's time I put you out of your misery,' Bernice said.

Her rage exploded without warning, blindsiding me.

'Hold him still,' Bernice said to Fester.

'Wait!' Samson shouted, fear etched into his features.

Bernice looked unimpressed by his outburst.

'I know why you're doing this. I get it. It's personal,' Samson said, trying to keep his voice steady. But his breath was shallow as he looked into Bernice's eyes.

'Too right it's personal. I've been dreaming about this moment and what it would feel like to get revenge for Roscoe since the day you murdered him. Let me tell you something. It feels fantastic! I'm on cloud nine knowing I'm about to finish you off.'

'I have a proposition for you. I'll sign over Eden's and everything I own in return for my life,' Samson said. He was in no doubt that Bernice meant what she'd said.

'I don't want blood money as compensation. Nothing's going to bring Roscoe back.' Bernice spat the words into Samson's face. Then she turned away from him and fixed her blue eyes on me. Her head was tilted to one side. She looked as though she was running an idea through her head before she focused her attention on Samson again. 'On second thoughts, maybe I was being hasty refusing your offer...'

Fester and I exchanged a worried glance. What the hell was Bernice doing? This wasn't part of the plan.

Samson gave her a smug smile. 'If you get my solicitor on the line, I'll instruct him to change my will with immediate effect.'

'That's fine, but I don't want your money. I want you to leave your entire estate to MacKenzie,' Bernice replied.

Samson looked like he was going to shit a brick at the thought of me being the sole beneficiary. But I knew more about the running of the club than he ever did so it made perfect sense that I should inherit Eden's. I deserved to have some security after everything he'd put me through. I'd be able to sell some of his assets or use them as collateral to pay off Arben and still have enough dosh left to last me the rest of my life.

* * *

Once the call was made, Bernice opened her Chanel handbag and took out a hunting knife. She grinned as she held it up to Samson's face.

'You didn't really think I had any intention of keeping my side of the bargain, did you?' Bernice sneered.

I breathed a sigh of relief. I'd been worried she'd lost her nerve. But Bernice was made of stronger stuff than that. And she was clever, too. Not only was she going to get retribution for Roscoe, she'd also secured my future.

'I should have known you wouldn't keep your word. Just for the record, if you'd have agreed to let me go, I'd fully intended to double-cross you. But you should know, if you go through with this, I'll come back and haunt you. I'll be lurking in every shadow. You'll never feel safe,' Samson spat.

Bernice hesitated for a second while she absorbed his threat. Samson stared up at her, his eyes silently pleading.

'You took everything from me when you killed Roscoe. So now I'm going to settle the score.' Bernice's hands were shaking when she crouched beside Samson and traced the blade along his skin. 'You brought this upon yourself. You started the war.'

Samson begged for mercy. Called for Igor and the guys. Called for Travis. Called for me. None of us were going to help him. His terror was palpable, but his fear suddenly turned to anger. His every instinct must have told him he was never going to survive this encounter, so he wanted to go down fighting. Seeing panic in our enemy's eyes was the sweetest retribution as Bernice got to work on him.

Samson screamed as Bernice etched her initials into both of his cheeks.

I was surprised he didn't call for help from the guys again, but I knew he wouldn't have wanted to appear weak.

Blood was running down his face and the handle of the knife. But I sensed there was more to come. Bernice paused for a moment as she studied his profile from every angle. Then she stuck her knee on his thigh, leaned in towards him and hacked off the end of his nose.

Bernice stood back to admire her handiwork. My stomach was twisting and turning. She'd totally disfigured the vain bastard. There was no sign of his bravado now. He was shitting himself.

'Take off his trousers,' Bernice said to Fester.

Samson started to buck like a mule, but it had little effect. My balls tingled when Bernice slit the skin on his cock and peeled it back like a banana. Samson cried out in agony. But Bernice carried on regardless. She was focused. Unshakable. When she slowly drew the knife across his throat, a spray of blood speckled my top before it started pumping out of the wound. His eyes grew wide. Then they began to close.

'Good riddance to bad rubbish,' Bernice said.

I forced myself to pluck up the courage to feel for his pulse. Check for signs of life before I breathed a sigh of relief. He'd duped us in the past, so I didn't want to jump the gun and start celebrating without being sure. I wasn't sorry to see him dead. Why would I be? I had a lot to gain. I couldn't wait to get my hands on Samson's hard-earned cash. I deserved the unexpected windfall for putting up with the shit he'd sent my way over the years. It felt good to finally be free of him. He'd suffered a horrible death at the hands of Bernice, which was exactly what he deserved.

'So what have you got to say for yourself?' Carly asked Travis.

'I'm s-sorry. P-please have m-mercy. I'll d-do anything y-you want in r-return f-for my l-life,' Travis stammered as tears streamed down his sun-ravaged face. 'I'll hand m-myself into the c-cops if you like or you c-can have everything I own, just don't kill me...' Travis broke off to glance sideways at Samson's lifeless body. Then he began sobbing like a little bitch.

I wondered what Carly was thinking as she glared at him. I'd be tempted to go with both of his suggestions. Shop the bastard and let him rot behind bars while she lived the life of luxury spending the fortune he'd amassed. That seemed like a fitting payback for what he'd done to her.

The sound of gunshots echoed around the room. When I looked down at my empty hand, it dawned on me that Carly had slipped the Glock from my grip without my knowledge. Her eyes were trained on the man who'd put her through hell as she pumped her abuser full of bullets. He bounced around in the chair as the slugs hit him in quick succession, sending chunks of flesh and bone flying through the air. My stomach somersaulted when some debris landed on the side of my face. I thought I was going to puke in front of everyone.

'You can stop now, doll. He's well and truly dead,' Fester said.

He placed his hand on Carly's arm to break the spell she was under. She turned away from what was left of Travis with thinly veiled hatred engraved on her features. Then she buried her head in Fester's chest. I could see her trembling. Her calm façade had slipped. An eerie feeling seeped around the large space as her heart-wrenching sobs filled the room. Justice had been served.

'We'd better get out of here,' I said.

Not just because there was no sense in hanging around a crime scene, but I wasn't sure how much longer I could hold my vomit inside.

46

DAISY

Wednesday 14 January

'How did you sleep?' MacKenzie said when he walked into Fester's kitchen.

'I didn't,' I replied, glancing up at him.

'All of this seems surreal, doesn't it? It turns my stomach to think how those bastards preyed on vulnerable women. I bet you were glad to see Samson suffer after what he did to you,' MacKenzie probed.

'I find it hard to talk about. The whole thing was traumatic. Is still traumatic. I don't think I'll ever get over it.'

I tore my eyes away from MacKenzie when I felt tears forming.

Travis and Samson didn't answer to anyone. They controlled women because they had money, which equalled power. The gender imbalance was skewed. It was a male-dominated industry.

None of us were brave enough to confront them, so they got away with abusing women. Abusing girls. I didn't have the strength or confidence to stand up to them. Fear had silenced me. I didn't have a voice.

Fame was synonymous with success. What people rarely talked about were the pitfalls. So many influential men were linked to women taking their own lives. Was that really the case, or were they killed because they'd outgrown their usefulness? It didn't bear thinking about.

'I need to see Mum and Lily. Will you come with me?' I asked, changing the subject.

'Are you sure that's a good idea?' MacKenzie quizzed.

'Probably not, but I'm worried Warren might have carried out his threat in retaliation of me doing a runner.'

'Look, I'm not trying to stir up trouble, but before you go, I think you should see a text Lily sent me while Warren was holding you,' MacKenzie said, tilting his phone towards me.

I was shocked that my sister had been so selfish. For as long as I could remember, Lily and I had had a terrible relationship. I'd hated her guts, blamed her for everything that went wrong in my life. I'd felt guilty about the way I'd treated her. I'd wanted to put things right. Make amends. But she'd thrown it all back in my face.

My family were weird. Dysfunctional. But we belonged together. Whether we got on well or not, we shared the same DNA, and at a time like this, I craved familiarity. I knew where I stood in the Kennedy household. I hadn't been blessed with Lily's lofty position, but none of that mattered now. After what happened with Warren, I didn't want to be out on a limb. We shouldn't have been letting Dad's death tear us apart.

* * *

My nerves started jangling as I turned the key in the lock. Lily and Mum stared at me in amazement when I walked into the kitchen. MacKenzie was two steps behind me. Even from the distance we were at, I could feel the bitterness radiating off them. Mum's warm welcome gave me a little taste of what was in store for me.

Mum marched across the room. I could see she wasn't happy, but I needed answers or I'd never find peace.

'What are you doing here? I thought I told you to stay away.'

I'd barely shown my face inside the house when Mum let rip at me. Her tone was hostile, which immediately got my back up.

'Whatever happened to putting family first? Where were you when I needed you? Off galivanting with him.' Mum looked down her nose at MacKenzie before she glared at me.

She wasn't the only one who was angry. I was boiling mad, too.

'While Lily was missing, I was preoccupied with trying to find her, so I pushed Dad's predicament to the back of my head. But it's clear that's an inexcusable offence in your book,' I seethed.

Dad's loss was too fresh. Forgiving and forgetting weren't on Mum's agenda. She was a professional grudge holder and never let anything go. She always had to have the last word.

I glanced over at Lily, but she looked away. My barbed comment must have hit a nerve. But she was spineless, so she buried her head in the sand instead of retaliating.

I wasn't born to shy away from an argument, but emotions were running high. If we went too far, it would fracture our family for good. That wasn't what I wanted. I'd been hoping Dad's death would bring us closer together, not drive a wedge between us.

'You have no idea what I've been through to protect you.

Warren threatened to kill you if I didn't do what he wanted,' I said to break the fingers of tension stretching out between us.

'Nobody asked you to stick your neck out for me. I don't want anything from you,' Mum snapped back.

No matter how much I disliked her at the moment, I couldn't have allowed that to happen. Animosity was flowing between us. We could barely be in the same room. I'd tried to extend an olive branch, but Mum had broken it in two. Fury bubbled inside me. I was fed up of pussyfooting around.

'Colleen told me she had an affair with Dad which lasted almost a year...'

Mum's expression turned from disbelief to fury in a split second. Our eyes locked in a power struggle. I was confident I wouldn't be the first to look away, but she was giving me a run for my money. Silence hung in the air between us. I could see the look of horror on Lily and MacKenzie's faces out of the corner of my eye. I'd dropped a clanger of monumental proportions.

Mum turned away from me and I saw her stiffen. Hostile body language was a red flag. It was so obvious she was reluctant to continue our conversation. Unlucky. I wasn't about to hold back.

'Not that I remember the incident, but I innocently walked in on them while they were going at it hammer and tongs by all accounts. How come I got the blame for Dad's affair? I don't get why you'd rather believe the lies he fed you than the truth your daughter told you.' I shook my head.

Mum spun around to face me with tears pouring down her cheeks.

'He wasn't lying. You were. Don't you dare speak ill of the dead,' Mum replied in a tinny, robotic voice.

'Why would Colleen have told me about this if it wasn't

true?' I locked eyes with Mum. 'There's no way she made it up. She was devastated when she confessed all to me.'

'How dare you go against my wishes and contact that woman!' Mum brushed off her sadness. She was livid.

I should have known she'd avoid answering the question.

'I'm glad I did. You'd never have told me otherwise, would you? The truth always comes out in the end,' I said through gritted teeth.

'Get out of my house and never come back. You're not welcome here. I can't stand the sight of you!' Mum yelled at the top of her voice.

I chose to ignore my mum's parting comment. After the way she'd behaved, I didn't give a shit if I ever saw her or Lily again. Mum wouldn't allow herself to lose face by backing down. Her stubbornness was stopping us from having a truce. It could be another thirty years before she let her grudge against me drop. I didn't have time to waste being bitter and twisted.

'That's fine by me, but you and Lily are on your own when it comes to paying Warren back. He kidnapped me over Dad's debt, and you did nothing to help me, so now the two of you can get on with it,' I fumed.

'You can't just wash your hands of the matter,' Mum snapped.

'Watch me,' I threw back at her before heading for the front door.

MacKenzie and I had just walked down the path when Lily came bursting out of the front door.

'Daisy, wait,' she called.

'You can save your apology for somebody who cares,' I seethed.

'I'm really sorry I let you down, but I couldn't leave Mum on her own. She needed me...' Lily's sentence trailed off. It hadn't taken long for her to run out of steam.

'I needed you.'

Lily cast her eyes to the floor. She couldn't look at me.

'At least I know where I stand now. Anyway, you'd best go back inside. Mum might need comforting over the nasty rumour I tried to spread. I don't doubt she'll convince you that Dad and Colleen didn't have an affair and that I made the whole thing up.' I shook my head. Lily snapped her focus back on me. Her eyes were wide. Her cheeks flushed. Her bottom lip was trembling. She was hiding something. I was sure of it. 'What's going on?'

Tears started pouring down Lily's cheeks as she stared into my eyes. 'I'm so sorry, Daisy. I should have told you before, but the longer I left it, the harder it was to come clean. I didn't think you'd ever find out about the affair. Nobody ever spoke about what happened. It was as though it was a bad dream...' Lily drifted off.

What the hell was she rambling on about?

'The reason you can't remember walking in on Dad and Colleen was because it wasn't you who caught them out. It was me, but Dad automatically assumed you'd opened the bedroom door as you were the more inquisitive twin so that put the idea in my head. I didn't want to get in trouble, so I kept quiet. I'm so sorry. Please forgive me.' Lily had trouble finishing her sentence. She was sobbing so much.

My head felt like it was about to explode.

'I can't believe you let me take the blame. All these years I've never been able to do anything right. But everyone thinks you're so fucking perfect. No, I won't forgive you. I'll never forgive you for this!'

I felt MacKenzie wrap his arm around my shoulder when I

buried my face in my hands. My world felt like it was crumbling around me as we walked towards the car.

'Please don't say that. I'm sorry, Daisy. Daisy... Daisy... I'm sorry...' Lily's voice faded into the distance.

'Chin up, babe. It could be worse.' MacKenzie turned towards me and flashed me his infectious smile when he got behind the wheel of Bernice's Jag. 'Don't let the bastards bring you down. Dwelling on it won't change anything. I never let myself get bogged down with shit. Life's too short. Sack it off and move on. No regrets. Lesson learnt. That's the way I roll.'

'Can you do me a favour?' I blurted out.

'Of course,' MacKenzie replied.

'I need to borrow Samson's Glock.'

MacKenzie tore his eyes away from the road and fixed them on me. 'Jesus, Daisy. What do you want the gun for?'

'I'm going to kill Warren as payback for what he did to me and my family. Otherwise, I'll always be looking over my shoulder. It'll be my final gift to my mum and sister before I wash my hands of them. Not that they'll ever thank me, but I won't double-cross them the way they did me.'

'I can't let you do that. It's too dangerous,' MacKenzie replied.

'It's not up to you. If you won't help me...'

'All right. All right. I know when I'm beaten. But if you're hell-bent on going through with this, let me give you a crash course on shooting to kill,' MacKenzie said.

47

DAISY

'Blimey! I didn't think I'd see you again after you shot through,' Raquel said when I appeared in the lobby of Warren's gentlemen's club.

She looked gobsmacked as she fixed her eyes on mine. She wasn't paying any attention to MacKenzie even though he was standing next to me.

'Is he in there?' I asked, gesturing to the door.

This place gave me the creeps, so I wanted to get this over and done with.

'Yes.' Raquel nodded her head.

'We need to see him,' I replied, looking sideways at MacKenzie.

Raquel waved us through without asking any awkward questions. When I pushed open the door I could see Warren's huge frame parked on a bar stool. He spun around when he heard our footsteps growing closer.

'Look what the cat dragged in,' Warren said, getting to his feet.

'I'm sure you know why I'm here.' My voice was cold.

'Can't say that I do,' Warren replied.

The sound of rapid fire shot through the empty room. Warren looked startled when the first few slugs hit his stomach. He glanced down at the blood seeping across the front of his shirt, bewildered by what was happening. My hands were trembling, but I kept pulling the trigger. I had to finish him off or there'd be no end to this. As I pumped him full of lead, Warren dropped to his knees as pieces of flesh sprayed in every direction before he splayed out on the floor in front of us, face down. MacKenzie put his hand on my arm, signalling for me to stop.

'I'm pretty sure he's dead, babe,' he said. I turned my tear-stained face towards his as I trembled from head to toe. 'Stay here while I check him. You can never be too careful.'

It was as though he'd just tapped into my thoughts and read exactly what was on my mind.

MacKenzie walked across the chequerboard tiles, littered with spent ammo and gore, being careful not to stand in the river of blood that was spreading further away from Warren's lifeless body. He crouched down beside Warren and placed his fingers on the side of the ogre's neck. He held them there for several seconds as his eyes roamed over the bullet-ridden torso.

'He's as dead as a dodo,' MacKenzie said, getting to his feet.

I'd thought revenge would taste better. Sweeter. But as I'd watched my enemy gasping for breath as he'd staggered around before dropping to the floor, all I'd felt was empty. It didn't feel like a victory. Just another loss.

'Come on, babe. Let's get you out of here. It's over,' MacKenzie said, snaking his arm around my waist and leading me away from The Beehive.

As we walked back to the car, I let out a big sigh. I couldn't let the dark cloud hanging over me ruin mine and MacKenzie's relationship before it'd had a chance to get off the ground. Time would move forward and I didn't want to get left behind. The only thing I could do was put the bust-up with Mum and Lily behind me and look to the future. There was only one way up when you'd hit rock bottom. I could sense better things were just around the corner.

This wasn't the way I'd wanted things to end. I'd had high hopes for a reunion. But I'd been the only member of the family who'd thought we should cling to our blood bond. I'd done everything humanly possible to put things right between us. Mum wasn't interested, and since Lily had confessed her dark secret, I wanted nothing more to do with her. But I wouldn't allow myself to hold a bitter grudge. It would rage out of control and eat away at my insides like a malignant tumour. MacKenzie was in my corner, so it wasn't all doom and gloom. Every cloud...

I didn't need to surround myself with toxic people. Mum and Lily were welcome to each other. But letting go was sometimes easier said than done. I owed it to MacKenzie to give it my best shot. It wasn't going to be easy, but I had the power to write my own ending. I couldn't let them get to me.

In the past, I'd been worried that I couldn't trust MacKenzie. But he'd surprised me. He'd stepped up to the plate and was going above and beyond to support me. Who knew what the future held for us? Only good things, I hoped. Wasn't it said they came to those who waited?

'Are you OK, Daisy?' MacKenzie asked, snapping me back to reality.

'I'm fine. You're right. I can't change any of this, so there's no point wasting precious energy on it,' I replied, tuning out the thoughts in my head to give MacKenzie my undivided attention.

'That's my girl.' MacKenzie's beautiful greeny-hazel eyes beamed with pride.

'What's done is done.' I gave him a half-smile.

'You said it, babe.'

I'd fallen head-over-heels for MacKenzie the first time I'd met him when Lily and I had auditioned for the gig at Eden's. Our eyes locked and I felt a sense of calm. Life was for living. It was too short to have regrets. I needed to cut out the deadwood and focus on the people who treated me well. The people who wanted me around. I'd lost everything – my entire family – but I still had Bernice and MacKenzie by my side. They were loyal and caring, and I knew for a fact they would never double-cross me.

MacKenzie leaned forward and placed his lips on mine. His kiss left me breathless. Things were looking brighter already.

* * *

MORE FROM STEPHANIE HARTE

Another book from Stephanie Harte, *Double Dealings*, is available to order now here:

https://mybook.to/DealingBackAd

ACKNOWLEDGEMENTS

Thank you for the brilliant suggestions, Emily Ruston. You are an amazing editor, and I've thoroughly enjoyed working with you again.

Thanks to everyone involved in the production of this book, especially Nia Beynon, Jenna Houston, Wendy Neale, Debra Newhouse, Jennifer Kay Davies, Colin Thomas, Ben Wilson, Gemma Lawrence and Chris Simmons.

Last but not least, a special shout-out to the readers, reviewers and bloggers. I value your continued support more than words can say. I hope you enjoy the book!

ABOUT THE AUTHOR

Stephanie Harte is the bestselling gang-lit author of seven crime novels set in London's East End. Stephanie taught beauty workshops at a specialist residential clinic for children with severe eating disorders for ten years. She also previously worked as a Pharmaceutical Buyer for the NHS and an international medical export company. She lives in North West London.

Sign up to Stephanie Harte's mailing list for news, competitions and updates on future books.

Visit Stephanie's website: www.stephanieharte.com

Follow Stephanie on social media here:

facebook.com/stephanieharteauthor
x.com/@StephanieHarte3
instagram.com/stephanieharteauthor

ALSO BY STEPHANIE HARTE

The Kennedy Twins

Double Trouble

Double Dealings

Double Cross

Boldwood

Boldwood Books is an award-winning fiction publishing company seeking out the best stories from around the world.

Find out more at www.boldwoodbooks.com

Join our reader community for brilliant books, competitions and offers!

Follow us
@BoldwoodBooks
@TheBoldBookClub

Sign up to our weekly deals newsletter

https://bit.ly/BoldwoodBNewsletter

www.ingramcontent.com/pod-product-compliance
Ingram Content Group UK Ltd.
Pitfield, Milton Keynes, MK11 3LW, UK
UKHW021309120825
7360UKWH00014B/97